THE REQUEST FOR PROPOSAL

IRA BELLACH

Dedication

For Risa, Andrew, and Mikayla

In loving memory of Thea

Preface

This novel is a work of fiction. Any resemblance to persons, living or otherwise, events, or organizations is purely coincidental and unintentional.

My desire for *"The Request for Proposal"* is to create a story for readers that inspires, gives optimism, uplifts, and hopefully entertains. Secondarily I want the *RFP* to shine a light on the need to elevate our collective social consciousness.

The *RFP* is a story of navigating life's unexpected twists and turns, sticking to one's inner guidance, and arriving at a place where a brighter future is achievable.

Within the *RFP* are numerous ideas (cultural, spiritual, philosophical, etc.), cloned from many writers, teachings, and thought leaders, none of which are proprietary or unique to the author. So many have contributed their ideas to shape the author's beliefs and world views. These beliefs and opinions are not intended to convert readers and are used solely as character and plot development mechanisms.

Introduction

For many, when life begins, we follow a standard path. We grow up, learn our livelihoods, find a mate, and raise a family. If we are lucky, we get to retire comfortably during the golden years before we depart.

We work to satisfy our own obligatory needs and wants, including our loved ones and culture. Life can devolve with unfulfilled expectations, where we ride a merry-go-round of responsibilities.

Such is the portrait of Jeremiah Baldwin's life—until everything changes with a winning lottery ticket. This opportunity to do whatever he wants miraculously falls into his lap, forcing him to decide what he would do now that he has an unlimited canvas to work with.

He immediately sets a new course according to a radical vision, and his life takes on a new trajectory of self-discovery and possibilities. This story is Jeremiah Baldwin's, and it reveals the choices he makes when there are no limits.

What would you do?

Table of Contents

THE REQUEST FOR PROPOSAL

Chapter 1
The Daily Commute

A recurring dream ends with a familiar, bellowing voice commanding, "Rise, come forth and lead the way." Too cryptic to interpret and too demanding to ignore, Jeremiah's eyes open, and limbs slowly begin to move.

It is an early November morning, 5:30 a.m. With the work preparation routine completed and the familiar unknown awaiting, the day begins to unfold. The sky is a sleepy elephant grey before it awakens with life. A sparse number of commuters are standing on a suburban railroad platform, anticipating their morning dose of transport to the big city. Today is just another day, starting with the daily trek to New York City, where dreams and responsibilities converge, providing the opportunity for a good life in the quiet paradise of North Shore Long Island.

The train rumbles into the station. Clusters of passengers are waiting to board the approaching train. They inch closer to where the doors will open. That prized seat near a window or on the aisle is the target. Half asleep, they can only wonder what the day will deliver, fulfillment or frustration, joy or torment, or another day of energy spent with little to show for it.

Jeremiah Baldwin is one of those sleepy souls angling for a seat. He'd been doing this commute thing for a good twenty years. He is one of the few who likes it. The Long Island Railroad, aka LIRR, allows him to ease into his day and decompress on the way home. One has to be crazy to drive in and out of the "city" every day, fighting other drivers over inches and wasting so much time stuck in gridlock.

Oh, and what about those excessive driving costs: gas, tolls, parking, maintenance, et cetera? For three hundred dollars a month, the railroad is the best deal, given the limited alternatives. The trains are rarely late to disrupt Jeremiah's routine. His commuter motto: early in, early out.

As the passengers squeeze into the waiting cars, Jeremiah finds his way to his usual place. He slides into a three-seat row on the right-side flush against the window. After shifting about and getting comfortable, Jeremiah pulls out his iPhone and headphones. He opens a podcast app and tunes to a meditation channel for quieting music, mantras, and serenity.

The regular slow, deep breathing and calming mantra, amidst the rocking train's quiet repetition, bring a heightened sense of relaxation. Before long, Jeremiah is unaware of time and space. He is in a dream state where an inner peacefulness conquers all knowledge of his earthly presence. Time has disappeared. Visions of light are sparkling. Occasional thoughts come and go. Stillness and tranquility abound, such calmness.

Suddenly, a violent jolt and the train lurches to a dead stop at its final destination: Penn Station.

The riders gather their belongings and head to the exits. A sea of bobbing bodies, clad in suits and manual labor attire, move in the direction of their appointed rounds. Jeremiah has a short two-block walk to his office. He orders a coffee through his smartphone and picks it up at the Thirty-second Street Starbucks. It is steaming hot and ready to go. He smiles at the barista and heads to the door.

It is less than a five-minute walk to reach the building where he works. Strewn on the sidewalk are at least ten homeless individuals wrapped in dirty blankets, tucked under cardboard box houses. They are spaced about twenty feet apart with suitcases and various possessions, marking off their reserved accommodations for the night.

This vision of poverty dampens the spirit, a wildly depressing way to start the day. It always gives pause for Jeremiah to take stock of his life. He quietly counts his blessings and is grateful for his good fortune, bewildered no less by the notion that in 2018, people still sleep in the streets of New York City, the "Greatest City in the World." As he reaches the door to his company's offices, he bypasses trash left behind by the dwellers from last night. In the doorway, another body quietly sleeps. Jeremiah gingerly steps over the motionless being, not wanting to create any disturbance.

Jeremiah rides up the elevator to the fifth floor. How ironic! Jeremiah works for a not-for-profit agency that provides housing for the homeless, and yet, there are more homeless here than ever before.

Chapter 2
At the Office

The elevator comes to a stop, and the doors open to a dark vestibule. Unlocking the door and entering 2-2-1-1 into a security keypad, a green light flashes, and Jeremiah pulls open the door. He walks down the hallway and switches on the lights. His office is at the end of the corridor, beckoning him forward. Entering his work sanctuary, he places his backpack on a chair and his coffee on the desk.

In his backpack are some folders, which he removes and places on the cluttered desk. He puts his iPhone in its charging station while slowly settling into a worn-out office chair. The computer is on, but the screen is black, and after a couple of keystrokes, a login page appears. A few taps on the keyboard, and he is in, ready to tackle the myriad of tasks carried over from previous days. It's only 7:14 a.m., and a whole day awaits, with routine and unexpected activities galore.

"Let's make it a good day," Jeremiah affirms to himself.

Jeremiah has been working for The Way Home for five years, responsible for its overall information technology. He has been in the technology and systems field, serving not-for-profit agencies for more than twenty-five years.

Every day is different. His charge is to make sure all systems are up and running correctly. Some days are smooth, calm, and relaxed; others chaotic and pressured.

Each day starts with a review of the numerous emails that came in overnight. They would find their way into topical folders or the trash bin if not read or responded to immediately. Then there is the review of system logs and computer files containing system messages that highlight any aberrations or problems. Today's survey shows nothing askew.

An hour has vanished. Jeremiah looks at his long project list. His pet project is his work in building and maintaining the agencies' internal data warehouse. He has created a comprehensive system that collects and processes operational and performance data used for managing the multi-faceted aspects of The Way Home.

It is still early, and no one has arrived other than Jacoby, the building's super, who is the only one around at this hour. His job is to make sure the heat and AC work depending on what time of year.

Atop Jeremiah's project queue is a new task to add a feature. It allows his users to drill down from reports and see further details below. The Way Home has twelve shelters, four thousand clients, and approximately six hundred employees, half of whom use Jeremiah's system every day.

Another hour has disappeared. Jeremiah has rewritten the code for a critical report, tested it, and installed it on the production server.

This task is checked off Jeremiah's daily to-do list with a red line drawn through the scribbled item. A high five to no one in particular, punctuating Jeremiah's delight. It's close to 9:30 a.m. now, and still, no one else is on-site. For Jeremiah, it's time for a break; he gets up from his desk, puts on his coat, grabs his iPhone, and sets out for a walk.

Jeremiah can't recall where he'd read that sitting for long periods had become the new smoking, so he tries to move about as often as possible. The weather always decides which route he will take—he has many different ones that measure ten to fifteen minutes a pop. Just enough to air out his head and get a fresh outlook for the next few hours back at his desk.

Jeremiah's favorite walks are to the Flower District on Twenty-eighth Street between Sixth and Seventh Avenues. New York is known for the way businesses cluster in the same general vicinities. Most notably is the theatre district, where Broadway dominates. The diamond district is on 47th. And so on.

Jeremiah sets out at a brisk clip, pedestrian traffic permitting, south on Sixth Avenue. At Twenty-eighth Street, he takes a right and stays on the north side of the street, navigating hordes of construction workers milling about joggers and other travelers on the crowded sidewalk.

There are plants, bushes, baskets of flowers, and bouquets as far as the eye can see. This block is a tapestry of floral splendor amidst the dusty city clutter, and a delight no less.

Jeremiah loves this excursion with the rich, vibrant colors, which have a way of engendering hope and optimism in him. He had also read someplace that being out in nature has a rejuvenating effect. If there is ever anything close to being in the plush countryside in the mid-town maze, this is it.

At Seventh Avenue, he crosses to the other side, and it's back to the office. More plants and a kaleidoscope of colorful grandeur equally decorate the south side of the street. The sights one sees while walking in this dynamic city are never the same. Daily, different people charge along to work in creative styles of dress.

Chapter 3
Back Home on Long Island

Time has an uncanny way of zipping by. Most people with office jobs in NYC can attest to this. For Jeremiah, time at work flies at warp speed.

Every day is different, never knowing what to expect. In the mornings, unresolved issues resume from the day before. Then there are the ongoing projects and tasks to help his colleagues. And the meetings, staff supervision, and vendor phone calls. Before you know it, it is time to start packing up to catch the train home.

Jeremiah arrives home safely after an uneventful train ride. Through the hallway and kitchen, he can see his wife Kate is watching late afternoon TV in the living room, diligently beading a necklace, a rush order she just received. She has been designing jewelry in her home-based business for over fifteen years. Her creative talents were not conspicuous thirty-plus years ago when they first met on a blind date. Over time, however, she has blossomed into a prolific artist with many devoted fans.

Often Jeremiah referred to Kate the governor of Long Island. She knew everyone, either from growing up on the island, summer camp, her single days in the city or from networking. She is a natural schmoozer and people gravitate to her like bees to honey. She is very health conscious with a trim athletic build, average height, sparking penetrating eyes and lovely shoulder length golden wavy hair.

Jeremiah's daughter, Harley, hasn't arrived home yet. Since graduating from college, she has been babysitting in Bethpage, waiting for her dream job to come through. Kate is nervous and impatient about her daughter not having a real full-time job in this competitive world. Jeremiah, on the other hand, respects Harley for following her heart. In twenty years, would it even matter? And if it did, Harley could chalk it up to a learning experience.

Ryan, Jeremiah's son, had long left the nest, working in the city for a thriving tech start-up in web advertising and content algorithms. Visits home for Ryan are few and far between; it isn't because of a lack of love or psychological issues. Ryan's ever-expanding job responsibilities and social life take priority over visits home.

Ryan and Jeremiah occasionally meet for lunch in the Flat Iron section near Ryan's office, not a long walk from Jeremiah's workplace. Kate often finds reasons to schlep into the city to drop off supplies at Ryan's Upper East Side apartment. Moms never stop caring for their kids regardless of how old they get, and Kate will not relinquish that role anytime soon. Was there anything else more important in life? Jeremiah, on the other hand, is okay with Ryan's independence. He feels it is a good thing.

Negative feelings were not the cause of their separation. It reminded Jeremiah of his own family. Jeremiah had grown up in Newington, Connecticut, not far from Hartford. He had a sister, and his grandmother had lived with the family until she passed away. Both his father and mother had worked professionally, so his grandmother ran the day-to-day operations of the house.

His father had been a senior executive at a local hardware manufacturing company, and his mother had worked in the state health department. He had been close with his family members, particularly his mother and grandmother. But not so much, though, with his father—their relationship was often strained if not outright difficult. At times, Jeremiah feels a certain aloneness, given they all had passed away. Nonetheless, his upbringing and predominantly happy childhood set the stage for the values he now embraces as an adult: family, community, and responsibility.

Chapter 4
There Must be More

For the most part, Jeremiah is content and happy with life. Nonetheless, sometimes he wonders, *Is this it?*

The mundane life is a small price to pay for having the best of both worlds: a good-paying job and a steady income that provides a comfortable lifestyle in the burbs. But is it worth it?

There are times Jeremiah feels his family takes him for granted. Maybe it is just that they are entirely unaware of his many sacrifices for their lifestyle. Regardless, he wishes they would show more appreciation for the contributions he has made. The Baldwin family is the typical Long Island family addicted to materialism, entertainment, and consumerism.

No matter. Jeremiah deals with these reoccurring thoughts and suppresses his self-righteousness as best he can. His upbringing taught him to be responsible, particularly for his family. But it sure would be a gift to be free from all the "have to's" that keep their merry-go-round spinning.

Deep in his heart, Jeremiah knows his destiny has more in store for him. But what? And how, when? It's late in the game to start over, or to start something brand new. This yearning for more has been

simmering for what feels like an eternity. Not quite ready to boil over—
or even sure if it ever will.

Jeremiah's reading of personal development books and
practicing yoga has re-awakened something within him. Ignited is a
hunger for more. Daily meditations produce a feeling that something
"bigger and better" comes without any visible timeline of its arrival.
Fortunately, there is an upside to this inner throbbing. It drives him and
consoles the vulnerability he often feels working in a youthful
organization close to retirement age.

Although he may be content with life, he is far from satisfied; he
expects more. But he waits patiently. Something more than a boring
retirement is coming. He knows it. He has felt it his entire life.

Chapter 5
"Say it ain't so, Sara!"

Sara Williams was the agency's new Chief Technology Officer. The previous year, she had come on board to create a more strategic approach for all information and systems. On paper, it seemed like a great idea. Jeremiah and the IT group reported directly to Williams.

On the surface, Sara was likable, coming off as genuine and friendly. Like Jeremiah, she was also a commuter, but took Metro North from Westchester. Her husband worked in New York as well, an attorney at a successful law firm. They had two young children.

Jeremiah had high expectations when he had learned that the new CTO was Sara. He and Sara had met a few years previously when she worked in government. She had interviewed Jeremiah for a job and ultimately asked him to come work with her. Jeremiah declined, but the offer enabled him to convince The Way Home to hire him for the position he now holds.

The job Sara had extended to Jeremiah did not fit. It was beneath his skill set, but Sara was desperate to get a body in the vacant slot. It should have been a clue to Sara's managerial talents, but Jeremiah never gave it much thought, given he never expected their paths to cross again.

As Sara settled into her new role at The Way Home, there were too many meetings and emails. Sara tried to come up to speed as quickly as possible. Almost immediately, her direct reports noticed disturbing qualities in Sara's managerial approach. She seemed to be mainly concerned with pleasing her boss, Len Oswald, the CEO, by reacting to his many needs and demands. Sara's impatience and slight nasty streak began to come out whenever she was frustrated.

Sara would continuously delay or cancel meetings with her staff. She hardly ever allowed the team to render feedback or opinions. The regular conferences took place in her office, where documents and folders piled a foot high on her desk. Though buried and over her head, she had been hand-picked by Len, who was oblivious to Sara's operational style. Her loyalty to him was all that mattered.

Sara did have a sweet side, though. Once she had returned from a family vacation at Hershey Park, she brought bags of *Kisses* to share with everyone. She had even got her direct reports extra-large *Kisses* in see-through packages. At Christmas, Sara would scurry around the office with gift bags for her team. She had her faults, but she was a decent woman.

Jeremiah was practical and able to get along with almost anyone. He tried to make the relationship work, and most times, it did. Sara knew Jeremiah was dependable, seasoned, and productive. Nonetheless, Jeremiah often bristled in Sara's meetings.

There were rumors that while Sara had worked in government, she had been demoted—twice. Some staff at The Way Home had even heard that Sara's nickname by her city colleagues was "Say It Ain't So, Sara," an indication of her rare accomplishments.

Then, there were other rumors that Len was frustrated with Sara and considered having her report to the new head of Human Resources.

Such were the dramas and dysfunction Jeremiah had to endure at The Way Home. From conversations with colleagues at other non-profits, he knew his situation was not unique.

Chapter 6
He's Got a Ticket to Ride

It's the morning of the 2018 mid-term elections—November 6th— and Jeremiah heads out for one of his routine morning walk breaks, just a stroll about his urban neighborhood. The temperatures are chilly, but not oppressive. This time the route is random, taking turns on impulse.

The idea of winning the lottery has crossed the minds of many New Yorkers. Jeremiah is no exception. Though the odds are ridiculous, the notion of having such insane amounts of money is tantalizing and liberating.

For years, Jeremiah would play the lottery when the jackpots grew large. After purchasing a ticket, he'd repeatedly wonder, *What would I do if I won?* Believing he could do anything was empowering. He called these "what-if" exercises his "lottery therapy."

Such a feel-good mood would overtake him from the trance of winning. A big smile would broadly appear across his face. Such joy! Such freedom, such *power*.

As he crosses the street, he eyes a kiosk with a neon lottery sign advertising the current jackpot: four hundred million. Feeling lucky, he pulls out two bucks and buys a quick pick. Folding the ticket in half and carefully stuffing it in his pocket. He quietly reflects on a regular appeal he makes—a prayer of sorts: *God, if you let me win, I promise to do whatever you'd have me do.*

Although the word God doesn't resonate with Jeremiah, given the archaic cultural connotation of an old, bearded man on a throne in heaven, it is a mnemonic for infinite intelligence, the divine field of possibilities and potentialities. No longer steeped in his religious upbringing, Jeremiah often prays; it is part of his spiritual practice. Prayer for him is like speaking to God, and meditation is listening to God.

He reflects further on the many things he'd do first when he won. If only he did!

Chapter 7
The Happy Camper

There are two framed pictures in Jeremiah's office: one of his kids together, and one of Harley alone. It's her high school graduation headshot, enlarged to 5 x 7. She looked a good ten years older than a high school senior, and whenever Jeremiah gazes upon her image, his mood brightens up, filling him with sublime joyfulness.

The father-daughter relationship they share is typical, but no less exceptional. Harley is trustworthy, honest, and loving. Jeremiah feels blessed to have her in his life.

Harley is still living at home, although it has been over a year since her college graduation. It isn't because of how hard it was getting that first job, as many kids complained. But she wants something precise and is willing to wait.

She has been going to sleep away camp in the Poconos for seventeen years. This past summer, she worked there as the Activities Director. She wanted a full-time, year-round position and was engaged in making that happen. It would mean moving to the Philadelphia area for the winter months, where the camp owner had set up shop. There, she and a small team would perform the necessary administrative functions to prepare for the coming summer.

Discussions for a full-time position are ongoing with the camp's director, and Harley hopes to start in early January.

Chapter 8
Lottery Dynamics

Jeremiah had bought a ticket to the Mega Millions game. Players pick six numbers from two separate pools. One had to select five different numbers between one and seventy and one (the Mega Ball) between one and twenty-five. Players could choose theirs or have the ticket machine randomly select the numbers on their behalf.

Jeremiah's numbers come up as:

5 – 16 – 27 – 44 – 58

The Mega Ball: **25**

Typically, when he buys tickets, he won't look at the numbers. It doesn't matter. To him, it is all random. One's lucky numbers have just as much a chance of winning as those selected by the machine. What counts is being in the game. And as they say in the advertisements: "You've got to be in it to win it."

On the day after the drawing held the previous night, Jeremiah always retrieves his ticket and compares it to the numbers reported at the lottery's website or mobile phone app. The result is almost always the same: a losing ticket tossed in the trash. Jeremiah is acutely aware that the odds of winning are nearly impossible, roughly one in two hundred and fifty-nine million. That doesn't stop him, nor the millions of others with equally insane dreams of winning.

Now and then, though, he matches the Mega Ball, where the paltry prize is only two dollars. One has to get the Mega Ball and at least one or more numbers; the more numbers matched, the higher the jackpot. And sometimes, he gets the Mega Ball and one number—this prize: four dollars. Either way, he "reinvests" his winnings for another ticket or two and eventually walks away with nothing.

Chapter 9
Beating the Odds

It's another day beginning like every other. A new morning, the day after a lottery drawing, with the promise that anything is possible. But before leaving the house for the train, Jeremiah follows his usual ritual as he opens his iPhone lottery app. He looks at the winning numbers and examines his ticket simultaneously, focusing on the Mega Ball; then, he looks at the jackpot for the next drawing, which would reveal if there had been a winner.

His eyes widen. His Mega Ball is twenty-five and matches the app, and the next drawing's jackpot is back down to forty million, indicating someone had won the night before. As he slowly reviews the rest of his numbers against the app, his heart begins to pump harder. One of the "regular" numbers matches, and another and another—*holy shit*—all his numbers match!

"Oh my God, I won," he murmurs and tentatively moves to the den adjacent to the kitchen, where he crashes into a larger-than-life sofa.

"Oh my God," he repeats about a dozen times.

"Oh. My. God!"

He sits there for what seems like hours, not knowing what to do, in shock and amazement, but still in a quiet, deep state of joy.

Not sure what to do next with this revelation, one thing is for sure: keep quiet. Figure out a plan. Slowly returning to Earth, he rises out of the sofa's comfort and walks carefully to the mudroom and his car waiting in the garage. He'd go into work as if nothing has happened, knowing full well his life is about to change in ways he can never imagine.

He pulls the car out of the garage, deliberately exits the driveway, and heads to the railroad station. Carefully sliding the car into a vacant parking space between a pick-up truck and an old beat-up Toyota Corolla, he puts the car in park and sits there. The radio plays soft classic rock. There are eight minutes before his train will arrive.

Jeremiah continues sitting there, unmoving and unaware of anything around him. A diverse collection of emotions run through him: confusion, wonder, uncertainty, surprise, anticipation, delight, and fear. Yes, fear. His life could go up in flames if he doesn't handle this judiciously.

The train pulls into the station, and Jeremiah doesn't move. Two minutes pass, and its doors close, and a moment later, it leaves the station. To no one, in particular, Jeremiah asks, "What am I going to do?" He was never one to engage in prayer, per se, but this is the closest thing to it. Instead, through his meditation, everyday affirmations, and oracle consultations, he would seek guidance on complicated matters when confronted.

If ever there was a complicated matter to work through, this was undoubtedly it. In the quiet of the car comes an impression, a thought, a perception.

This is the kind of problem we want; we crave. Relax! Trust yourself. You will figure it out.

Remembering his petition to God about winning when he purchased the ticket, a gentle calm floods his consciousness. *God came through for me; he will continue to do so.* He takes a deep breath and lets out an audible sigh. It feels good, consoling; he repeats it, and again, feeling more centered—his mood shifts. *I can do this. It will all work out fine.*

A jarring alarm blares from the next train approaching the station. Jeremiah snaps out of his trance and prepares to leave his car. He opens the door, resolved to come up with the right plan for himself and his family. It will take some time and effort, but it will all work out just fine.

After all, he just won the freaking lottery.

Chapter 10
What would you do?

How much money does it take to be happy, comfortable, and secure?

The metaphysical answer would be none. But here in the twenty-first century living in the affluent USA might require a small fortune. A million dollars today does not go as far as it used to. One cannot even buy a one-bedroom apartment in NYC with a million dollars! But four hundred million, before taxes—now that's a different story. One hundred or even fifty million would be completely life-changing.

So, how much is one hundred million?

One hundred million is equal to one million hundred-dollar bills! Or ten thousand packs of hundred-dollar bills.

One pile of bills is .43 inches high. The vertical distance of ten thousand stacks of hundred-dollar bills equals four thousand and three hundred inches, or three hundred and sixty-eight feet, about the size of a thirty-story building.

Staggering! Jeremiah is often prone to think about this kind of nonsense.

Undoubtedly, he could get by with a lot less than one hundred million, let alone the estimated one hundred and sixty million take home after taxes, et cetera.

So, how much would it take? Really, how much would he need?

Doing some quick calculations, Jeremiah arrives at a budget he feels would work for him and his family to live comfortably for the next twenty years. It would include:

- $300,000 annual spending allowance totaling $6 million

- Miscellaneous transition costs (attorney fees, etc.) of $1 million

That is all. Rounding up to ten million, safely squirreled away in the bank, could easily cover the Baldwins for the next twenty years. Plus, there is plenty of room for a second home in Florida. Would they need more? Are there any deep, unfulfilled, burning desires? Jeremiah's hypothetical budget has enough wiggle room; it could expand to twelve or even fifteen million—or even more.

For now, with ten million off the top, Jeremiah has about one hundred and fifty million left, which would be available for anything else.

So, what to do with that much? Does he go completely hog wild and spend it like there is no tomorrow? That would seem so misaligned with any sense of decency.

Does he now become a serious investor, buying properties, collectibles, and cars, hoping to enlarge his wealth over time? That would be a new job. Perfect. Win a bunch of money and need to manage it or oversee money managers.

Another option is to become a philanthropist and donate to decent places where some good could come about. That, too, would become a new job. However, the big difference in giving grants to worthy charities would produce tremendous benefits in the community and a deep sense of fulfillment.

And then, when in doubt, Jeremiah could develop a hybrid approach, where he could do it all—be a philanthropist, be an investor, and live a carefree life traveling and enjoying his newfound wealth.

So much to think about and to consider. One thing is evident to Jeremiah: he wants something simple and easy.

Chapter 11
Ava Starling

You could say that Ava and Jeremiah are "recent" friends. They had met earlier that summer in an online chat. Ava Starling was a professional astrologer on the south shore.

There had been something in a book that Jeremiah had read which sparked his interest in astrology. In theory, a chart might disclose why he "came here" and for what purpose. At the time of one's birth, the planets' locations were supposedly very informative in revealing one's life goals, personality, dispositions, and understanding one's soul intentions.

Kate loves massages, and Laura Tyson is a local masseuse whom Kate visits whenever her back bothers her. Jeremiah once asked Kate about an astrologer, and she recalled that Laura was into that sort of thing and had even raved about Ava. She highly recommended her.

Jeremiah checked out Ava's website. She had been doing astrology readings for over twenty years, offering natal charts, relationship advice, psychic readings, Reiki sessions, and more. One could book hourly or thirty-minute sessions with varying prices. There were many pictures on her website, giving it a real New Age feel. The vibe was positive. Hence, Jeremiah made an appointment online, and so began their relationship. He waited two weeks with great anticipation.

The day of the reading finally arrived. Jeremiah was at his laptop promptly as scheduled. After fumbling with the phone so he and Ava could also talk, they were ready to start.

Following some brief chit-chat, Ava explained aspects of the planets and their positions in Jeremiah's chart houses. He listened intently but was clueless, not knowing the meaning or context of this alien language. No matter.

What fun. Ava chattered away enthusiastically in a friendly, perky manner. Her knowledge was impressive even though Jeremiah had no way to judge its legitimacy.

Ava first shared Jeremiah's sun sign, Sagittarius, a person whose personality is vibrant, curious, and exciting, one who values independence and freedom. Sagittarians are brave, truthful, and adventurous. Sagittarians are also fire-signs, which tend to be passionate, dynamic, and temperamental.

One's "rising sign" is how people see you, and for Jeremiah, Ava announced, his sign was Aquarius. Further, she shared, "You may be well suited to work with large groups of people, major organizations that have concerns of a humanitarian nature. You may also get involved with science or politics. You have a strong social conscience and may be adaptable to scientific innovation and working with advances in technology."

Incredible, thought Jeremiah, considering where he worked.

Lastly, Ava revealed that Jeremiah's moon sign, his inner self, was Pisces. Pisceans are known for their sensitive emotions. Their empathic and psychic abilities can help them channel intuitive feelings and dreams into creative mediums like art, music, or dance.

Jeremiah's head was spinning at all these revelations. Some of Ava's statements seemed spot on, and others offered some explanation as to how Jeremiah's life had been playing out thus far. But what did it all mean, and where was it going?

Now that the generalities were over, Ava went deeper. She indicated that Jeremiah had been carrying a large wound, a profound hurt, presumably from a parent—his father. There was much need for healing. Jeremiah knew full well that what Ava had stumbled upon was true.

His father had been old school, critical, and most challenging to be around. They had a rocky relationship. For complete healing, Ava recommended the forgiveness of Jeremiah's father.

Jeremiah would also need to release his suppressed anger—surrender and accept the past. In so doing, he would be honoring and valuing himself. All essential in the healing process.

"Wow," was all Jeremiah could say. "This is too much." *Was this coming from his chart or her psychic sense?* Intuitively, he knew he'd need to deal with these issues if he were to move forward.

Ava suggested Jeremiah write a letter to his father, even though he'd long passed. "Strongly tell him how he had failed you," she directed. "Hurl all the accusations and blame you have held inside about how he let you down, and don't hold back. Give it to him with both barrels! And with your letter finished, go to bed and on the next day, burn it. This ritual will release the hurt you have been carrying all these years."

Jeremiah was all in. In a few days, he would write that letter when he'd be in Montauk for a short vacation with Kate.

Ava had more. She mentioned that she saw tensions at work, and things had been uncomfortable and intense. *How true!*

"But next year will be better. A new work opportunity may arise with someone from the past," she added. "You are very intuitive, Jeremiah. Pay attention to your dreams. Keep a journal. Try Kundalini Yoga—it will help fast track your personal growth." Lastly, she offered, "Build a network of like-minded people. I also see public speaking for you. In six to eight months, you will be a completely different Jeremiah."

There was a lot to process. Who was this woman, and where was she getting all of this information? Some of it sounded so good, and some seemed too unbelievable. They continued to talk and slowly wrapped up the session, which had run over by fifteen minutes.

When the reading was over, Jeremiah felt inspired. He sat at his laptop for a while, regurgitating in his mind all that Ava had said. In the days following, he tried to digest what he'd learned from her. She had reinforced his yearning for personal growth and gave him a strong sense of support and validation. She was a brand-new friend who believed in him. Here was someone, a confidant whom he could lean on as he transformed into the new Jeremiah.

Little did he know how these new insights would shape his thinking in the months to come.

Chapter 12
Anonymous in New York

It is 3:56 p.m., and Jeremiah gets to track sixteen at Penn Station for the next train home with four minutes to spare. He has managed to make it through his day without spilling the beans about his big secret. He settles in his seat and dozes off before the doors even close. The train is only half-filled. In a blink, he wakes up as the train passes the Woodside stop in Queens. No more than ten minutes have passed, and his power nap is over. He sits up, wondering how to occupy himself for the next forty minutes of his trip.

Grabbing his cell phone from his jacket, he opens the Safari app and Googles "Claim lottery anonymously." A list of websites matching his request appears, intermingled with ads for various irrelevant services. He scrolls through, opening some, reading bits and pieces, then returns to the list.

It turns out that only six states allow lottery winners to claim their prizes anonymously, and New York is not one of them. The state's legislature approved a bill, but Governor Andrew Cuomo opposed it and indicated he would veto the measure.

As he continues surfing different sites, Jeremiah finds an interesting one—*The Lottery Lawyer*—located on Long Island, no less. How unbelievable, a lawyer specializing in helping lottery winners, and he's in Jeremiah's backyard. Is this a scam? He scrolls through the site; it seems legit. They are not disclosing any details regarding fees. For more information, one needs to complete an online form.

He finds more information from other websites, where winners can create a legal entity called a trust to claim their winnings and another to distribute the money—a strategy that requires an attorney. So, it seems that maintaining one's anonymity is doable in New York with a lawyer and a couple of trusts. He would need to discuss this with the Lottery Lawyer or an attorney he might retain independently. But who? Is this Lottery Lawyer trustworthy, and should he call him? What will it cost?

Before Jeremiah can resolve his questions and get to the new book in his backpack, he types the lottery's web address into his phone. He navigates to the Mega Millions page. Surprisingly, now, it shows that his winning ticket's actual jackpot has increased to four hundred and thirty million from four hundred. He now has thirty million more in winnings.

Nothing has changed significantly. Another thirty million comes out to about twelve million after taxes. Nonetheless, it's good news and provides more flexibility for Jeremiah in deciding his future with the winnings.

Chapter 13
Why Not Give It Away?

On the surface, the idea of being a multi-millionaire is very appealing, bringing total financial freedom. But the reality is different. Jeremiah believes he'd have so many demands placed upon him without anonymity. And that his newfound wealth could be a burden and out of his control. He had heard too many stories of winners who squandered away their fortunes.

There were even more stories of "friends" and family members who took advantage of vulnerable winners. Jeremiah could say no and be labeled selfish—or worse. He did not care about people's judgments, but it would be exhausting.

All across the world, there is so much struggle, division, and suffering. There are no buttons to push to resolve this tragic reality. Jeremiah knows he can only change himself. And as an example of being the best version of himself, he might touch others to do the same.

If there were more compassion, understanding, and forgiveness in the world, maybe he would need to demonstrate it. In doing so, a utopia of sorts could be achievable. Such a new world might enable everyone to realize the pursuit of happiness and their elusive dreams.

Though a hippie notion, these thoughts are sincere. So are the impressions Jeremiah has of his new calling. Instinctively, he is being drawn in a radical direction—his prevailing altruistic mindset leads him to do something philanthropic with his newly bequeathed fortune. His actions will demonstrate the values he feels the world needs.

What if he donated his winnings to a human services organization with progressive programs to help those struggling with poverty?

It isn't so much the idea of the impact the money would have on the recipient agency. That is important. But equally significant is the selfless gesture of Jeremiah's actions and how they would provide healing.

His act could also elevate the consciousness of all those who witness this scenario play out.

He wants his family to feel proud—would this colossal act of charity succeed in that, or would they be embarrassed? Would they embrace his vision and idealism? Would this example of generosity be viewed as a divine act or a delusional publicity stunt?

These are just some of the thoughts running through Jeremiah's mind. He'd begun to trust his intuition a long time ago. He would sort it out eventually, but he knows he is on the right path for now.

Chapter 14
Breaking News

Kate's morning has been hectic. She ran errands, including a small grocery shop and a brief stop at the post office. She needed to send out a couple of orders and pick up more priority mailing boxes. The holiday season is rapidly approaching, and the requests for jewelry gifts are piling up by customers who want to get ahead of the looming shopping crunch.

She has just finished lunch, a toasted whole wheat sunflower bagel with melted cheese, and is on the couch in the living room, ready to start work on a large bracelet order for a new store in New Jersey. All thanks to Rachel, an old friend who had referred the new account to her.

The empty house is both pleasant and creepy. The quietness means she can plow ahead with her work without interruptions, except for the occasional phone call. But often, it is too quiet. Kate needs to turn on the TV for some background noise. Sometimes there is a show she likes, and she will half-heartedly pay attention to it.

Before long, the late afternoon sun is dimming. Kate has caught some of The Ellen DeGeneres Show. The doorbell rings. It is probably Desmond, the UPS guy. Kate is always online ordering beads, supplies, and personal items. Thank God for next-day delivery!

The newly arrived package is small, a few thousand gold beads offered by a Chinese company on Etsy. She dumps the contents into a nearly empty container of similar stock. Picking up the remote, she starts channel surfing. There isn't much to watch except for the news and weather. She lands on channel two, the CBS station in NYC, just in time for the weather update.

The forecast calls for clear skies, partly sunny, and mild temperatures. The broadcast then shifts to the usual murder and mayhem — "Breaking News" about a fire in the Bronx and the heroic saving of an elderly couple on the top floor of a burning building. The screen then flashes a large graphic: *$430 Million* with a giant question mark.

The reporter comes on the air. Excitedly, she says there had been only one winner of the lottery drawing the night before. It is not unusual for news stories to cover big lottery jackpots and winners. But this story is different. The ticket came from a kiosk in mid-town Manhattan.

Kate pauses from her work. The reporter continues, indicating they have learned the kiosk's location is on Sixth Avenue near Thirtieth Street. That is not far from Jeremiah's office. Kate does not dwell on it and continues listening. The screen shifts to images of the exuberant kiosk manager who had sold the ticket. The reporter presses him for information on who had bought it.

The manager remarks, "Some guy with a baseball cap, I think. I don't know. We sell a ton of tickets every day—who knows who he is?"

The reporter turns back to the camera with a microphone in hand and asks, "Who knows who he is? Who is the big winner?"

Kate flips to ABC and then channel four. Similar stories about the unidentified lottery winner are also airing. They are making too much of this; the drawing was just last night! So typical of the TV news. But still, who is this lucky person?

Chapter 15
The Next Day

Since Jeremiah had learned that he won the Mega Millions Lottery, he has not shared this tidbit with anyone. No one! Who to tell? Who to trust with this? Kate is trustworthy without exception, but she loves to gab with the girls. No, he has to wait before telling her.

Often on TV, big winners would come forward immediately. "I'd buy my mom a house," some would say. Others would exclaim with uncontrollable glee, "I'd quit my job, pay off my debts, and go travel around the world." As the media would share these details about the lucky winners, financial planners, attorneys, and all sorts of deal makers would be swarming and scurrying to find out more about the winners to make their pitches.

Jeremiah wants no part of that. He will maintain control over his destiny and his anonymity the best he can. People's beliefs on what he should do would be outright annoying. Others' opinions and self-interests are of no concern to him. He'll figure it out, and if he needs any help, guidance, or advice, he'll seek it on his terms.

He imagines Kate exploding with ideas on what to do next, ideas like moving to a new house or getting a second one in Florida and maybe one out east. She would want new cars for herself and the kids. To be sure, a complete wardrobe make-over would be in the mix. All those restaurants they could try.

There is no end to how creative Kate can be when spending money with no limits. Jeremiah can easily see her on her iPhone with non-stop emails, texts, and calls with girlfriends; the mom network completely abuzz with: "The Baldwins were Lottery Millionaires!"

No, it isn't going to play out that way. Jeremiah will craft the right plan for his family. He'll be in complete control, and no one will know that he had won. He wants to be smart about this; work out all the details. He is a planner by nature and lives by the old saying, "Fail to plan, plan to fail."

But he has to tell someone. He could call Eli, his close college friend and tax preparer of many years. Or maybe he'd seek out Robbie, the lawyer who did the legal work on his "ReFi" ten years ago. He'll wait to tell Kate until he has at least some concrete ideas for a tighter plan. Still echoing in his mind, *Who can I share with now? I need to talk to someone!*

It's 9:45 a.m., and Jeremiah decides to act and texts Ryan: "Supp?"

"NM pops," Ryan responds.

They go back and forth for a while, finally agreeing to meet for lunch later at a burger joint halfway between their offices. The morning quickly passes, and before long, Jeremiah is sitting at a table in wait mode.

Ryan strolls into the restaurant, passing the bar with his signature cocky walk, hoodie over his head, unshaven for about a week in jeans and a tee. Oh, to be a superstar in a hot high-tech start-up!

They order their meals and exchange trivial details about friends and family and what's going on in their respective universes. Finally, Jeremiah can no longer contain himself. He asks Ryan, "What would you do if you were the winner of that large Mega Millions jackpot?"

Ryan can see a slight difference in his father's eyes, a twinkle of sorts, and recalls the newsfeed on his smartphone about one winner in the recent Mega Millions drawing. A lucky soul had purchased that winning ticket and not far from where they are sitting. He says nothing.

There is a pregnant pause that seems to last an eternity. Slowly, looking Ryan directly in the eyes, like they are the only two people on the planet, Jeremiah utters in a soft but firm voice: "I won, Ryan."

Ryan stares back.

"I won. I did. No joke. I won."

Ryan can't believe it. His dad is not above pulling his leg; he's done it too many times before.

"No, really, I won the lottery!"

Silence. The two of them are just sitting there. Finally, Ryan says, "You're kidding, right, Dad?"

"Nope."

Another pause.

"Did you tell Mom?" Ryan asks in a tone of half believability.

"Nope."

"What about Harley?"

"Nope."

Ryan then asks meekly, "So what are you going to do, Dad?"

"I'm seriously considering giving it away!" Jeremiah proudly announces.

"Are you crazy?"

"Well, not all of it but a lot!"

"You're still nuts, Dad!"

"Listen, Ryan," starts Jeremiah. "I plan to work out all the details. You are the only one I've told so far. Promise me you'll keep this only between us—this is going to be good. I know it. I need you to keep quiet, though, okay?"

Ryan cannot believe what he is hearing. He wonders how he might handle being an instant millionaire. What would he do? His dad has always been levelheaded and a straight shooter. *How could he consider giving away a fortune? What about Mom and Harley? And what about me?* For the moment, at least, he will appease his dad.

"All right, Dad. For now, this is just between us. I won't say anything to anyone, and don't *you* do anything!"

They continue to sit in silence, both with vacant looks on their faces. Ryan then signals the waitress, who has been hanging out with the hostess at the bar, patiently waiting for the two of them to settle up and leave.

She brings the check, and Ryan pays it, but not before giving a bewildering smirk to his father that says, *"Why am I paying for this?"* Both Ryan and Jeremiah get up and head to the door.

Outside, the two agree to talk later, hug, and turn their separate ways to leave.

"Remember, Ryan, not a word to anyone!" reminds Jeremiah.

"Love ya, Dad," returns Ryan.

Chapter 16
Ruby Miller

The Way Home is one of the largest organizations of its kind in the city. In the Finance department alone, there are about twenty accounting types. How ridiculous this seems to Jeremiah. Why is so much staff needed in finance when his department only has four?

One of the recent hires in finance was a friendly but often very busy woman initially hired as a temp. Ruby Miller's desk was on the floor beneath Jeremiah's, near his boss's office, where he'd see her whenever there were those dreadful meetings with Sara. They rarely talked, just exchanged friendly smiles in passing.

To accommodate the ever-changing organizational dynamics, the office manager regularly changed staff seating assignments. Ruby is now sitting a few cubicles down from Jeremiah's office, where they have had more opportunities to get acquainted.

Jeremiah confronted her one day by the copier machine, saying, "You always seem so happy. What's up?" Ruby proceeded to share her philosophy in an elevator speech manner, riddled with spiritual overtones. Not knowing whether she was delusional, on drugs, or just enlightened, Jeremiah did like what he'd heard, and thus began their new friendship.

Chapter 17
Many Questions and No Firm Answers

The idea of giving away a majority of the lottery winnings is sticking with Jeremiah. Getting all the family members on board, however, will take time and some serious selling. But the decision is not theirs. They will come around at some point, for sure, once they fully comprehend Jeremiah's vision. A vision he is still in the process of formulating. He will not necessarily need tenacious persuasion to get their support. In time, they all have to—and will be—on the same page.

What should the framework be for making this all happen? He wonders. How does one go from just having a winning lottery ticket in their pocket to all that cash in the bank, then making a tremendous gift to a worthy organization without anyone knowing it is him? That is the goal. The dollar amounts don't matter. The key questions on how to accomplish Jeremiah's wild vision are:

- How to stay anonymous? Would trust(s) do it?

- How to decide who should receive the gift? What about an RFP?

- How to "come out?"

- How much money to give away?

How much to donate could turn out to be the most difficult decision of all. There are a few permutations that Jeremiah could go with:

- Gift x% / keep y%
- Gift 100% with a 10-year contract with the recipient
- Keep most; give away a small percent
- Keep much; distribute arbitrarily

The most important metric for deciding a recipient should be the maximum social impact achievable. Not easy to judge! The more money donated, the bigger the results—theoretically.

Until the lottery prize is claimed and safely deposited at the bank, nothing can happen. For now, Jeremiah can only plan and refine his strategy. Once the funds are under his control, things can start happening. He is contemplating approximately one million for expenses. Maybe Robbie Winthrop, his attorney, could be the overall "project manager." Having Robbie would be a significant selling point for Kate. And possibly a PR person or a crisis manager would also be wise to have on the team?

Even with all the outstanding questions and decisions to be made, Jeremiah is comfortable and confident. Things are coming together. He knows unanticipated situations will arise, and he'd handle whatever comes up unexpectedly. He is sure, too, that life as he knows it will change but has no idea how so. This planning effort is an attempt to manage change, not be the object of it.

Jeremiah ponders further that this would be the right time to intensify his yoga and meditation practice. Maybe this would also be an excellent time to pray?

"Yes, indeed." He chuckles.

Chapter 18
Robbie Winthrop and Eli Fleming

As Jeremiah is about to go out for lunch after his Thursday morning team meeting, his iPhone buzzes.

A text from Ryan: *Supp? You tell Mom yet?*

Nope, everything cool? Replies Jeremiah.

Yeah, when r u gonna?

Maybe tonight or maybe tomorrow … IDK.

You want to be there with me? offers Jeremiah.

Ryan: *Nah … maybe FaceTime?*

K … we'll see … ly … bye.

Ly.

Jeremiah puts his iPhone down. He returns to the questions he's been asking himself as to how he'd pull off this crazy idea. He will need help, a few "trusted advisors." His family and friends are too close to remain impartial. He will need support in legal, financial, and marketing.

He pauses and reflects on who he could potentially recruit. He needs a fixer! Not the sleazy, shady "Michael Cohen" type—someone who can help make all of this happen, someone who is reliable. After another pause, he softly pounds his fist on the table, remembering his earlier thoughts, and murmurs, "Robbie!"

Jeremiah had already figured he'd need Robbie Winthrop's legal services. She is a natural. She's been a close family friend for years, but not too close. As an attorney, she is a pit bull, despite her diminutive size, and had advised Kate and Jeremiah on the refinance of their mortgage years ago, handling all the details expertly. This project is not the same as a mortgage transaction, yet it requires a high degree of trust, which Robbie can deliver. She is smart, can think on her feet, and will never take no for an answer unless, of course, that is her intent. With certainty, Jeremiah decides he'll reach out to her.

Before Jeremiah's non-profit career, he had worked for a leading NYC bank and two brokerage firms. He knew several bankers, brokers, and financial advisors from his past, but none were popping up as possible choices to help. Rising from his chair, he stares out of his office window. Who could he rely on for financial advice? Then he remembers his old friend, Eli.

Jeremiah and Eli Fleming were in engineering school together back in the day. They continued to be good friends afterward, and both went on to get master's degrees at Pace University in lower Manhattan. Eli majored in tax, and after graduation, he got a job as a budget and project analyst at Con Ed. On the side, he prepared taxes for friends as a hobby. It quickly grew into a second job. He'd done the Baldwin's taxes for more than twenty years. Whenever Jeremiah needs advice, financial or otherwise, Eli is one of the first he consults.

Jeremiah feels more at ease now that he has lined up two trustworthy contacts to help him. He will also reach out to JP Morgan, where he has a few accounts. Though the bank is massive, they had done well over the years, even though he was a small client.

Jeremiah intuitively feels that he will need some banking assistance, but is unsure how much. He makes a mental note to call his account manager at JP Morgan in the next couple of days.

Chapter 19
What's an RFP?

In Jeremiah's brainstorming on identifying a recipient for his charitable gift,

an idea flashes to him—why not an RFP? In the simplest terms, an RFP is a competitive bidding process, short for "request for proposal."

For transparency purposes, when a business wants to make a significant purchase most economically or undertake a large project, they often seek bids from multiple potential vendors.

Jeremiah had prepared many RFPs at previous jobs. He had done one for an enterprise phone system when he worked at a non-profit in Queens. He'd also used RFPs to select contractors for two past relocation projects.

Why not use the RFP approach for choosing the appropriate organization to receive his grant? thinks Jeremiah. That would work! And hopefully, it would also make for a less emotional and controversial decision. Setting forth the essential criteria necessary to determine the worthy organization with an RFP is the first step.

Chapter 20
Getting Legal

Jeremiah hasn't seen Robbie for some time. The last time was at a new restaurant that had opened recently in the mall. Kate and Jeremiah had run into Robbie while waiting to be seated. She was with Jeff Barron, her "roommate," for the past ten years. It was always good seeing them, such a hip, with-it couple.

Robbie spends much of her time on Long Island, where she has an office, or in Florida, where she has a condo on the water in Boca. Jeff is an orthopedist with a thriving practice with multiple offices in Nassau County. They are both savvy and grounded, not the typical successful couple; very authentic. Both had been previously married.

Jeremiah pulls out his iPhone and opens his email app, where he begins composing an email to Robbie. He isn't sure whether she is in Florida or up north, but an email will help get the ball rolling and get her on board with his project.

TO: Robbie.Winthrop@RobbieWinthropLLC.COM

FROM: JBaldwin@GMAIL.COM

SUBJ: Checking in!

Hey Robbie, I hope all is well with you and Jeff! I was wondering if we could meet up sometime soon. I have an exciting project which may need some of your wise legal counsel. Are you on Long Island these days? Please advise your availability.

Talk soon.

Best,
Jeremiah

After checking his message for typos, he hits SEND, and the email disappears.

Turning to some work documents, Jeremiah dives into a folder outlining a critical task requiring his attention. Within ten minutes, his phone buzzes; a new email has arrived. Reopening his app, it is a reply from Robbie.

Hi, Jeremiah! All good here. Yes, I am up north for the next few weeks. Sure, I'd love to meet. What's up? 😊

They go back and forth a few times, with Jeremiah telling her there are too many details to go into now. Finally, they agree to meet at her office in three or four days—the date and time to be confirmed.

Jeremiah puts his phone down, preparing to get back to his work tasks. A wave of satisfaction comes over him. He knows he'll get Robbie in his corner, and things will move ahead. Everything is going to work out just fine.

Jeremiah pauses. There are many more things to cover from his list, but he needs a break for now. There is always tomorrow to resume work on the RFP.

Chapter 21
Lunch with Ruby

The next day at the office, Jeremiah is finishing up a small project for the fundraising team. Ruby walks past him on one of her routine trips to and from the copier machine. He signals to her, and she glides into his office.

"You have plans for lunch today?" he asks.

Shaking her head, they agree to meet at 12:15 at Speedy's, a nearby café.

Located at Thirty-second Street and Broadway, Speedy's is open for breakfast, lunch, and dinner, where one can order meals from the menu for take-out or eat-in. There is a seating area upstairs, very spacious, and Jeremiah retreats there often for a peaceful lunch. Customers can also select from the many "grab and go" choices, but Jeremiah regularly opts for the salad bar, which offers hot and cold dishes that change daily.

As Jeremiah is closing his take-out container and heading to the register to pay, he sees Ruby coming in the front. Pointing to the different food stations for Ruby to visit, she winks, acknowledging his cue.

"I'll get us a table upstairs. You get yourself some lunch, okay?" Asks Jeremiah.

Ruby smiles and walks toward the menu board with the different specials of the day. Upstairs, Jeremiah has found an empty table by the window overlooking the street below. After quickly checking his phone for emails and messages, he sits down and opens the box containing his meal. He stares at its contents: steamed vegetables, baked salmon, three avocado slices, and Kalamata olives.

Ruby comes up the stairs and heads to Jeremiah's table, in the corner where they can eat and chat without being disturbed. As she sits down in front of him, she says, "I've never been in here before. What a find!"

"I know, right! I've been coming here for a few years now. The food is so tasty and no more expensive than any other place in the neighborhood."

They both dive into their lunches, famished from a morning of concentrated work back at The Way Home. Ruby starts to relate some recent episodes concerning her sister and sixteen-month-old nephew. Her sister is a twin, but the two of them are vastly different. They both live in the city, and Ruby goes to visit practically every day.

The conversation then shifts to the office, where they both comment on all the new staff and the cramped working conditions. The Way Home is growing, hiring out of control, and stuffing new employees wherever space is available.

Outwardly Ruby is warm and friendly. She has a happy glow about her. As the two of them have become more familiar, Jeremiah has learned that they both share similar spiritual interests and that Ruby is a psychic with solid mediumship abilities, or so she has told him. They could chat for hours, time permitting, flip-flopping student and teacher roles as they discuss books and topics concerning meditation, angels, metaphysics, God, and more. Jeremiah intuitively has complete trust with Ruby and feels no reluctance in confiding in her.

"Ruby!" Jeremiah begins, moving their attention to a new topic. "I want to tell you something, something unbelievable, something extraordinary."

"Do tell. What's going on, mystery man?" replies Ruby playfully.

"Well," Jeremiah begins weakly. "I don't expect to be at The Way Home for very much longer. I intend to be moving on as soon as I get a few things in place," he says proudly.

"That's great! Where are you going? New job?"

"Not exactly. I have a new project that will require my full-time attention. I don't think I will be able to do both at the same time."

"That sounds so exciting! What kind of project?"

Stalling a bit to find the right words, Jeremiah finally replies, "I am planning on giving away about one hundred million."

"No way! That is unbelievable. How can that be?" Ruby quizzically asks, with the wheels in her head now spinning fast.

At this point, Jeremiah thinks that maybe Ruby's psychic abilities may not be all that great, but then she blurts out, "That wasn't you who won the big lottery prize, was it?"

With his confidence restored in Ruby's psychic gifts, Jeremiah replies, "Damn, there's no keeping anything from you, is there?" Jeremiah wears a huge smile that Ruby matches.

"I knew something was up," she says. "You've been acting a little weirder than usual. That is so crazy!" And then she starts hurling questions at him: "How are you going to do this? When? What does your family think? Who knows about this? Have you given notice yet? Oh my God! Can I come? Are you sure about this?"

"Slow down, Ruby! I just won! I don't have all the answers yet. I only wanted to tell you, that's all." He pauses. "I don't know how 'can I come?' will play out, but I do want you on my team, whatever that means."

Ruby smiles, saying, "Good."

"And another thing, Ruby. No one knows about this yet. I want to remain invisible, however this unfolds."

"Got it. Mum's the word. Not a peep from me. Your secret is safe!"

Over the next five minutes, they finish up their meals and clear away the table, depositing the empty paper plates and containers in the garbage bin. Quietly, they descend the steps and exit the café.

In the shadows of the tall building from across the street, they exchange farewells, with Ruby heading off to run an errand and Jeremiah back to the office. Like a felon who has just confessed, a feeling of relief surrounds him. He is feeling less alone with his new adventure. Who better to have along on this wild ride than Ruby?

Chapter 22
Conversation with Kate

It's just after dinner—if microwaving leftovers counts as dinner. When it comes to food, Kate and Jeremiah have vastly different preferences. However, both prefer fast and easy. Soon they will retire to the living room to catch their daily fix of Alex Trebek and Jeopardy, the usual entree into the night's entertainment schedule of network programming. If nothing appeals to them, then it's Netflix, HBO, DVR, or On-Demand.

A commercial break offers senior citizen medications and "reverse mortgage" promotions. A trailer for the eleven o'clock news highlights the question everyone is asking: "Who is the winner of the big lottery prize?" Here is the perfect opening for Jeremiah to lay the foundation for getting Kate on board.

"Kate, what would you do if we won?"

"Oh, I don't know. Probably pay off the house, buy something in Florida, maybe a place in the Hamptons. Travel. I'd get a dog, for sure! Why? Did we win?" she asks jokingly.

"That's cool. Would you ever consider something radical, something really over the top? You know, like setting up a charity or giving much of it away to a charity, hypothetically, of course?"

"Whenever anyone uses the H-word, it worries me. But since we haven't won, what's to worry about?" She laughs. Continuing, she remarks, "Yeah, I'd consider something radical as long as I got some serious play money out of the deal. There's a lot I'd like to makeover around here."

"That's good to know. So, if we win, we'll need to do some real negotiating. The dog is not a deal-breaker!" Jeremiah answers.

They both smile and drift back to the TV screen. Jeremiah, having gauged her level of possible acceptance, is more at ease. Kate will not be a problem, so long as she gets her share, whatever that might be. His thoughts swirl. He needs to get cracking on getting this together. The sooner he has some money in the bank, the sooner Kate can support whatever he proposes.

Chapter 23
Working in Non-profit

Jeremiah has worked for three non-profits, The Way Home being the third. In an interview for his first non-profit job, he had asked the interviewing president and chief of operations, "What is the difference between a for-profit and a non-profit?"

The short answer given, "Nothing—just accounting rules—it's a business!"

That agency was Adults with Developmental Disabilities, an organization in Queens that directly renders services to consumers or clients. ADD's president was an autocratic tyrant who ultimately got pushed out by his board of directors for questionable business practices. Though it had been an excellent steppingstone for Jeremiah's career, it had been very toxic. While there, though, Jeremiah had learned much.

ADD became his launchpad to move up to the Community Fund, a trade association serving other non-profits located in Manhattan, where his responsibilities increased significantly. The Community Fund raised money from donors and distributed them to smaller direct service organizations consistent with its mission. Jeremiah spent over fifteen years at the Community Fund through four "regimes" and finally left in 2013, a down-sizing casualty.

The Community Fund was very different from ADD. It was more professional, less entrepreneurial, and much more political. After about fourteen months in transition after being let go, Jeremiah finally ended up at The Way Home. At first, The Way Home had a family business flavor, evolving into a more business-oriented operation. That lasted about two years until a new CEO, highly political, came aboard, replacing the current CEO, who suddenly decided to retire and pursue other lifestyle interests.

When working at a non-profit, one must embrace doing more with less. As in any business, the organization's leadership dictates the environment's tone and culture. Since NPs are dependent on donations or grants, it is challenging for them to say 'no' to unexpected requests or demands from donors, even if they are way off point with the non-profit's mission.

One might assume that those who work in non-profit are more humanitarian, but that is not so. Just like for-profits, some are committed and dedicated, and some are not. Some NP staff are career-oriented, and others are only there for the paycheck. At some NPs, management empowers employees, and at others, not at all. It is a function of the organization's leadership sense of trust and personal security.

When Jeremiah first started working at The Way Home, it was a professional dream come true. But as time went by, things changed. Increasingly The Way Home was becoming a place where staff—particularly at lower levels—would only follow directions to avoid recriminations, seldom taking any initiative. As a result, the day-to-day way of work was reactive, sometimes chaotic, and pressured.

This work pattern was counter-intuitive to Jeremiah's sensibilities for an efficient organization operating like a well-oiled machine. He struggled with trying to maintain the vision of a workplace that empowered and valued staff. No easy task, but his evolving personal awareness kept calling him to stay at it. His professional gifts were unique and being at The Way Home was his means of rendering valuable, necessary services.

Chapter 24
A Plan is Born

Having had a few days to contemplate, Jeremiah now has a better sense of what he will do. His vision is taking shape. It is early, and he is at work where he can think more clearly. He pulls out a pad and starts to outline what will become version one of his plan:

1. Get Robbie Winthrop onboard with the RFP concept

2. Get Eli Flemming as his financial advisor

3. Steps to be taken by Robbie:

    a. Confirm anonymity can be achieved via trusts

    b. Create trust(s)

    c. Meet with the lottery officials to verify expectations

    d. Schedule collecting funds

4. Develop a banking relationship

5. Key RFP steps:

    a. Define a rollout for the RFP

    b. Identify potential NPs to solicit

    c. Create a process, applications, forms, etc.

6. Make the RFP announcement

7. Collect the funds and deposit them at the bank

8. Issue the RFP

9. Work through the RFP process

10. Decide and announce the winner

11. Distribute funds to the selected winner

It seems straightforward enough, but nothing is ever easy. Jeremiah had learned that a long time ago. Still, this is an excellent, high-level plan for now, and as with any project, it will require revisions as the process unfolds.

One element missing from Jeremiah's plan is Kate. How will he get her to embrace the RFP idea fully? The uncertainty keeps gnawing at him. She has to be a full partner, buying into the RFP positively. Jeremiah has trusted her for a long time on so many other things. And she has trusted him. He will need to uncover that one thing that will get her on board.

He pauses and recalls when he first met Kate and how quickly their relationship had advanced. After a few weeks, he was sure she was the right one for him and considered asking her to marry him. He was uncertain she'd say yes and ultimately had to have faith and trust her.

Now, he'd have to do the same thing.

Chapter 25
Enlisting Some Star Power

A couple of months after Jeremiah's astrology reading with Ava Starling, he had received an email inviting him to a four-week class about astrology for beginners. He was curious and figured it would be a fun and easy way to learn more, given how ignorant he was on the principles of how astrology worked. So, he signed up.

He was one of three students who had registered for the webinar with Ava. In the first class, he and only one other male showed up. Ava went into teacher mode and described different aspects of the Zodiac and their meanings. She explained the houses or positions where one's signs would appear. It was interesting, but Jeremiah was not connecting the dots. Nonetheless, he enjoyed the session.

The following Tuesday, at seven p.m., he promptly logged into the webinar. This time, he was the only one, and Ava focused solely on his planets, doing what she referred to as a transit reading. How wonderful, one hundred percent of her attention was on him, answering his questions as they arose. In the end, Ava asked for Kate's birth date and place and offered to do a compatibility chart the following week. After the session, Jeremiah gathered Kate's birth information, and the next day emailed it to Ava.

Again, on weeks three and four, it was only Ava and Jeremiah for the readings. Ava went through the compatibility chart. She noted that Kate was creative and exceptionally social, and they both had excellent chemistry. Ava saw no speed bumps in their relationship; their future together looked secure for a long time to come.

In the fourth and last session, Ava discussed the new moon arising the next day, advising Jeremiah that it was an auspicious time to set intentions for the coming month. She also informed him that she saw significant changes in the year ahead, a most exciting time.

"Don't kill yourself at work; they don't appreciate what you do."

More personal exchanges followed, and the growing friendship blossomed. They promised to stay in touch at the end of the session and then closed with warm wishes.

As agreed, they did stay in touch via emails every few weeks or so. In addition, Ava had a YouTube channel and posted videos on different esoteric topics. Jeremiah would sometimes watch with much curiosity but little comprehension.

It has been almost three weeks since Jeremiah had won the lottery, and he has succeeded in keeping his secret close to the vest. He had told only Ryan and Ruby. Although his friendship with Ava is in its infancy, he feels he can trust her, particularly given she had predicted "big changes" and an exciting time ahead in their last astrology class.

Reaching for his laptop, Jeremiah opens his Gmail account. He composes an email to Ava, telling her he'd like to talk with her about a couple of things, either in-person or via FaceTime. The message is short and straightforward, without any drama or cause for alarm bells to go off. He hits SEND, and off it goes.

Ava and Jeremiah connect via FaceTime the next day. Jeremiah is in his office with the door closed, and Ava is in her studio, where she conducts readings and broadcasts her webinars. It is about 8:30 a.m., and no one appears to be in yet at The Way Home.

After some chit-chat, Ava asks, "So, what's been going on with you?"

Ava's hair is pulled back in a ponytail. Her face glows as if she just had a facial. Jeremiah jumps right in, saying, "Remember my last reading when you said big changes were coming? Well, you have no idea how right you were!"

"Whoa, that is too much. What are you saying? I am dying to hear more. What kind of changes? What's happening?"

"I'll get to the specifics, Ava, but you have to promise me you will keep this a secret. What I'm going to tell you is huge. Unbelievably huge. And I am only telling you because I trust you."

"Jeremiah, I'm touched that you place so much trust in me to want to share something so important to you. Yes, of course I will keep your secret."

Jeremiah pauses and then asks, "Remember the reports that someone in New York won the lottery?"

Stupefied, she stammers, "No. I mean, yes, I remember. Tell me it's not you."

Jeremiah looks back, smiling.

Growing impatient, Ava says, "Really? No? Jeremiah?"

Jeremiah admits he is the winner and says, "And what's more, Ava, I have a plan—or at least a reasonable idea—of what I'm doing with the winnings. And it's radical. People will be kind of totally freaked out, though."

Ava is stunned. Finally, she replies, "I know you're *not* kidding, but this is too hard to believe." Pausing, she continues, "What kind of plan? Nothing stupid, I hope. If I recall, that was one of the largest jackpots ever."

"Exactly. I figure there is no way I'd ever use it all. So much of it could evaporate if one…" Jeremiah drifts off. "To be set for life, I need to plan intelligently. So here is my plan."

Catching his breath, Jeremiah continues, "First, I am getting an attorney, a friend of mine. She will establish an anonymous trust, so I can claim the money without anyone knowing my identity. That is crucial! I plan to give away a lot of the money to a charity. How much? I still need to decide that. Maybe half or three quarters, but I assure you not all of it."

Ava is still with him, and this is making sense. It is not over the top.

"I am going to put together a team and a process to select the charity to receive the donation."

"What kind of process?" Ava asks.

"It's called an RFP—a request for proposal. Typically, it's where organizations compete for a project or job. In this case, it will be charities bidding for the donation. As part of the RFP, we will announce our intentions to donate to a worthy organization. Organizations will then need to apply. Finally, there will be an interview process where selected candidates will have the opportunity to make their case for why they should get the donation."

Ava is processing this. It's making sense. Radical—but not crazy.

"You know, Jere?" Ava starts, shortening Jeremiah's name for the first time.

"That's not half bad. I like it. You are doing something very cool. Just make sure you take care of yourself. And don't let this get out of control."

"Exactly, that's my intention," replies Jeremiah.

Still thinking, Ava finally says, "I love it. It's great! You're something else, Jeremiah. What a great idea! You will do just fine. No doubt, big changes are coming for you."

Jeremiah is feeling pleased and empowered. He asks, "How does this sit with my chart?"

Checking Jeremiah's last reading, Ava replies, "Very well! You are entering a period where a project like this is favorable. Luck is on your side. Be very comprehensive in your planning. There is alignment in your chart to do this. Go for it, Jeremiah!"

Jeremiah is thrilled and more self-assured. Deep inside, he knew this was good. But having Ava's blessing is the icing on the cake. He would move forward now, full steam ahead. Time to bring in the lawyers and accountants!

"That's awesome, Ava."

"I know, right?"

"One thing?"

"What?"

"You're on my team, yes?" Jeremiah asks.

"Absolutely!" Ava exclaims.

They continue to chat a bit longer before hanging up and agreeing to talk more about the RFP soon. Jeremiah is flying. Confirmation from Ava is very affirming. He settles back, daydreaming about this and that related to what's next and how things might play out. There are so many unknowns and aspects to be worked out, but Jeremiah's confidence is high. With Ava—and soon Robbie—on board, things are looking good.

Chapter 26
No News is Good News

It's hard for the media to let a good story die. The Mega Millions Lottery win from earlier in the month is one such story.

Recent news reports had revealed nothing new since the previous announcements that someone in Manhattan had won. Not a peep. That didn't stop the NYC TV stations. They would just run an update with nothing new to report. They would re-run their earlier segments and comments with heightened curiosity and speculation. And so, they did.

Kate is home, her MacBook on her lap, and the TV is on in the background. She has just purchased something at Amazon; she loves Amazon Prime. It allows her to find whatever she wants to buy, and with one click, presto—the package is delivered the next day.

As she navigates to her Gmail account, she looks up at the TV as it turns to the midday news. The reporter is giving an update on the lottery story, questioning where and who the winner is.

As she pauses, she recalls the strange conversation she had had with Jeremiah a few days prior when he had asked her what they might do if they won. She can't place it, but she has a strange feeling. It isn't unusual for Jeremiah to go off into bizarre topics or ideas. And probably everybody is asking themselves, what would they do? Still, it felt strange.

Suddenly, Kate's phone rings, her attention diverted with a jolt.

"Hello," she answers sweetly, turning on the phone after the third ring.

It's her mother, and she goes down a rabbit hole of conversation for the next ten minutes.

Chapter 27
Sitting Down, Legally

The sign in the lobby reads Robbie Winthrop, Attorney at Law. She has a small office in a medium-sized commercial office building on the Long Island Expressway service road in Plainview. Her office suite has an unattended reception area and three rooms: a private office where Robbie spends most of her time, a decent-sized filing room, and a conference room for real estate closings and client conferences.

Before Jeremiah can plop down in a chair, Robbie charges toward him with arms outstretched, ready for a big welcome hug.

"How are you, darling?" she says. "And how is your beautiful family?"

They exchange pleasantries as Robbie guides them into the conference room. Jeremiah has always admired Robbie. Such a sharp cookie. Managing as a single mom after her divorce, she has sustained her small, but thriving legal practice.

"Things are great with Kate, the kids, and me. And you, my dear?" Jeremiah responds.

"No complaints here!"

As they get settled at the conference table, Robbie at the head and Jeremiah to her right, Robbie asks, "So, what can I do for you?"

"Robbie, I have this special project, and I want you involved. I will need your expertise on a few fronts and your wise counsel overall."

Without hesitation, he continues telling Robbie how he'd won the lottery and that he wanted to claim the prize anonymously through a trust—and lastly, relating his intention to gift much of the winnings to charity through his request for proposal idea.

Her response: "Wow. That is some special project." Without any apparent concern, she continues, "That all seems doable. A trust or two is not a big deal. We will need to meet with the lottery to agree on details, like anonymity and a possible announcement. I don't think you should be at such a meeting. Your idea of using an RFP is an innovative way to choose a recipient. You will need to have a sound approach for rolling it out and working it through to the final winner."

Jeremiah sits quietly, taking in Robbie's remarks. He is pleased she has not brought up any serious issues. Her calm responses only underscore his initial impression that she is the right person for his legal needs.

"I'd be happy to work with you on this, Jeremiah. Absolutely. Your basic plan seems sound. But keep in mind that there will be a lot of noise and unforeseen things coming up, particularly in the media. So, I'll do everything I can to achieve your goals and insulate you from being exposed."

"Good. As far as a lottery meeting, I agree I don't need to be there. I have a trusted friend and tax advisor who can be in my place. We'll figure those details out another time."

Robbie has another thought: "Maybe we should reach out to the lottery sooner than later. You know, get a sense of how they handle this sort of thing?"

"Good idea, Robbie."

"Okay, I'll get on it," she promises.

"This is wonderful. I'm so glad you're with me on this, Robbie. I cannot tell you how much it means to me."

"No worries, Jeremiah. No biggie at all."

He smiles. They have covered all the items that have been floating in Jeremiah's head.

As Jeremiah heads to his car, he feels more empowered. Robbie has embraced his ideas. He feels relieved that she didn't laugh him out of her office. *I'm not crazy, after all,* is his parting thought.

Chapter 28
Thoughts of Work and God

With Jeremiah's new RFP project now taking shape in a tangible way, he still needs to contend with his day job at The Way Home. There are meetings, conference calls, audits, budget reports, and site visits, among the many unforeseen demands on his time to help his colleagues with technology issues.

The Way Home also has some large shelter projects under construction, which require IT planning and support. They are building four shelters in Brooklyn, one in Staten Island, and have four conversions ongoing in Manhattan and Queens.

But the big project they have been pending for months is the potential headquarters relocation to Harlem. There have been numerous delays because the landlord and The Way Home cannot agree on leasing terms. Relocating all systems and infrastructure requires much planning. The IT team would also need to transport all the desktop computers and office equipment for more than one hundred employees. It is an enormous project, and it appears to be close to happening soon.

Not surprisingly, there would be a lot of pressure to accomplish the move seamlessly. It is frustrating given the low IT staffing levels. Maybe they would get some short-term temps or interns for some of the menial tasks, but that would only help in the interim.

It is also frustrating working with Jeremiah's colleagues. Departments operate in silos. There seems to be no enterprise-wide holistic management perspective. As a result, staff would panic for assistance and services at the last minute— they rarely anticipate their needs.

These experiences support the case for skipping an RFP process altogether. Jeremiah can easily avoid dealing with other non-profits; they probably have similar issues as The Way Home.

Not only are these job aspects weighing on Jeremiah—at some point along the line during his regular lottery bets, but Jeremiah would often make implied deals with God. There were no words exchanged, only his thoughts and impressions that God would agree to allow him to win the lottery, but only if he did something benefiting humanity like setting up college funds for the poor or letting the money "pass" through to a charity.

No one could know about this "deal"—it would label Jeremiah as a crackpot. Or would it? Who would believe he made a non-verbal, unwritten deal with God without even a handshake? What if the press got a hold of this somehow? And what would happen if Jeremiah reneged on his part of the deal? How might God retaliate?

What would Kate think of this deal with God? How Jeremiah tortures himself with such absurd thoughts!

His cell phone rings, slapping him back to reality. It's Harley. He answers, "Hi, honey, what's up?"

Chapter 29
"Hey man, I need your help."

Eli had retired from Con Edison about a year and a half ago. He and Jeremiah didn't keep in close contact, just an occasional phone call or email. Mostly, Eli would send jokes to a group of their buddies. And often, this might generate a thread for a day or two.

Since retirement, Eli continued with his tax preparation practice; his busiest time was the first four months of the year. Throughout the rest of the year, Eli might be traveling the country visiting one of his three daughters, skiing, or just hanging out and enjoying life as a retiree.

Whenever Jeremiah wants Eli's opinion on an idea, he doesn't hesitate to pick up the phone. Having just met with Robbie, he is en route to the gym, an excellent time to make hands-free calls from his car.

Jeremiah dials Eli, and via Bluetooth, a ringing sound comes through the car's speakers from his iPhone. Two rings later, and Jeremiah hears Eli's voice say, "Hello?"

"Hey man, how are things?"

"Just peachy," comes Eli's signature response. "And you, Jeremiah?"

"Awesome, Eli! Listen, I have a bit of a situation here, and I am going to need some expert financial advice and thought you would be able to fill the bill."

"Sure, is everything okay?"

"Well, Eli, to tell the truth, things couldn't be better," continues Jeremiah.

Eli has known Jeremiah for over forty years and begins to suspect something unusual in Jeremiah's voice. Jeremiah has always been a very positive person, but there is something extra today.

"What gives?" Eli asks.

There is a long pause.

"Are you there, Jeremiah?"

"I don't know how to tell you this, Eli," Jeremiah finally replies.

"Well, spit it out, man!" Eli returns with a growing tone of impatience.

Another long pause.

At last, Jeremiah says in a sober tone, "Okay, but this is on the down-low. So you cannot tell anyone. No one at all can know. Okay?"

Eli is bursting with anticipation and impatience, wanting to know what is happening here with his old friend. "Yeah, sure, fine," he agrees reluctantly, only to get Jeremiah to continue.

Slowly Jeremiah starts, "Eli, you are not going to believe this. And I swear I am not bullshitting you. It's just that…" and Jeremiah trails off.

"What is it, Jeremiah, for crying out load?"

"Eli, the impossible has happened. A total freaking miracle has just fallen into my lap."

Eli's mind is now racing. If it were a new job, Jeremiah would have just come out with it. Perhaps he is retiring, muses Eli. Maybe he is getting a super sweet package. Possibly, it is a new job with some fantastic organization or CEO. Or perhaps one of his kids is getting married to some zillionaire? Maybe Kate's business is finally taking off with a substantial new account. None of these scenarios seem that extreme to justify Jeremiah's strange behavior.

At last, Jeremiah abruptly interrupts Eli's thoughts, half laughing, half whispering, "I won, Eli! I won the big Mega Millions Lottery; you know the one from a few weeks ago. All of it! Four hundred and thirty million! I won!!"

Eli is stunned. Over the years, he and Jeremiah would pool together and play the lottery, never winning more than a few dollars. But they had always dreamed of a "big payday."

"That's awesome, Jeremiah! The odds of winning are crazy! You are one lucky dude. Someone upstairs must really like you or have a big job for you to do," responds Eli enthusiastically.

"I know. It's crazy. I haven't told many people, just a few I trust. I am still coming to terms with this and want to have a solid plan before I do anything," continues Jeremiah.

"That's wise, Jeremiah! Very smart to make a plan first. You know I'm not the jealous type—just don't forget your old buddy, Eli," replies Eli gleefully.

"I am going to need your help, Eli. I will need some expert advice on a lot of different things. And don't worry—I'll take good care of you!"

"Sure, absolutely, Jeremiah."

"I have to go now, Eli. But let's meet soon. Maybe you can come to the city for lunch or something? And please, keep this quiet, okay?"

"No worries. I'm here. Whatever you need, don't hesitate to ask."

"Good. Talk soon. Bye."

"Bye."

Chapter 30
Guess What, Kate?

Having done much thinking about the RFP, it is time to bring Kate in on it for real. Besides Kate's creative side, she is a caring and generous person. She loves her creature comforts, though, and can never get enough escapism. Kate is also very interested in holocaust history and has read almost every book on the subject.

Jeremiah believes she can align with his desire to make a real impact with his lottery winnings. Perhaps sharing the prize with those in poverty will appeal to her. He trusts his intuition, and his wife; she is righteous, open to doing good deeds and mitzvahs. She'll go for this— it just needs to be presented in a way she can relate to, and in a way, she will be happy with the outcome.

Deeper within the recesses of Jeremiah's mind is the idea of writing a book about this whole unbelievable story. It would be fun and something he's always dreamt of doing. Of course, there is also the potential for additional income if it sold, but that does not matter.

However, the book idea might only scratch the surface. Jeremiah's story of winning the lottery, the RFP, and distributing a fortune to charity would make a great movie! Kate would love that! She could be a producer and become deeply involved in all aspects of the project. That could be one way to go—the movie.

Should he start with the movie idea and roll back to winning the lottery, or start at the beginning and end with the movie?

Either way, it would be a lot for Kate to take in. Regardless, Jeremiah needs to dig deep to bring her along on this adventure. He trusts his instincts—it will be fine. Besides, Robbie, Eli, and Ruby are on board. How crazy can this be if three people who Jeremiah highly regards think this is workable?

Ryan has come home for dinner. He has a doctor's appointment the next day on the island. Jeremiah is mustering the confidence to share the obsession that has consumed him over the past few weeks in the living room.

Finally, he says to Kate, "Guess what?"

He starts at the beginning and doesn't get too detailed. His approach is straightforward, easy to understand, bulleted points about the RFP, and possible book and movie ideas. While pacing the room, he reinforces that they must do something of substance. He makes a point that they will have tens of millions to do whatever they want.

Lastly, he concludes by saying how their lives will change forever, no matter what they do. So why not do something remarkable, something phenomenal? Then, whatever the decision, they will never be in need.

Chapter 31
Kate Responds

Ryan has not heard all of this before. He sits quietly, contemplating. On the other hand, Kate is flabbergasted, her mind racing between euphoria and her husband's lunacy. Finally, she states emphatically from the couch, "This is crazy, totally insane! Why not just take the money and donate some of it to a few charities you know and like? Why go through such an elaborate undertaking?"

She has a good point, thinks Jeremiah.

Still, he tries to explain his rationale. "This RFP thing has a sense of real adventure. It will engage so many more people, much more so than just quietly making donations. I know it's not the usual way, but why not? It could be fun and exciting! Think about the impact it would have on society if done right."

Finally, he says, "Besides, from a place deep inside me, I feel called to do this in this way. I have always wanted to make a difference in my life. The RFP is how I will do that. Please trust me," he pleads. "We will have many partners in this, and we will not regret it—I know it—I swear to God!"

The silence in the room from Jeremiah's big announcement is deafening. It seems to last an eternity. Jeremiah cannot tell if Kate is on board or is going to kill him. Ryan doesn't say a word either; he knows better.

Finally, Kate starts laughing.

"You know, Jeremiah, I can't believe this whole thing and that you are going through all these machinations. True, a hundred and fifty million is a lot of money. And we could get by on fifty, or even less. But, on the other hand, it seems so hard to take the path you are inclined to follow."

Ryan and Jeremiah say nothing.

"I could go either way, I guess; keep it all or give away much of it," she continues.

Jeremiah jumps in, saying, "I have spoken with Robbie on this. She doesn't think I'm crazy!"

Kate doesn't say anything, but Jeremiah can tell she does not like hearing that he has spoken to Robbie first.

"And Eli is going to be advising me, too. So, you will also be key in all of this, I promise."

She stares blankly back at him, not knowing what is best.

"And another thing, Kate. And I know this part will sound even crazier, but collecting the money and awarding it to a worthy charity would make for a great book and an even greater movie if we successfully pull this off. Publishers and Hollywood would love this story. They'd be all over it. And you would be responsible for all of that. And it wouldn't cost us a dime."

"You're right. That is even crazier. Interesting, but still nuts."

Jeremiah can tell she is chewing on the movie idea.

"Okay, Kate, you don't have to commit now. Just keep an open mind—we are not doing anything immediately. Just trust me and keep it quiet. That's all I ask. I am not one hundred percent sure this is a smart move, but I am willing to see where it goes. Know this one thing for sure: our lives will never be the same, no matter what we do."

She nods.

Jeremiah walks toward Kate, and she rises. They hug. A fragile agreement of sorts is in place. All the while, Ryan can only spectate, and then they all move to the kitchen, debating dinner possibilities.

Chapter 32
The Request for Proposal

With everything out in the open with Kate, it is time to start working through the details. A request for proposal will be the vehicle for Jeremiah's project to donate most of his lottery winnings. He will need to construct a framework, process, and sundry documents required to actualize his vision. He starts feverishly writing down all the details that have been incubating in his mind.

The RFP framework should involve a broad solicitation of at least two to three hundred non-profits in the health and human services sector who will be required to complete a brief qualifying questionnaire.

Jeremiah's team will select at least ten NPs who submitted the qualifying questionnaire to complete a second, more in-depth application. Of the ten-plus agencies that follow through with the second questionnaire, Jeremiah and his advisors will choose three or four finalists. They will then participate in in-person interviews or Skype meetings.

Jeremiah has decided to limit his focus to NYC only. He has also determined that he will need:

- A selection committee

- A rules and requirements document

- A list of potential candidates and means of getting the word out

- An announcement document for the RFP with a web address to obtain the qualifying applications

- A qualifying questionnaire, a second questionnaire, transmittal letters, and evaluation forms

- A post office box

- A timeline and various press statements

Jeremiah's selection team will assist in determining the recipient and double as his workgroup to accomplish various tasks. While the RFP process progresses, Jeremiah intends to continue working at The Way Home as if nothing unusual is afoot. His committee will include:

- Kate

- Robbie Winthrop, attorney and point person

- Eli Fleming, financial advisor

- Ava Starling

- Ruby Miller

And there may be one or two other team members, perhaps from Jeremiah's contacts in the non-profit world. One name pops up first: Elizabeth Gilbert, the current head of the NYC Housing Coalition, an advocacy group whose members are providers of shelters, apartments, and crisis centers. There is also a similar advocacy group for health and human services. Maybe someone from that organization could join the committee or, at the least, help provide candidates for the grant.

Next, Jeremiah grabs another notepad and starts scribbling on a blank page. In the center at the top is written:

THE RFP RULES

He stops. He needs a name for this whole thing, so he drops the pad and pen, gets up, and paces about the room. One idea that comes right away is the Wayne Dyer grant, honoring and commemorating the recently passed and renowned self-help author and teacher Jeremiah has been following for years. Jeremiah's great-grandfather's name surfaces as another alternative. None of these ideas are profoundly inspiring to Jeremiah. He sits back down in a chair, reclining back and staring up at the ceiling for minutes. Then it strikes him.

THE "RISING-UP" GRANT

He likes it well enough and will stick with it for now. If the selection committee has a better idea, so be it. So Jeremiah goes back to his pad. He crosses out THE RFP RULES and writes THE "RISING-UP" GRANT RULES, and begins outlining:

- Must be an NYC non-profit agency in the health and human services sector

- Must have annual revenue of $50 million or more

- Must have twenty or more years of providing services

- Applicants are required to complete a preliminary qualifying application and deliver it by mail within two weeks to a specified post office box

- Those applicants who are selected will be required to complete a second application and return it by mail within two weeks

- Of those who complete the second application, the selection committee will choose three to four candidates for in-person interviews

- The finalists' CEO, CFO, and Chief Program Officer will attend interviews

- All decisions are final and subject to the discretion of the selection committee

"Great," considers Jeremiah. He sketches out a rough timeline following the grant announcement:

THE REQUEST FOR PROPOSAL

THE "RISING-UP" GRANT TIMELINE

- Issue qualifying application—allow two weeks to complete and return

- Evaluate qualifying applications and select ten semi-finalists—two weeks

- Issue second application—allow two weeks to complete and return

- Evaluate second applications and select four finalists—two weeks

- Schedule in-person interviews—two weeks

- Select grantee—two weeks

According to this rough timeline estimate, this entire process will take twelve weeks minimum, but it's good to go for now.

According to Jeremiah's outline for the Rising-Up grant, he will need two questionnaires. First, he will want to know the standard identifying applicant information like the agency's name, annual revenue, years in service, mission, and contacts. Additionally, answers to the following questions will be necessary for framing each candidate's profile.

THE REQUEST FOR PROPOSAL

QUALIFYING APPLICATION

- What impact is your organization making?
- Describe your organization's culture.
- What makes your organization the ideal recipient over all the other applicants?
- Describe what your employees like about working at your organization.
- Describe how your organization achieves operational excellence.
- How would you use $100 million, and what impact would that have on the people you serve and your organization?
- Describe your CEO's management style.

SECOND APPLICATION

Give some examples of how your organization has successfully collaborated with other non-profits, government, etc.

- What is the greatest challenge your organization has faced recently, and how was it overcome?
- Describe your organization's staff development policy and programs.
- Describe the nature of your current funding sources.
- Name and elaborate on the three most significant aspects in today's world that affect our ability as a society to operate more effectively?

- And how does your organization and its mission relate positively to improving those aspects?
- These are excellent questions. There could be more later. And which should go with which questionnaire?

Jeremiah takes a deep breath and sighs loudly. Second thoughts are lurking: *Maybe I should decide more arbitrarily on who to select. Or maybe I should keep all the winnings. This RFP project is going to be a big job!*

Chapter 33
Checking in with the Team

Jeremiah had not mentioned his intention to donate most of the jackpot when he told Eli about winning. However, now that he has a better idea of how he'll proceed with the RFP, he wants to get Eli's thoughts about it.

After three rings, Eli picks up and greets Jeremiah. They exchange the usual pleasantries. Getting to the point, Jeremiah starts by saying, "So Eli, I wanted to fill you in a bit on my thinking about what I am planning so far with the lottery money."

"I'm listening," replies Eli.

"Well, first, I plan to give away a large chunk of it to charity and keep the rest. I'm not sure of the actual numbers yet. I estimate the take home after taxes would be about one-seventy, and I am thinking about giving away, say, a hundred to one-twenty."

"Wow, that's a big donation!"

"True, but do I need more than fifty or seventy million? I don't think so."

"I know, but…"

"But nothing. Why be a *chazir?* What difference would it make, keeping fifty, seventy-five, or one hundred, let alone all of it? I doubt any. The more I get, the more headaches I will have."

Without letting Eli interrupt, he continues, "Whatever the amount I decide to donate, it will be to a worthy charity. I will set up an RFP to choose a charity from NYC's health and human services sector."

Eli is taking this all in and, after a few moments, replies, "Well, if you are going to give away money to a charity, your RFP idea sounds okay. Why not just donate to a Jewish charity or a non-profit you know or have had some experience with?"

"I suppose I could do that, but I don't have many connections with Jewish charities. I am most familiar with health and human service organizations, having worked in them for over twenty-five years. There are many agencies that I am familiar with that would make excellent candidates.

"That sounds reasonable," responds Eli.

"And here is the crazy part: this is a good story. Good enough, I believe, for a book or even a movie. All of which could be a lot of fun and profitable."

"You've been thinking very hard about this. Just stay focused for now on collecting the money and determining who to donate to."

"You're right. That's why I will need your help, Eli, to navigate through all of this. Right now, these are just ideas taking shape. I plan to have a selection committee—you will be on it, okay?"

"Sure, but I don't know much about charities," answers Eli.

Multiple thoughts bombard Jeremiah. He will probably have to compensate the committee. He will also need a distribution trust for expenses and sundry distributions in addition to grants. And Eli will need to create an accounting system to keep track of transactions. Finally, payments to committee members will need to be either lump sums or annual pay-outs to minimize tax consequences.

"Good. Don't worry about your lack of experience with charities; it's your common sense that I want," acknowledges Jeremiah. "Not sure you ever met Robbie Winthrop—she is my attorney and is also on the team. She is setting up a meeting with the lottery on Long Island. She will need you to go with her, Eli."

"No problem."

"And there will also be a meeting at the bank in NYC; I will need you there as well."

"You sure are going to keep me busy. I'm supposed to be retired." Chuckling, Eli continues, "No big deal. Just let me know where and when."

"Great. Tell me, do you think I'm nuts with this RFP thing?"

"Nope, not at all. Sure, it sounds a little wacky since it's unheard of, but it also sounds very viable. It could be a wild ride."

They both laugh.

"Many thanks, amigo. I'll be in touch. Ciao!"

"Bye."

They both hang up, and still with his iPhone, Jeremiah texts Ruby.

Hey.

Hi, Jeremiah. What's up? she replies.

Remember when I said I wanted you on my team when we had lunch? Well, I'm planning on creating an RFP to select the charity that will receive the donation— I want you to help me with that, returns Jeremiah.

Yes, I remember. What do you need me to do? writes Ruby.

Most importantly, be on the selection committee, helping me decide who gets the donation—and helping in other ways where needed, somewhat like an assistant and advisor.

Sure, no problem! Whatever I can do to help, you just say the word, responds Ruby.

Super! Thank you so much. More to come :), Jeremiah closes.

Jeremiah releases a deep sigh and settles back, comforted, knowing he has two allies he trusts and values. Glancing at his watch, he sees he's got enough time to catch an early train home. He straightens up his desk and gathers his belongings before heading to the door. Hopefully, a peaceful weekend awaits with quiet time and some rest, maybe a movie and a nice dinner.

Chapter 34
Family Time

It is the Saturday before Thanksgiving. Everyone is coming home for the weekend. Both Ryan and Harley have plans with friends much later in the evening. In the meantime, they will order dinner from one of the local Italian restaurants.

It seems the ideal time to discuss the RFP and inform Harley of the lottery win. It could be dicey, though. Harley has a way of reacting to things without the full benefit of life experience. She might think it's idiotic to give away so much money. That is the probable judgment most people would conclude upon hearing Jeremiah's intentions for his lottery winnings. He even suspects that Ryan and Kate are in that camp as well but are just hiding it.

Nonetheless, to not include Harley now in all that is happening would be a big mistake. She would be pissed. Jeremiah can picture her saying, "You told Ryan, but not me? You always ignore and overlook me!"

He will sit tight until she is home and then tell her—he wants to do it in person.

They place their order for pick up, and twenty minutes later, Jeremiah leaves to retrieve dinner. He is back in ten minutes. Kate has set the table. She takes the large bag containing the meals, empties the to-go containers onto dinner plates, and puts them on the table. Included in the order are rolls with butter, and Kate deposits them in the table's center. Harley places one-liter bottles of Diet Coke and spring water next to them and puts glasses and silverware at each seating.

The meal doesn't last more than five minutes. Ryan gobbles down his serving almost immediately, with Jeremiah a close second. Kate and Harley just pick and do not finish their portions. Ryan is still eating samples from Harley and Kate's plates. Kate refills her water glass while reviewing her plans for Thanksgiving and all the things she needs to get done.

As Jeremiah gets up to make coffee, Kate takes some fresh fruit from the fridge for dessert. With the platter situated on the table, Jeremiah begins to tell his story of the lottery. For Ryan and Kate, it is a review. Looking over at Harley, she sits there riveted.

He discloses that he had won, including the amount and his entire plan. However, he keeps it short and sweet, not getting bogged down on small details.

To his surprise, Harley takes it all in very positively. She thinks the idea is sick and wants to be a part of it. She doesn't mention anything about not hearing the news sooner. Ryan, on the other hand, starts challenging the rationality of donating so much.

"Why give away more than half? What if we run out someday?" he asks.

Jeremiah says, "First of all, it's not we, the four of us. It's we, the two of us, me and Mom. And second: forty, fifty, maybe seventy million is a lot of money! I can assure you we will never run out, no matter what we do. This plan has the opportunity to grow into many other possibilities. There is a great story here for a possibly best-selling book or movie. I bet some people would pay handsomely for this story."

Ryan is smiling, not entirely buying Jeremiah's pitch, but chooses not to pursue it.

"Your mom and I will come to a decision on what to do and how much to keep after we get more professional advice," continues Jeremiah.

Kate interjects, "I'm still on the fence on this. However, I can see arguments for keeping it all and for making a large charitable donation."

"Well, I think it's dope, Dad! You are a genius," Harley adds.

They all crack up laughing.

"I don't know if I'd say that. But I trust my intuition here, and it is telling me this is the right way to go. Just trust me. We will work out the amounts and details," Jeremiah says. "Oh, and another thing: if we run out, it's our fault for being wasteful and poorly managed."

They all nod and smile at each other, knowing there is no issue here. Anyone would die for this kind of problem.

Chapter 35
A Walk in the Park

Julie Stevenson is probably Kate's best friend, depending on how one might define a best friend. She is like a sister to Kate. They have a long history, growing up in Jericho.

Julie is a successful mom, as strange as that sounds. Of course, being a mom isn't considered a career, but if one were to look back on Julie's life, she had succeeded in managing a household and raising three adult sons. Her second grandchild is on the way. And she had celebrated her thirty-sixth wedding anniversary to Jack over the summer.

She hasn't had an easy life, per se. Although she enjoys all the comforts, being married to a doctor and living in Long Island, her life is often in constant turbulence. Raising three boys was a lot of work. There were bar mitzvahs, preparing them for summer camp, getting them through high school and into college, family holidays, vacations, weddings. She also takes care of her aging mother.

In some sense, Julie is like a family manager/mentor for Kate. She is someone Kate can reach out to for tips, ideas, and suggestions when she needs advice for any family matter. Julie has seen it all.

Regularly Julie and Kate go walking in a nearby neighborhood park as part of each other's exercise routines. During these walks, they catch up on whatever is going on in one another's lives. It also provides them an opportunity to vent, rant, complain or share current concerns either of them might have.

As they walk, Kate feels compelled to confide in Julie and tell her everything. Could Julie keep quiet about the lottery and Jeremiah's plans to donate the winnings? She is conflicted. Julie is terrible at keeping secrets, but Kate, nonetheless, trusts her deeply.

Their conversation drifts to Julie's anecdotes about her new one-month-old grandson.

"Julie, I need to tell you something important, and you can't tell anyone, not even Jack!" Kate begins when Julie pauses.

"Kate, you know you can trust me to keep a secret," is Julie's reply.

They both stop and look at each other and start laughing.

"No, really, this is very important. Please promise me and don't make me regret telling you!" Kate insists.

"Okay, okay, I promise. I won't say a word to anyone. I promise," Julie pledges.

"Good."

Slowly, Kate begins to relate the details around Jeremiah's win and pending intentions. Next, she gives a vivid account of what has transpired thus far. Finally, she shares how undecided she is, despite her agreeing with Jeremiah on his plan.

Julie is amazed. Never has she heard such an incredible story. Winning the lottery is unreal enough, but giving it away? That is ridiculous.

"I can't believe you would let him do that," Julie finally says. "I've never heard of anything so crazy. Winning all that money and then just giving it away?"

"We wouldn't give it all away—we'd still keep a sizable chunk for ourselves," replies Kate.

"I don't care. It makes no sense to me! You've got to stop him. Jack knows some good lawyers. Get a restraining order!"

"Julie! Really? I don't want to go that route. We need to work this out ourselves," Kate vehemently protests. "Julie, don't go nuts on me with this. We will figure it out, and it will be just fine. I just needed to share this with you, my dearest friend. I trust Jeremiah's sensibilities."

Julie answers, "I'm not sure I do. Don't be naïve. Think about what you could do with *all* that money!"

Kate is at a defining moment with Julie. Julie is coming from a place of fear while Kate, not so. Kate is realizing the contrast and is growing more confident in Jeremiah's intentions.

"You know Julie. Everything is not always about the dollars. We will probably wind up with about fifty million when all is said and done and doing a tremendous mitzvah at the same time."

Kate knows they won't agree on this, at least for now. She closes with, "I know you disagree with me. And I, too, still have my doubts. Just don't do or say anything to anyone. I'll let you know what we decide when we do. Okay?"

Reluctantly, Julie concedes, "Okay, Kate. No worries."

Chapter 36
Trust Me

As the lawyer on the team, Robbie's charge is to create two trusts for Jeremiah. She had taken a class in trusts and estates back in law school, but that was some time ago. *How hard could it be?* she wonders.

Back at her office, she Googles: *how to claim lottery winnings through trusts*. Many results appear. After rummaging through the results, a revocable trust seems to be the best way to go. She also checks her law books on specialty contracts, powers of attorney, and letters of authorization.

After about an hour of studying, Robbie has the steps to create a legal structure to collect the lottery funds and keep Jeremiah anonymous and protected. First, he will need to sign a power of attorney (POA), giving Robbie the authority to act on his behalf. Second, he will need to provide a letter of authorization (LOA) instructing and authorizing Robbie to do the following:

- Create a revocable trust (Trust 1) for the collection of funds from the Lottery

- Create a second trust (Trust 2) for the distribution of funds collected in the first trust

- Sign the winning lottery ticket to claim the winnings on Jeremiah's behalf. She will surrender the signed ticket and a notarized original of Trust 1 to the Lottery for registration and to claim the winnings

This approach assures Jeremiah's anonymity. The lottery will only see Trust 1, which has no reference to Jeremiah. The POA will enable Robbie to execute all the necessary tasks to collect the lottery money. And the LOA will document that Jeremiah is the rightful owner of the lottery ticket and Robbie's authorization to complete the various tasks on his behalf.

Trust 1 will be named "The Rising-Up Collection Trust." The specific elements of it are:

- The Settlor (creator of the trust)—Robbie Winthrop, the attorney acting on behalf of her client

- Trustee (responsible for the trust)—Jeremiah's Bank

- Trust Res (assets or property of the trust)—lottery ticket & collected funds

- Beneficiary—Trust 2

Trust 2 will be named "Phoenix Warehouse Trust." Its elements will be:

- Settlor—"The Rising-Up Collection Trust"

- Trustee—Jeremiah's Bank

- Trust Res—The lottery winnings

- Beneficiary—Jeremiah Baldwin, his family, his associates, and grantee(s) of the RFP

The final step required will be to file the completed, notarized trusts with the Mineola County Clerk's Office, a mere formality.

Immersed in warm satisfaction, Robbie lets out a sigh. It is not complicated but lays out a viable solution to the problem, and she has done it! With the two trusts designed, it is time to execute.

Grabbing her iPhone, Robbie shoots Jeremiah a text: *Hey Jeremiah, good news! Figured out the structure for the trusts; will prep today. We should meet up for you to sign docs as soon as I have completed them.*

Jeremiah does not respond right away, but when he does, he sends a big smiley face. A second message is sent to her immediately afterward: *You go, girl!!!!!! I am free all this week. Just say when.*

Robbie replies: *OK, let's shoot for tomorrow early afternoon,* with a big heart emoji.

Done, confirms Jeremiah.

Both Robbie and Jeremiah are smiling, though geographically, they are miles apart. Nevertheless, it is coming together, and they both know it will work.

Chapter 37
Thanksgiving 2018

Jeremiah is awake. It's Thanksgiving morning, around five a.m., the usual time he gets up. But today, he does not have to go to work or do anything other than assisting Kate in preparing their Thanksgiving meal.

As he lies in bed, mind wandering, Jeremiah decides to go into the den and meditate in the early morning quiet. His meditation time is often the most satisfying experience of his day and almost impossible to communicate to anyone who hasn't experienced it. Sitting, he focuses only on his breath, receiving a level of stillness, being at pure peace with connectedness and oneness to the infinite energy of the universe.

Fifty minutes pass in a blink of an eye. Jeremiah reflects on the day ahead—Thanksgiving—and what it means to him as he comes out of his deep calm. He has many things for which to be thankful. The lottery win, however, is not at the top of his list.

He starts ticking off the list, firstly, this divine relationship with the creator, his higher power, the source of all, who he connects with through his mediation and prayer. This relationship is the engine for his life, and all that follows. Then, finally, he pauses and wonders whether he'd be as thankful if he weren't so blessed with good fortune. But, of course, the answer is yes with trust and faith, the two final pieces that complete this cosmic puzzle called reality.

Jeremiah's thoughts descend back to Earth to more tangible things. His health is excellent, with no diseases or illness, no ailments, or issues. He has love in his life from Kate, Ryan, and Harley. He is thankful for their home and having a job that sustains them and fulfills him professionally. In addition, he has friends and interests.

He thinks back to his mother and father, who have enabled him to be the man he is today. He silently sends them a message of appreciation and gratitude for all their love and support.

And then there's my mind, abilities, and all the opportunities I enjoy, Jeremiah thinks. He pauses, feeling pure joy—so much for which to be thankful! *Thank you, Lord!*

After a few minutes, it's time to get moving, but first, some coffee. Then a little exercise and off to run those last-minute errands Kate has itemized for him.

Thanksgiving this year is a small dinner at home, just the Baldwins and Kate's mom. Nothing fancy, only the annual event without any frills. The same as years before, the menu is a roasted turkey, baked salmon, sweet potatoes, steamed string beans, and some salad to start, an array of soft drinks, and dessert: ice cream and apple pie to complete the meal.

The menu hasn't changed in almost twenty-five years. Kate handles everything, and Jeremiah pitches in wherever he can. In other words, he does what he's told. And as usual, his primary task is to slice the turkey.

When Jeremiah has returned from the gym and the store where he picked up the extras from the list Kate had left on the counter, Kate is in the kitchen, arranging the dinner table. The TV is on, and occasionally she looks over to see images of the Macy's Thanksgiving Day Parade.

The turkey has been roasting for only an hour, but its aroma already wafts throughout the house. Harley and Ryan are home but have not yet made appearances; they are sleeping or watching television in their rooms.

In previous years Kate's brother and sister-in-law would come, but this year they declined. Instead, they had opted to go on a cruise to celebrate their fortieth wedding anniversary.

Before long, it's three o'clock, and buzzers in the kitchen are going off. Kate's mom arrived shortly before, and Jeremiah and Ryan are watching a football game in the living room. On the coffee table are some appetizers. Harley is in the kitchen, talking to her grandmother. Ryan hollers, "So when are we going to eat, Mom?"

"A few minutes. Now go wash up," is the reply from the kitchen.

The table looks like a picture in a lifestyle magazine. The "good china" shimmers in the reflecting glow of the adjacent lit long stem candles, and the five of them take their seats at the table. Harley complements Kate on how beautiful the flower arrangement looks.

As the food arrives, the conversation ceases as everyone starts serving themselves. Soft moans of satisfaction come as the sampling begins. Everything tastes fantastic—Thanksgiving is the unanimous favorite holiday of the year.

Quickly their meals are consumed. Only Ryan reaches for seconds. No one else is hungry for more. Kate comments on how it takes so many hours of preparation, and in ten minutes, it's over. As they sit and wait for dessert, Harley asks no one in particular, "So, what are you thankful for this year?"

Every year this question gets raised at the Baldwin dinner table. The responses are routine but genuine. Ryan is thankful for his exciting job that makes it possible for him to travel internationally and live independently in NYC. Kate is grateful for their life together and hopes things always remain the same. Her mom is just happy to be with everyone this year. Finally, it is Harley's turn—she is thankful for her parents and their home.

Now Jeremiah states that he can only say that he is grateful for this life, even with all of its ups and downs. Then, getting philosophical, he rambles on, saying how, without the darkness, how would we know the light? And he says he's most thankful for his loving family. Turning to Kate's ninety-year-old mother, he says, "Mom, we have a little secret to tell you."

"Oh, I love secrets," Kate's mom replies demurely.

"We won the lottery a few weeks ago, and we are set for life," Jeremiah declares.

"Oh, that's nice. So now you won't have to work so hard," Mom replies kindly and takes a sip of her coffee.

Everyone laughs softly, and dessert dishes start circling. Soon they are done scarfing down the sweets, and the clearing of the table begins. Kate moves to the sink to prep the dishwasher, and another Thanksgiving sunset begins.

Chapter 38
A Trip to the Lottery

About three weeks have elapsed since Jeremiah learned of his lottery win. Everyone agrees that he should not attend the meeting with the lottery officials. His mere presence might give away that he is the actual winner.

Attending the meeting from his team are Robbie, Eli, and Ruby. They are meeting a deputy commissioner named Steve Granson. Jeremiah had Googled Granson, not finding much other than an old LinkedIn page in need of updating. Ruby and Eli will be joining Robbie at the lottery offices on Zeckendorf Boulevard near the Roosevelt Field Shopping Mall. The plan is for Jeremiah to pick them up at the Mineola train station and drive them to the meeting.

The lottery offices are in a drab one-story building near the entrance to the Meadowbrook Parkway. When Jeremiah arrives with Eli and Ruby, Robbie is already waiting in her car ten minutes before the three o'clock meeting.

Robbie, Eli, and Ruby had not previously met each other in person but had talked on the phone the day before to prep for the meeting. They all get out of their respective cars and converge near the building entrance, exchanging greetings. As Jeremiah remains in his car, his heart begins to race; he is nervous for no reason he can explain. He watches as his three partners disappear into the building, hoping for no wrinkles or surprises.

Robbie checks in with the receptionist, informing her that the three have an appointment with Mr. Granson. The woman behind the plexiglass partition picks up her phone and dials him. After about ten seconds, she speaks, her words barely audible. She turns back to the trio and instructs them to enter the adjacent locked door and that a conference room is located two doors down the hall on the left. The receptionist nods in the direction of the loud vibrating buzz from the doorway; Eli lunges to grab the doorknob.

Casually they walk to the appointed room and go inside. There is a long table with chairs evenly placed around it with enough space for at least twenty people. The room is empty. They congregate at one end near the door and randomly take seats on the table's far side. A woman and two men enter in a couple of minutes, wearing business attire appropriate for a government agency. Granson is the older man. His title at the lottery is Director of Claims. The other man is a junior attorney, and the woman is Granson's assistant.

Granson is lean, about six feet tall. He is wearing black horn-rimmed glasses and sports a closely cropped gray goatee. He appears to be in his mid-fifties. Robbie starts by introducing Eli and Ruby, and Granson does the same with his team.

Getting to the point, Robbie indicates that she is an attorney representing a family trust. The trust owns a winning lottery ticket, and the family intends to claim the prize anonymously, with the funds going into the trust.

Granson replies by saying that this is a scenario the lottery has dealt with previously. His assistant is taking notes recording all the statements from everyone present.

Robbie then asks, "Mr. Granson, I assume we will need to supply you with a copy of the trust document when we return to claim the winnings. Can you assure my clients' confidentiality?

"Yes, we will need a copy of the trust, and as I have mentioned, Ms. Winthrop, we have done this before. I'd say we have had over a hundred trust winners and have never had any breach in confidentiality."

"But Mr. Granson, this is the big Mega Millions drawing from a few weeks ago," returns Robbie.

Granson and his associates are stunned. There has never been a giant Mega Millions Lottery claimed by a trust at their office before—this is a first. The silence that hangs over the room lasts for only about ten seconds but feels like an hour.

"I see," Granson finally answers.

"Would the lottery be amenable to providing us with a signed affidavit guaranteeing my clients' confidentiality?" Robbie counters.

After a long pause, "We've never done that before, but I don't see why not. I will need to take that up with the senior director," is Granson's measured response.

"So, for now, let's assume you can provide us with an affidavit. What are the requirements needed to collect the winnings?" Robbie asks.

"There are only two requirements. First, you will need to submit a notarized original copy of the trust. Second, you will also need to surrender the ticket, signed by the trust's beneficiary or by the attorney acting on behalf of the trust," Granson replies. "Upon receipt of the trust and the signed ticket, we can process your claim and then register the transaction at the County Clerk's Office. Once that is completed, usually, within the same day, we are free to disperse funds. Then, we can wire the funds to your trustee's bank."

"When do you think we can have an answer on the affidavit? By Monday or Tuesday next week?" asks Robbie.

"Yes, that seems doable," Granson replies.

"So, if we have the ticket and copy of the trust to you by Wednesday, you should be able to process, register and close by Friday, next week?" Robbie inquires further.

"Yes, I believe so," concludes Granson.

"Great," Robbie chirps. "We will start getting the requirements together for you and will follow up early next week on the affidavit. By the way, Mr. Granson, will there be any announcement regarding the claiming of the jackpot?"

"Usually, with trust winners, there is no public announcement," Granson replies.

"Excellent," says Robbie.

"Well, I guess we have covered everything. If you have any additional questions, please feel free to call or email me," closes Granson, handing Robbie his business card.

Eli and Ruby had said nothing the entire meeting, but they are pleased with the outcome. All six get up from the table to leave the room.

Robbie thanks Granson and his colleagues for their time as everyone disperses. The meeting had lasted only twenty minutes, and Robbie had accomplished everything she wanted. She does not feel the affidavit will be an issue and probably not even necessary. In the parking lot, the three get into Jeremiah's car for a quick de-brief.

Chapter 39
A Trip to the Bank

Harry Mitchell, a wealth manager at JP Morgan, manages relationships with wealthy individuals for the bank. Jeremiah has a small trust that his mother had set up for his kids many years ago. Its size has declined slowly over the years due to distributions to cover college expenses. The current value is close to one hundred and fifty thousand.

Jeremiah had called Harry earlier in the week, and they agreed to meet at his mid-town office on Forty-second Street. As Robbie, Eli, and Jeremiah patiently wait in the reception area, market updates keep flashing on a flat-screen TV screen on the wall.

After about ten minutes, a tall attractive woman—Harry's assistant—walks over and announces they should follow her, at which point she escorts them to a small conference room. Harry is seated at the head of the table.

Harry offers everyone coffee or soft drinks after they are seated and introduced. All choose water, and the assistant leaves the room to retrieve the refreshments.

Jeremiah starts by explaining that Robbie is his attorney handling the creation of a trust. However, he does not share what the intent of the trust is. He then states that Eli has been his tax preparer for many years and has advised the Baldwins on numerous financial matters.

Harry is surprised by this meeting's nature; the existing trust has been dwindling over the years. He is curious as to where Jeremiah would get the money to fund a new trust. Robbie can see Harry's curiosity and steps in by saying, "Jeremiah is planning on receiving a large settlement soon."

Harry's eyes are smiling. More assets are coming under his care, he envisions. "Are you at liberty to provide any details on the nature, size, and timing of the settlement?" he asks.

Robbie's response is quick and emphatic. "The Baldwin's have retained me in this matter because the nature of the settlement requires the utmost confidentiality."

"I understand. If anything, JP Morgan values our clients' privacy above all else. I can assure you that we apply the strictest measures for confidentiality in matters such as this," replies Harry.

"Good. I can tell you now that we are looking for your firm to be the trustee of a new trust for Jeremiah Baldwin and his family's benefit. The settlement is to be one multi-million-dollar payment, and we expect it soon—within a week or so," Robbie counters.

She has opted to keep the lottery aspect private for now. There is no reason to reveal that detail if it isn't needed to get things started. And Robbie does not mention the RFP either, which is entirely irrelevant to the new trust relationship.

Not knowing the settlement's true nature, Harry can only assume it is an insurance settlement or perhaps a lawsuit involving Jeremiah or one of his family members. Frankly, he doesn't care how, why, or from where the cash will come. He only cares that it is new money.

Harry nods. "This all seems pretty straightforward. When you have a new trust agreement document completed, forward two notarized originals to me, and my office will establish a new account for you. When the funds are available, you can wire them directly to the new account. We will send wire instructions to you when the new account is set up. Once funds are received, they will be placed in an interest-bearing account until you have your investment strategy in place. We can also assist you with that. At the time you initiate the transfer of funds, please call me, and we can schedule an investment strategy meeting unless you'd like to do that now."

"We will reach out soon to schedule a meeting and determine how to invest the funds," Jeremiah interjects. "Our main priority is to get the funds here first."

"Agreed," replies Harry, and the whole table nods. Jeremiah looks around at Robbie and Eli. All are registering that there is nothing further to discuss.

"That's it, I guess," Jeremiah remarks. "Thank you, Harry, for your help on this."

"Any time, Jeremiah. Don't hesitate to call me if anything comes up. It is our pleasure to be of service to you and your family. And thank you for this opportunity."

They all rise and shake hands. Harry slowly escorts his visitors to the elevators, where they say their goodbyes. As the elevator doors close, Harry waves.

Eli turns to Jeremiah and Robbie and says, "Well, that went smoothly. No questions and no hiccups. Just the way we wanted it. Smart not mentioning the lottery."

"Yeah, not bad for twenty minutes," agrees Robbie.

"When he sees the huge credit in the account, he's gonna shit!" Jeremiah quips.

They all laugh as the doors open. They walk out of the building, head to the street corner, exchange farewell hugs and handshakes, and pledges to talk soon. When the light changes, they cross the street and merge into the pedestrian traffic, moving down Sixth Avenue to their respective next assignments.

As Robbie settles in on the train back to her office, she texts Jeremiah, asking him if he can swing by later to sign the power of attorney, letter of authorization, and the lottery ticket. He replies almost immediately and says he'll be at her office at around five o'clock. Robbie pulls out a newspaper with their next step set and starts reading as the train picks up speed.

Chapter 40
A Stylist's Point of View

It's ten past eleven on a chilly grey Monday morning, and Kate is late for her standing appointment with Ron Messina. Ron has been cutting Kate's hair since before Ryan was born. Not only is he a fabulous hairstylist, but he is also an all-around good guy—friendly, down-to-earth, and astute.

As Kate rushes to the vacant chair waiting for her, Ron signals for her to get her hair rinsed first in the rear of the salon. Five minutes later, she is back in the chair, and Ron places a salon cape around her.

She is still conflicted with all the lottery stuff. Regardless of Jeremiah's leanings, should they give away a fortune or keep it all for themselves or somewhere in-between? Should she try to stop him legally, as Julie had suggested? Maybe she should just flip a coin. Or perhaps she should just surrender and let the universe decide?

She'll confide in Ron, she reasons. He has always been discreet over the years with secrets and advice.

"So, what's new, darling?" he cheerfully asks.

"Oh, you know, the usual. What about you and Mark?"

"Same. Mark wants to buy a condo in South Florida," replies Ron, referring to his husband's latest great idea.

They continue catching up on kids, TV shows, and movies. Then Ron's phone rings. He answers it, giving Kate a few minutes to frame how she will tell him.

When he returns, and after he pledges to keep Kate's secret, she begins to share all the details about their new pending fortune. She relates how Jeremiah is stuck on giving away a lot of it, plus his ideas about an RFP, book, and movie.

Ron lets Kate ramble on without interruption or questions. Her story is unbelievable, but he has no reason to doubt her. If anything, Kate is truthful and no-nonsense, not like some of Ron's other clientele. She is practically out of breath when she finishes.

"So, what do you think, Ron?" asks Kate.

"Wow! That's a lot to digest. I don't envy you."

"Well, what would you do?" presses Kate.

"Here's my take," starts Ron after a pause. "This world we live in today is so crazy. Isn't it great when something incredibly miraculous comes along? Why don't you and Jeremiah be that miracle? Do you need all that money?" He pauses again, then continues, "Listen, Jeremiah is no fool. You've had over thirty years with him. Right? You could be in for an amazing, fun, wild ride—if you play it right, particularly the movie and book stuff. You have nothing to lose. That's my sense. What the heck? Go for it!"

"I'm just afraid that if this ever got out—that we are the ones behind this—people will judge us and think we are stupid," returns Kate.

"Since when has that ever been important? You go the other way, and people will still judge you with stuff like 'they should have blah,

123

blah, blah.' And they will be all over you for handouts and all kinds of schemes and opportunities. That would be even more insane, right?"

"I guess you have a point," replies Kate and retreats into thought.

Ron then says, "Kate, you need to ask yourself: what is the source of those doubts? Are they coming from a place of fear or love? If they are coming from fear, let them go."

Silence surrounds them for a few minutes, only filled by the clipping of scissors. Ron's last point is something to think hard about, acknowledges Kate, still deep in thought. The conversation picks up again, shifting to the status of Kate's mother's health.

Ron is done cutting Kate's hair and grabs a hairdryer to blow away cuttings on the protective gown covering her. As she gets up, she slips a twenty into his top drawer, and they exchange their closing words.

Ron leans in and says, "Honey, don't worry. You'll figure it out. Trust your intuition—and your husband. It's all good. It will be fine."

He smiles, and they hug goodbye. Kate heads for the exit, feeling a bit more confident.

"We'll see," she says to herself.

Chapter 41
It's Official

Jeremiah has left work early and manages to catch a 3:43 p.m. train to the island. As agreed, he heads straight to Robbie's office to finalize all the paperwork.

When he gets to her office, he goes straight to the conference room, where Robbie stands alongside five stacks of documents. Post-its are visible on each pile, indicating its recipient: one for Jeremiah, one for the bank, one for the lottery, one for the County Clerk's Office, and one for Robbie's files.

Robbie moves to Jeremiah's stack, where two completed, notarized trusts rest: one for collecting the funds and one for disbursements. She hands the power of attorney document to Jeremiah for his signature. As he signs, she gives him the two-page letter of authorization, outlining all the assumptions of their legal arrangement and the tasks Robbie is to perform. He reviews it thoroughly.

Jeremiah turns to Robbie and solemnly says, "You know, there are two Ts in 'lottery' in the second paragraph?"

"Shit! Really? I had spell-checked it three times!" is her instant defense.

"Just kidding," returns Jeremiah, smirking as he signs.

"Not funny, Mr. Baldwin," responds Robbie with a crooked smile.

Robbie places the three documents in a large envelope and hands the envelope to Jeremiah. They go through the same signing process of the papers in Robbie's stack.

The bank stack has the two completed, notarized copies of each trust in a large envelope labeled *Bank*. The County Clerk's pile, marked *CC,* is just like the bank's. The last stack has a lonely completed, notarized trust placed in a large envelope labeled The Lottery for the *lottery*.

With the paperwork completed, they sit down at the table with Robbie at the head and Jeremiah to her right. Jeremiah pulls out a manila folder from his backpack. In it are three pages stapled together with the heading: THE RFP. It outlines the RFP's description, rules, timeline, and other details that Jeremiah had sketched out, including the applications and roll-out plan considerations.

"Here, Robbie. I have put down on paper what I see for the RFP so far," he states as he hands the folder to Robbie.

"Good—I'll look it over later tonight and give you my thoughts."

"And I also have my ticket for you. You need to sign it and include it when you visit the lottery folks."

Taking the ticket from Jeremiah and looking at it for a moment, Robbie says, "Do you realize that this little piece of paper is worth hundreds of millions of dollars? Totally beyond reason." She turns the ticket over and places it in front of her on the table. Picking up a pen on the table, she signs *Robbie Winthrop, Attorney at Law*.

"Guess that does it," she says, getting up with the ticket and dashing out of the room. A minute later, she returns with two copies, front and back of the original, one for her and one for Jeremiah. She puts the signed ticket in a small envelope and places it in the larger one designated for the lottery. "This will all go into the safe until I meet with Granson. Next up: sending the bank and the County Clerk their packages tomorrow and dropping off the lottery documents and ticket at the lottery, Wednesday. By the end of the week, we'll be complete with this part of the adventure."

"You know, Robbie. You've done an amazing job taking care of all of this!" Jeremiah proclaims.

"Aww, Jeremiah, you're just saying that because it's true."

They both laugh. "No, really, Robbie. I can't thank you enough."

She smiles.

They both rise and hug while saying goodbye. Jeremiah heads to the door while Robbie gathers up the envelopes.

Over his shoulder, he says, "Have a great night, Robbie!"

"Talk soon, Jeremiah."

Chapter 42
Strange Dreams

That night, Jeremiah retires early after his long, busy day. Kate is still up watching the Jimmy Fallon Show. It isn't long after his monologue that she too starts to fade and migrates to the bedroom. Within minutes of her head hitting the pillow, she is asleep. Jeremiah is out cold, sleeping like a baby.

Jeremiah dreams every night. Often, he wakes in the morning with vivid recollections of what had occurred. Today, he awakens to recall the dream he just experienced.

Jeremiah is grabbing a quick bite to eat at the On Parade Diner in Woodbury. He walks into the main dining room, where he sees his mother and grandmother sitting in a booth by the windows. It is late afternoon, and nonetheless, they are ordering breakfast meals, pancakes for Grandma, and an omelet with home fries for mom.

A few minutes later, a disheveled young couple walks in and sits in the next booth. They inform the waitress that they haven't eaten in two days and have no money. Unsympathetically, the waitress tells them that they will have to leave. The meals for Mom and Grandma arrive. They immediately get up from their booth and give their plates to the couple, telling them, "Here, have ours," and then they fade out.

Rarely has Jeremiah's mother—and seldom has his grandmother—appeared in his nightly visions. The images are so distinct. He feels warmth and comfort. The dream is positive, but he isn't sure what it means. Perhaps it is a prophetic message of sorts, possibly, something about being charitable and how his mother and grandmother support such acts of kindness.

Kate, also, is a nightly dreamer, but usually, she does not recall hers. Jeremiah cannot remember the last time she had told him of a dream she'd had. In the morning, Kate wakes with a jolt, having had the strangest, most animated dream in a long time. It was so colorful, with the most beautiful Beatles soundtrack playing in the background.

> *Kate is in Hollywood, making a movie. The script in her hand has THE RFP written on the cover page. She is having a conversation with her father and Reese Witherspoon, who is starring in the movie. Without any fanfare, Steven Spielberg walks onto the set. She is in shock. Spielberg praises her and Jeremiah; he thinks their story is fantastic. He tells her to call him if she ever needs anything, hands her his card, and moonwalks offset.*

Kate is beyond words as she sits up in bed. This dream was all about what has been going on with Jeremiah and his RFP. If there were such a thing as a sign, this is undoubtedly it—tears stream down her face. Jeremiah had left for work hours ago. She needs to talk to him in person. That will have to wait until tomorrow evening when they are both home again.

Chapter 43
Moving Forward

Robbie had created the two trusts. The letter of authorization (LOA), power of attorney (POA), and winning ticket are all signed. She has completed reviewing all the documents for the fourth time and is satisfied that they are in order. There are five packages:

- One for the bank containing two notarized originals of each trust

- One for the County Clerk like the bank's

- One for the lottery with a notarized original of the collection trust and the signed original winning lottery ticket

- A complete set of documents for Jeremiah

- And a package for Robbie's files containing an original of each trust and copies of the LOA, POA, and a copy of the signed lottery ticket

Being a notary, Robbie had also notarized each trust, simplifying the process. She will overnight the bank and County Clerk their packages and drop by the lottery tomorrow to personally deliver their package. These many documents, copies, and notarizations are like a real estate closing but so much more fun.

The FedEx office is only two miles from Robbie's. She reaches for the package she had prepared for the bank. In it, she places a handwritten note reminding Harry Mitchell of the points they had discussed. She inserts the envelope into one for shipping, addressed to Mitchell as per his business card. She also prepares a shipping envelope for the County Clerk's package, the address she gets from her contacts app.

Ready to go, Robbie grabs her coat and keys and heads out to her car. Her Beamer is parked in a reserved space in the building's garage in the basement. As she exits, she notices that traffic is very light, and within what seems like seconds, she is pulling up in front of the FedEx office.

She gets out of her car and enters the shop. No one is around. Then a young woman appears from a back room, wearing a name tag with *Annie* on it, offering to assist Robbie. It is simple: complete the mailing slips for each package and scan them with a barcode label gun. After a few keystrokes on the computer, Annie asks for a credit card. Robbie pulls a Visa from her purse, gives it to Annie to swipe, and a receipt pops up almost immediately. Annie hands it to Robbie.

Easy peasy—with another task done, Robbie turns to leave, thanking Annie for her help. Robbie pulls out her iPhone and a piece of paper with the lottery's phone number on it after getting back in her car. A pleasant voice comes on after two rings, announcing that the caller has reached the NYS Lottery office. Robbie gives her name and asks to speak with Steve Granson.

"One moment, please," says an unknown, pleasant voice.

In less than a minute, she hears a click, and then Granson says, "Hello, Ms. Winthrop. What can I do for you?"

"Hi, Mr. Granson, I am calling to follow up on the matter we discussed last week regarding the confidentiality affidavit. You mentioned you were going to speak with your Senior Director about it," proceeds Robbie.

"Yes, I do remember, and in fact, I did speak to her about it just yesterday. She is fine with us drafting an affidavit guaranteeing your client's confidentiality," he replies.

Robbie is delighted. Since she had formalized the two-trust strategy, she is certain Jeremiah's anonymity is secure; the affidavit is the icing on the cake, but not essential.

"We can have it ready for you tomorrow morning," he continues.

"That will be fine. And I can come by in the afternoon with the signed ticket and a copy of the trust," answers Robbie.

They agree on a time, one-thirty, then exchange farewells. Robbie closes her phone. Everything is coming together as planned.

Chapter 44
Dream Analysis

As Jeremiah's train approaches the Hicksville station, the clouds lighten up, and the rain turns to a light mist. The last two days have been trying. There had been much haunting him. He still holds some negative thoughts about how he'll navigate life as a lottery millionaire. He is uncertain how he'll be a non-profit patron. And the RFP's success looms with considerable ambiguity. It is all so overwhelming.

As Jeremiah finishes listening to a podcast, he experiences a small *aha* moment and begins to feel more positive and confident about his circumstances. One thing is sure: he feels guided to make the right moves and decisions at the right time, regardless of the outcome.

Then appears a spectacular rainbow with vibrant, dramatic curves. Admittedly, this is a sign, a confirmation of sorts, a divine tap on the shoulder indicating, *"You got this!"* Empowered, he hops off the train at his stop and heads home.

A few minutes later, Jeremiah walks into the living room, where Kate is watching TV. She greets him with a kind smile as he sits on the couch. He begins to tell her about the stunning rainbow he just saw, which has now dissolved. He tells her that he, too, has been feeling conflicted about the lottery win and that maybe they ought to take the money and forget the whole RFP idea. And then, this incredible rainbow appeared, and it feels like a sign that they are on the right path with the RFP.

"Kate, I also had this dream last night, which sure seems like another mystical indication that the RFP is the right thing for us to do," offers Jeremiah. He tells her about his dream where his mother and grandmother are at the diner, and they give their meals to hungry, needy strangers. "It sure seemed like they were trying to tell me that giving away what we have is something we should do. Well, anyway, that's how I interpreted it," adds Jeremiah.

"That's interesting. The rainbow and the dream," replies Kate with interest. "You know, I had a crazy dream last night too. My father, Reese Witherspoon, and Steven Spielberg were all in it. I was making a movie about the lottery and the RFP, and Spielberg said he thought our story was amazing," she continues. Jeremiah, listening, smiles inside. "I hadn't thought much about it, but that also sounds like some kind of validation," says Kate.

"Yes, it does," confirms Jeremiah.

"It's just I've been so concerned, Jeremiah, about what people might think and say about the crazy Baldwin's giving away a fortune. I guess that doesn't matter. What matters is what we think, and if we think it's a good idea, I guess it is."

"Yes, Kate, that's all that matters. And besides, you have a movie you've got to make, and you can't do that unless we complete the RFP," jokes Jeremiah. He gives Kate a big hug and says, "Let's get going on this RFP thing!"

Kate nods. The RFP is a go.

Chapter 45
Back to the Lottery

Since Jeremiah had re-emerged in Robbie's professional life with his lottery project, the RFP tasks highlight her daily activities. Today will be significant—it will set the RFP and all the planning, thus far, into high gear. Pulling out of the parking garage, the clock on the dashboard in her car reads 1:05 p.m.; she will be at the lottery offices with minutes to spare. She plans to get in and out, ten minutes max.

Robbie is sitting at the conference room table where she had been the previous Friday at exactly one-thirty. In walks Steve Granson, alone, with a pad and manila folder. He bends to shake hands, warmly greets Robbie, and sits across from her.

From her tote, Robbie removes a large envelope with *The Lottery* prominently inscribed on it. Opening the envelope, she extracts the collection trust and hands it to Granson, saying, "Here is an original, notarized trust for my client's claim."

Granson takes the document and browses through it quickly, not revealing any opinion or judgment. "This looks straightforward enough," he finally says, not mentioning anything about the trust's strange name: The Rising-Up Collection Trust.

Reaching back into the large envelope, Robbie pulls out a smaller one marked *ticket* and hands it to Granson, saying, "And here is the signed winning ticket to the November sixth Mega Millions Lottery drawing."

He takes the envelope, removes the ticket from inside, and examines it, front to back. Nodding, he declares the claim is in order. From the manila folder he brought with him, he pulls out a single two-ply page with CLAIM REPORT boldly printed at the top. There are multiple boxes, and he checks them all off, indicating Robbie has met all the requirements. And now, the claim is ready to be processed.

Signing the receipt, he then tears off the top sheet and places it back in his folder, then hands Robbie the bottom copy. Robbie scans it to make sure Granson had checked the box, indicating that the claimant has surrendered the actual ticket. Granson then retrieves from his folder a single-page letter on NYS Lottery stationary marked CONFIDENTIALITY AFFIDAVIT and hands it to Robbie. She quickly reviews the document, noting the senior director's signature. It looks satisfactory, even though it most likely won't be needed.

Pointing to the trust and signed ticket, Granson states, "I think we are all set, Ms. Winthrop. I will submit these to the claims department to register your claim. I expect we will complete this by noon tomorrow, at which time I will call and inform you accordingly."

"Good," says Robbie, "after I receive your call, I will follow up with an email with my client's bank wire instructions."

"Perfect. Upon receipt of your wire instructions, we will send you a secure online transfer request to authorize us to make the wire transfer. Upon your authorization, we will initiate the transfer, which should complete within twenty-four hours. You will receive confirmation notifications from us for the transfer authorization, transfer initiation, and transfer completion via email. All I need now is your email address, Ms. Winthrop."

Robbie removes a business card from her tote and hands it to Granson. With their meeting concluded in precisely ten minutes, they both rise and shake hands. Leaving the room, Robbie heads to her car. Robbie's phone rings as she exits the expressway. It's Harry Mitchell from the bank. He informs her that he has created the two trust accounts and will be forwarding her the wire instructions for the collection trust.

After squeezing into her parking space at the office, she texts Jeremiah: *Bank accounts set-up. Lottery claim filed. Moving forward!! Money to transfer tomorrow!!*

Chapter 46
Key RFP Steps

The RFP plan was simple if broken down to its most basic elements: (1) rollout, (2) identify a shortlist of candidates, and (3) select a winner.

So, what's my rollout plan going to be? wonders Jeremiah. Broadly, it is to get the word out and direct interested non-profits to visit a website for more information, instructions, applications, et cetera.

The RFP plan is not rocket science—at least, it doesn't have to be. Once the word is out that there are funds up for grabs, non-profits will circle like sharks detecting blood. There are hundreds of NYC NPs in the health and human services sector. Jeremiah will have Robbie send an announcement to a couple of charity publications, requesting they share it with their subscribers. Robbie will also reach out to the Human Services Consortium in NYC and other trade groups for assistance; maybe they can inform their members.

Jeremiah had previously arrived at the name "Rising-Up" for the RFP. He is sticking with it. He will brand the website and any other related materials with it.

Selecting a winner for the grant will involve a filtering process. Starting with a large pool of potential applicants, maybe one to a couple hundred. They will complete a short application that will reduce the number of possible candidates to about a dozen. That group will complete a second, more detailed application, and from those, four will advance as finalists for interviews.

The selection committee that Jeremiah had assembled would determine which NPs would advance to the final three or four, including the ultimate winner. In the end, though, Jeremiah will reserve the right to override any of the committee's decisions.

It all seems simple enough, but as Jeremiah knows from past experiences: the devil is always in the details. And until they get going, there is no way of knowing what demons might be lurking.

Chapter 47
Registered

As Steve Granson had assured Robbie the day before, once the lottery registers her claim successfully, he will be calling her. He had indicated that the registration should take no longer than a day, and when completed, they can initiate the process of transferring funds to the trust.

Robbie's phone rings at 11:50 a.m. "This is Robbie Winthrop. How can I help you?"

"Hello, Ms. Winthrop, this is Steve Granson from the lottery calling. I am happy to report that we have successfully registered your client's lottery claim."

"Hi, Mr. Granson. That's wonderful. I will forward you my client's bank wire instructions as we had discussed."

"Good. I look forward to hearing back from you soon," responds Granson.

"Thank you, Mr. Granson, for all of your assistance in this matter. You have made this quite easy."

"You're quite welcome, Ms. Winthrop. We do our best. I'm happy you are pleased."

Now, the wait begins. By this time tomorrow, Jeremiah will have his winnings safely deposited at his bank.

Later that evening, while Jeremiah is clearing the dining room table, his phone rings. It's Ava, and she says sadly, "Hi Jeremiah." A phone call is unusual; ordinarily, she communicates either by email or text.

"Hi Ava, what are you doing?" asks Jeremiah.

She replies, "I feel terrible. I need to pull back from being actively involved with you on your donation project. I need to spend more time with my daughter. She is having some challenges at school, and I need to pay more attention here at home. I hope you understand."

Surprised by the call, Jeremiah replies, "I'm sorry to hear that, Ava. No worries. Your daughter's needs should come first!"

"I know, but I still feel like I am letting you down."

"Don't worry about it. I understand. I'll be in touch with updates, and if things change, you are welcome to come back in."

"Thank you, Jeremiah. I'll let you know if anything changes. Good luck! Talk soon."

Well, that was a surprise; now I'll have to find someone to fill in for Ava, thinks Jeremiah.

The wheels in his head start turning. Who else can he recruit? No one surfaces immediately, and then he recalls his old work friend from The Way Home. What about Morgan Sunstein?

Chapter 48
Money in the Bank

Harry Mitchell is in his office, staring at two computer monitors with numerous charts and figures blinking. It is a very organized display of market activity and trends to inform portfolio managers, like him, the status of their clients' holdings with instant results.

Such is the way of twenty-first century, computer-based money management. Harry is having a good day; the market is up three hundred points, and all of his clients are showing green.

His phone rings, startling him back to the real world. It's the wire transfer department calling to alert him that the new trust account he set up has just received a rather large credit. Harry thanks the clerk, hangs up, and then opens a new screen to see his accounts' recent transactions.

He scrolls down a long list of his clients until he comes to The Rising-Up Collection Trust. He clicks on the *transactions* tab. A window opens, revealing a matrix with numerous columns. There is only one entry with today's date, and the credit column shows $172,022,356.07.

Holy cow, thinks Harry, *that is one heck of a settlement!*

Reading more, Harry sees that the source of the credit is NYS Lottery. Harry has very wealthy clients, and large amounts of money are not uncommon for him. But a lottery winner—this is a first.

He calms down but is still in disbelief. All of Harry's clients are on speed dial. With a couple of taps on his phone, it rings Jeremiah. When Jeremiah picks up, Harry admonishes, "So when were you going to tell me, Mr. Lottery Winner? I almost had a heart attack."

They are both laughing.

"Listen, believe it or not, this whole thing has been quite stressful for me," Jeremiah says. "Do you realize what I'm going through to keep this quiet?"

"And you couldn't be straight with your old friend Harry?"

"Hey, I had to have a little fun. I knew you'd find out soon enough. I take it the money arrived."

"Yup, all one hundred and seventy-two million."

"Awesome!" says Jeremiah as he maniacally starts fist-pumping. He has finally gotten to this point in his plan, and now with the money is in his account under his control, things will start happening!

"You can say that again," Harry chimes. More laughter.

"That is freaking awesome! Well, park it somewhere safe. We'll figure out a game plan later," instructs Jeremiah.

"Okay. You have any more surprises up your sleeve?" asks Harry.

"If I told you, they wouldn't be surprises," answers Jeremiah.

Harry has no idea what Jeremiah is planning. But he will find out in due time. Laughing with Jeremiah, Harry closes with, "Okay, Jeremiah, talk soon."

"Bye, Harry. Thanks for calling."

Without a moment's delay, Jeremiah texts Kate. *We are now millionaires! $$ arrived. Harry just called.*

Kate replies, *YIPPEE!*

Gonna ask Robbie to stop over for a toast, OK? Replies Jeremiah.

Sure. And tell the kids!

OK, Xoxo, closes Jeremiah.

Jeremiah leaves a voice message on Robbie's cell phone: "If you are free later, please stop over for a toast—we got the money."

Jeremiah then sends a similar group text to Ryan and Harley.

Shortly, his phone buzzes with Robbie's incoming message, stating she'll be over at seven. Ryan sends his regrets; he has a date but is happy to hear the good news. And Harley has confirmed she will be home to celebrate.

On the way home, Jeremiah stops at a local liquor store to get a bottle of champagne. While at the register, Jeremiah dials Eli. When Eli picks up, Jeremiah softly speaks into his phone, "I'm now a millionaire. The money has arrived."

"Bravo!" is all Eli says.

Jeremiah closes with "Ciao, amigo." They both hang up.

Chapter 49
Share the News

The celebration "party" is a short, very intimate affair: Kate, Harley, Robbie, and Jeremiah. They raise their champagne flutes and share their delight in reaching this point. Jeremiah's toast is simple; he thanks Robbie for her assistance and praises Kate for her support. Harley beams, so proud of her dad.

Their celebration meanders with the sharing of pleasantries and thoughts of what potential of having millions of dollars. Jeremiah begins to move the empty glasses onto the counter, and as Robbie leaves, Kate tidies the kitchen. Harley has retreated to her room to watch some mindless reality TV. Jeremiah has much to do in the next few days. Tonight, however, he will only update his advisors on today's long-awaited event, his plans, and a prospective date and time for them to all convene.

He opens his Gmail account and starts composing an email. The "to list" includes Kate, Robbie, Eli, Ruby, and Ava; Jeremiah will need to reach out to Morgan Sunstein as a possible replacement for Ava. The subject line states The Rising-Up Grant – Selection Committee Update. And the body of the email reads:

Dear friends,

I am happy to inform you that we have achieved phase one of the Rising-Up grant. My bank has received the lottery money today.

The immediate next steps are to (1) announce to a few charity publications, (2) inform non-profits of the grant, and (3) create a website for the application process. I plan to get this done over the weekend as best I can.

We will be convening in the next couple of weeks to review the applications received, discuss future tasks, etc.

I am grateful to all of you for your support and assistance.

Yours,

Jeremiah

That should do it. A brief status update with indications of things to come without too much detail. Jeremiah rereads the message a couple of times, checking for typos and grammar. It looks fine, and off it goes.

Chapter 50
Rumors of a Lottery Winner in the News

Almost four weeks have passed, and the November 6th lottery winner hasn't come forward to claim the prize. As a news item, this story has pretty much gone dark. Nonetheless, it sits in the parking lot on the editor's follow-up storyboard at various media outlets and gets resurrected on slow days.

When one network broadcasts an update, the other majors usually follow. Today is one such day where WABC decided to remind viewers that the Mega Millions winner from November 6th is still "at large." They replay old footage and taunt viewers with the same graphic: WHO IS THE LUCKY WINNER?

What is new this time is that the reporter shares that ABC has been in touch with the lottery office in lower Manhattan. On conditions of anonymity, an official discloses that rumors are circulating within the lottery. A winner has stepped forward through an attorney on Long Island. No further details are given, making it seem unlikely the public will ever learn the winner's identity. Nonetheless, the report has re-ignited even greater interest and speculation.

The reporter states that there had been many cases in New York where people have claimed their winnings through legal vehicles called trusts that shield their identity. The reporter also says that determining the "owner" of a trust used to claim a lottery prize is not impossible, but it would require much research.

Closing out the segment, the reporter promises that ABC will investigate further the winner's identity and report any findings they might uncover.

Jeremiah has been watching, attentively, wondering: could they find out it is him?

Jeremiah is confident that his strategy is ironclad in protecting his identity. But is it completely foolproof? Don't trusts have to be filed in court? Yes, Jeremiah recalls being in Robbie's office. There were five stacks of documents—one, with the two trusts, was for the County Clerk's Office in Mineola. Conceivably then, a resourceful analyst could research these newly registered trusts, which are a matter of public record. A bright person could find both trusts and piece together the paper trail and determine that Jeremiah is the ultimate beneficiary and, therefore, the winner.

Jeremiah shudders and does his best to put this unlikely scenario out of his mind. It is too late now. All the documents are completed and filed. He will leave this up to the universe and hope no one outside his inner circle will ever find out.

Chapter 51
Announcing the Giveaway

The next day, after having received the lottery funds, Jeremiah and Robbie are in high gear. They are at Robbie's office early Saturday morning, as they had agreed the night before. They draft a concise communication announcing the RFP. It reads:

The Rising-Up Grant

Robbie Winthrop & Associates, LLC is pleased to announce the creation of a grant to donate $100 million to a not-for-profit organization, in New York City in the health & human services sector.

Interested applicants can obtain additional information on the requirements, application process, and deadline at the following website:

www.Rising-Up.com

She prints two copies of the announcement on her letterhead. Later in the day, Jeremiah will FedEx it to The Chronicle of Philanthropy in Washington, DC, and Philanthropy New York in New York City. These are two well-respected publications.

With the announcement prepared, Robbie asks what their plan should be for contacting non-profits. Jeremiah is aware of the Human Services Consortium, a trade group that advocates for NYC non-profits in health and human services. Undoubtedly, the HSC will want to assist in attracting funding to one or more of its constituents.

Robbie looks up their website and obtains the executive director's email address. She then drafts an email introducing herself, her firm, and her client's intent to make a substantial gift to an NYC NP as per the announcement she will attach. Robbie asks if the executive director would circulate it among the HSC membership.

Jeremiah will have to quickly create the Rising-Up website before Robbie can send her email to the HSC since the announcement references it.

He goes to the WordPress site, where simple, low-cost websites can be designed and built literally within minutes. WordPress also allows Jeremiah to establish a domain name. He and Robbie agree that they will send the email to the HSC later that afternoon. In the meantime, they go and grab a bite, and while they are out, they will also stop at FedEx and send out the announcements to the philanthropy publications.

While in Robbie's car after lunch, en route back to her office, Jeremiah's iPhone buzzes, alerting him of newly arrived messages. There are two, both Ava and Ruby, acknowledging his update from the night before. Both are very congratulatory. Ruby states how she cannot wait for the committee to meet.

Jeremiah ponders this. Now that the cash is under his control, he needs to consider a few things. Expenses will start very soon. For example, he should pay Robbie something. She has done a lot of work so far and deserves some compensation. There will also be other sundry costs to cover. He will have Harry move some funds from the collection account to the distribution account for these and other expenses.

Maybe he should quit working at The Way Home? Yes, perhaps he should devote his full attention to Rising-Up? He makes a mental note to get Kate and Robbie's take on this.

As Robbie and Jeremiah are riding up the elevator to her office, Jeremiah opens with, "Robbie, I have been thinking. I feel you are entitled to some compensation for all you have done on this project so far. What do you think?"

"As usual, Jeremiah, you're right," she replies half-jokingly with a big grin.

"Okay, I'll take care of you," he promises as they exit the elevator.

They walk to Robbie's office door. Robbie unlocks it, and they proceed straight to her private office. It's 2:45 p.m., and Robbie wonders where the day has gone. She gets behind her desk, and Jeremiah sits in the guest chair across from her. Jeremiah opens his phone and begins texting his kids. Robbie opens her Gmail account and scrolls to the draft email for the HSC.

She looks over to Jeremiah and says, "I'm sending the HSC email now. Okay?"

Jeremiah replies, "Let's do it." Robbie presses SEND, and with a whoosh, the email is on its way.

Chapter 52
The HSC Steps Up

Robbie returns to her condo after having had a session with her personal trainer at the gym. She feels invigorated and alive. Her plans for the day are simple: rest up and enjoy. She will go through the Sunday papers, shower, and then meet with some friends for brunch.

Sitting on her sofa, she pours through the *Times* business section. Then she picks up the lifestyle section. In the background, the TV quietly runs the Sunday morning political shows. Her coffee cup is almost empty, so she rises to refill it in the kitchen.

While in the kitchen, she instinctively grabs her phone to check her messages. Emily Jordan, the executive director of HSC, has responded to the email Robbie had sent yesterday.

The email is very upbeat—she agrees to help however she can. She has already sent Robbie's email and announcement to the HSC membership of around two hundred and fifty organizations. Emily also states that she has also forwarded Robbie's email to Beverly Watson, the executive director at Housing for All, a similar trade association as HSC focused on non-profits involved with homelessness.

Emily and Beverly are long-time friends, and Emily is confident Beverly will also send the email to her members. Emily also pledged she'd forward the announcement to other colleagues and asked Beverly to do the same.

It is just the kind of response Robbie wanted. With maybe three or four hundred potential applicants so far, they are off to a good start. Perhaps this will go viral if the media picks up on it. They should receive a good pool of possible recipients. Two to three hundred submitted applications seem realistic. Now, they will wait and see.

Robbie dials Jeremiah. Getting his voicemail, she leaves a message. She knows he'll be happy with this update.

About an hour later, Jeremiah retrieves the voicemail and is pleased to hear that HSC has circulated the announcement. With his focus back on the RFP, Jeremiah remembers his call with Ava and decides to phone Morgan Sunstein.

Probably one of the classiest people one could ever meet, Morgan has been in the fundraising department for five years. She has worked for many non-profits and knows her way around the sector. And she can fundraise! Morgan has the most incredible gift for engaging people, a great deal of life experience, and wisdom. She will make the perfect addition to Jeremiah's team.

He makes the call, and after they have caught up, having not talked in weeks, Jeremiah explains his confidential matter in vivid detail. Morgan is speechless, but thrilled at the same time. She agrees to join the team and promises to be at the upcoming selection committee meeting.

Chapter 53
Announcements Received

Ominous, foreboding, dark gray clouds greet a cold and blustery Monday morning in NYC. Sleepy office workers are stumbling into their jobs. FedEx delivery guys, though, are catching their second wind; they'd been making their rounds for hours now. Smitty, a fifteen-year veteran at FedEx, exits the Forty-third Street office of Philanthropy of New York, where he had just delivered the Rising-Up announcement. It is a little past nine-thirty a.m.

A similar experience has occurred in Washington, DC, at The Chronicle of Philanthropy. At the Chronicle, Robbie earmarked the announcement to the managing editor's attention, and at Philanthropy New York, she had sent the parcel to the director of communications. It does not take long for the respective packages to find their way to the appropriate desks. Once received, the curious recipients immediately open them and read the announcements.

The Rising-Up announcement would resonate, given the two organizations are always looking for a good story, an attractive opportunity for their constituents. Both the Chronicle and PNY will do further digging, and if nothing negative surfaces, they'll run a piece on Rising-Up.

The managing editor at the Chronicle is a man named Ben McIntosh, who recently came aboard. His previous gig was in marketing for a large consumer goods company in Virginia. He is intrigued; even though the Chronicle is more national in scope, a hundred million dollars would catch anyone's attention. He picks up his phone and dials the number on Robbie's letterhead.

Robbie answers in two rings. It is 10:45 a.m. McIntosh introduces himself and explains why he is calling, and Robbie is delighted. They chat for ten minutes, with Robbie verifying the announcement's authenticity and successfully selling the Rising-Up grant's intentions. McIntosh is on board. He assures Robbie he'll post the Rising-Up grant opportunity on the Chronicle's homepage. He also promises to forward it to his circle of relevant contacts once he receives a PDF from Robbie.

The result is similar for Philanthropy New York, but one better. Robbie receives a call from Cindy Saunders, director of communications at PNY. The conversation is the same as the one with McIntosh, except Saunders promises to also circulate the announcement to PNY's members in addition to her professional contacts.

After both calls, Robbie, to express her sincere appreciation, immediately fires off emails with an attached RFP announcement. She is on cloud nine. Not only is this happening the way she had envisioned, but it is also happening quicker than she had hoped it would.

Of course, she needs to share this and quickly sends an email to Jeremiah, informing him of her earlier calls. She turns her attention to her day job and puts Rising-Up aside for now. Time to double-check her punch list for a property closing tomorrow morning.

That evening, Cindy Saunders of PNY is with her college roommate, Karen Goldman, who now works in public affairs news at WCBS-NY. They are having drinks at their regular meet-up spot. The waiter serves them as Cindy wraps up her report on her four-month relationship and how she feels it has legs. But only time will tell. Karen then goes into graphic detail about her upcoming wedding next September. Both are happy about how their lives are unfolding.

Besides the social aspects of drinks, Karen also values these get-togethers for the possible tidbits she can use on the job. She does them with lots of her contacts in government and the non-profit sector. It is her way to get insights and scoops for stories that might otherwise go unnoticed.

"So, how's the job going?" queries Karen, shifting subjects.

"Fine, I guess."

"Anything new or exciting happening?"

"Funny you should ask..."

At that point, Cindy relates the strange package PNY received that morning blindly addressed to her, containing an announcement for a one hundred million grant. When she investigated it further, calling and Googling the attorney involved, she felt it was legit. But it still looks pretty unusual, a huge grant by an anonymous donor. Usually, donors want credit and recognition. When she discussed it with the VP of member services, they agreed to post it on their website and share it with their members.

"That is interesting. No clue who's behind it?" asks Karen.

"None."

They continue chatting about work experiences, drifting back to social topics. They are close to finishing their second glasses of wine when both start getting ready to leave. They agree to meet up, "same time, same place," next month.

As Karen gets into a cab, her thoughts turn to the strange blind grant announcement Cindy mentioned. So unusual, she reflects, wondering if there is any connection to the Mega Millions Lottery win last month. She will speak to Frank Martino, the lead on the lottery story that CBS is following.

Chapter 54
The Media Churns

While on his daily commute into the city, Jeremiah sends a text to Robbie, asking for her bank routing and account numbers. He states that this is needed so Harry Mitchell can wire her some money for all the assistance she has provided. To Jeremiah's astonishment, he receives a reply with the requested information and a big smiley face within five minutes. It's not even six a.m., and Robbie is already up and checking her iPhone.

When Jeremiah gets to his office, he emails Harry to transfer one million dollars from the collection account to the distribution account. He also provides Robbie's bank information and instructs him to wire her ten thousand from the distribution account.

Uptown at CBS's headquarters, Karen Goldman is getting coffee and yogurt in the employee commissary. As she pays for her breakfast, Frank Martino walks toward the register to pay for his bagel and coffee.

"What a coincidence, Frank," Karen says. "I was going to call you later this morning. Got a sec?"

"You know, Karen, there are no coincidences," he replies, chuckling.

He nods consent to her request, and they both head to an empty table in the considerable seating area. "What gives?" he asks.

Karen relates her encounter from last night with her friend at PNY and that there is an announcement floating around for applications for a one hundred million anonymous grant.

"Wow, that's a lot of dough! And anonymous, too," is his response.

"I know. You are following that lottery story; you think there might be a connection here?" asks Karen.

Frank is deep in thought. Finally, he replies, "Who knows? Could be. I'll look into it."

Karen hands Frank a folded piece of paper. On it is written the web address for the Rising-Up grant. "Check this out when you can," she instructs. He nods.

As they finish up and head to the exit, Frank says, "Thanks for the tip, Karen."

"Sure, Frank. Let me know if you come across anything."

Across town, in a medium-sized bullpen where the NY Times metro section reporters work, Joyce Chen is on her computer surfing the web. She has about a hundred sites she checks weekly for small items or updates, possibly useful for new news stories or follow-ups to existing ones. Philanthropy New York is one of those sites she regularly checks. There, on the PNY homepage, is the announcement for the one hundred million Rising-Up grant.

"That's a big prize," she says to herself. In the announcement, there is a link to a website for more information. Clicking on the link, her page refreshes, and she finds herself staring at the site Jeremiah had created. She reads through all the pages with interest. Chen is making notes and prints a few, particularly the contact page, which has Robbie's office number. She makes a mental note to call Robbie after the morning staff meeting.

Meanwhile, Robbie has been in her office for hours, trying to complete some lingering projects. She wants to free up her work queue to have more time to spend on Rising-Up matters. She has just returned from the bathroom and sees a blinking light on her office phone, indicating a voicemail.

She presses play. It is someone calling inquiring about the grant. The caller says nothing further other than they'll try again later. The game is on. Robbie then shoots Jeremiah a quick text, "We just received our first indication of interest, an unknown caller!"

Meanwhile, over at the Times, Joyce Chen's staff meeting has ended. She has just returned from the cafeteria on the third floor with a cup of coffee. She puts on her headset and punches in Robbie's phone number. There is ringing, but no answer. Finally, a voicemail announcement plays. Joyce reluctantly leaves a message requesting a callback and hangs up.

Chapter 55
Who is Jeremiah Baldwin?

Located across the street from the municipal court complex in Mineola is 240 Old Country Road, the home of many county departments. Most of the Nassau County Clerk's operations are here in a 60s styled, six-story office building. Consumer Affairs, Board of Elections, Comptroller, Department of Assessment, the Human Rights Commission, and numerous title companies are also here. The energy radiating throughout the building is reminiscent of the DMV—a slow-moving, methodical bureaucracy.

County residents conducting business enter the Clerk's office on the first floor, where interactions with the public occur. However, the real work transpires in the basement offices, where county employees perform document reviews, registrations, filings, and more.

Being budget-conscious, the support staff is lean, with only three full-time managers and two part-timers, usually college students from nearby Hofstra. Today, Danny, a law student graduating in May, is the only one working. He is an outwardly friendly but complicated and conflicted curious type; he is going through a final review of recently registered trusts and electronically filing and archiving them.

He has been at the County Clerk's Office for two years, and the income has helped offset his staggering graduate school expenses. Not surprisingly, his acquired student debt to become an attorney keeps him up regularly at night with fitful nightmares. Often, angry childhood memories and disillusionment fill his waking mornings. He lives in a two-bedroom apartment in Bellmore, a few miles from his mother's house. His parents divorced when he was in middle school.

With no one else in the office, the peaceful solitude is calming. Danny can attend to his tasks without any distractions. It is 3:30, and with only eight trusts left to do, he should be able to finish within an hour. He takes the first one from his inbox—the Peterson Family Trust—and quickly scans it while making notations in a spreadsheet that the beneficiaries are Nancy and Craig Peterson. Done! Next: The Rising-Up Collection Trust. *That's an unusual name*, thinks Danny. Again, making notations, the beneficiary is the Phoenix Warehouse Trust. That's also a strange name and just as bizarre, one trust being the beneficiary for another. No matter.

The next one is for the Milton Katz Trust beneficiaries: Lorraine Michaels and Robert Katz. The Keith Parker Trust follows. Next is the Phoenix Warehouse Trust. Danny pauses—that name is familiar. That's it; he looks through the entries in his spreadsheet. The Phoenix Warehouse Trust is the beneficiary of the Rising-Up Collection Trust. Quickly, he examines the document further. And the beneficiary of Phoenix Warehouse Trust is Jeremiah Baldwin. Thinking for a moment, he concludes—this Jeremiah Baldwin guy is, therefore, the rightful beneficiary of the Rising-Up Collection Trust!

Why two trusts instead of one? Something strange for sure, but why? Danny will dig deeper later, but for now, he wonders why there would be two trusts filed the same day, with one as a beneficiary of the other. He grabs them both, hurries to make photocopies, puts the copies in his backpack, and settles back to work. Within twenty minutes, he has finished all his work. Getting up from his chair, Danny reaches for his coat and belongings, turns off the lights, and heads out for the day.

Chapter 56
More Media Gyrations

Back at CBS, Frank Martino is in his office, rummaging through his business cards of contacts. In today's digital record-keeping era, one would think Martino would have an app for this or use Microsoft Outlook, like everyone else. But no, he's old school. He finally finds the card.

It is a tattered, crumpled beige card with the New York State logo prominently displayed. The name on it is Julio Lopez, Managing Director at the NYS Lottery, Long Island Division. Martino had met Lopez years ago when he first started covering lottery stories. Lopez was always coy but would share inside information whenever he could. He insisted on never being credited as the source—no trace back to him. His position was that any press about the lottery was good for business, as long as it was favorable.

Frank picks up the phone handset and dials. After speaking to the receptionist, she transfers the call to Lopez's secretary. She informs Frank that her boss is on the phone, and if he waits, she will connect him. He agrees impatiently. After a few minutes, Frank hears a few clicks and then a deep voice, "Hey, Martino, I was wondering when I'd be hearing from you."

Frank laughs, saying, "Nice to speak to you, too, Julio. How are things at the lottery?"

"Things are all good here, Frank. What's on your mind?" responds Lopez.

"We got a tip on the winner of the big lottery win last month," comments Frank.

"We haven't reported anything reported about a winner," answers Lopez.

"I know; that's why I am calling. Did a winner come forward?"

"Not exactly, Frank."

"What does that mean?"

"Promise to keep this quiet?"

"I always do," replies Frank emphatically.

Lopez then says, "We processed the claim, but not by an actual ticket holder."

"So that means it was either a lawyer, legal entity, or corporation?"

"Correct."

"So, which is it?"

"A lawyer."

Having visited the Rising-Up website, Frank asks, "That lawyer wouldn't happen to be a Ms. Robbie Winthrop, would it?"

Lopez is slow to reply, and finally, he says, "You have some sources, Frank."

Bingo. Frank has what he needs.

"Julio, is there anything else you can tell me?" asks Frank.

"Not really," replies Lopez.

That's okay thinks Frank. He has enough to run a story update.

Frank thanks Lopez for his time and promises to buy some tickets for the next drawing. Lopez laughs and hangs up. Frank sits back in his chair—this is great. He has enough for a follow-up. He hastily drafts a piece that will get reworked by the production staff and rushes into his boss's office. They have plenty of time to make the afternoon broadcast.

To Frank's displeasure, his boss wants more. They need confirmation that Winthrop is, in fact, the one who claimed the lottery prize. His off-the-record source at the lottery is not sufficient. CBS needs to confirm that Winthrop claimed the winnings before broadcasting that the grant and lottery win are connected. "Get her on the record to confirm she was the one," Frank's boss hollers as Frank leaves the corner office.

Chapter 57
Quitting Time?

The RFP is in full swing, and the money is in the bank. Maybe it's time to leave The Way Home? Those are the thoughts swirling about in Jeremiah's head for days.

He is undecided about how to proceed or if this is even the right time. If so, how much notice should he give? Should he offer to be a consultant to make the transition smoother? Perhaps, speaking with Sara, his boss, might help. How should he play it? Sara would probably go running immediately to Len Oswald, given she never did anything independent of his blessing.

It should not be such a big deal. Maybe speaking with Kate and Robbie first would help frame a strategy for raising the topic of his departure from work? He could also ask Ruby for her thoughts.

Jeremiah had been in his office for a few hours, completing a report due for one of The Way Home's donors. His iPhone is on his desk when it buzzes—a new Gmail from Harry. The bank has successfully transferred funds to Robbie. Jeremiah replies with a big thank you and then sends Robbie a text, *Check your account … $$*. Ten minutes later, she replies, *You are the best! Thank you! Thank you! Thank you!* Jeremiah's reply, *You earned it, and this is only a down payment. More to come!! XO.*

Jeremiah stands up and stretches. Needing a break, he walks out of his office over to Ruby's cube. "You want to take a walk?" he asks.

"Sure. Give me five minutes to finish up. I'll meet you by the elevator," Ruby replies.

They ride down the elevator and turn left out the front door, and head toward Fifth Avenue. Crossing Sixth Avenue, Jeremiah gets to the point and asks, "Is now the right time for me to leave The Way Home, now that I have the money and a plan?"

"Probably. What is there to stay for?"

"That's what I think. I want to leave without a lot of disruption. You know, a smooth transition. I've built a lot of good stuff for them and would hate to see it all collapse just because I am no longer there to support it."

"That makes sense. Maybe you should speak to Sara and tell her you are thinking of leaving, but don't give too many details. You know, like you want to pursue personal interests or it's time to retire. You want to come up with a transition plan."

"Yeah. I was kind of thinking something like that, too."

They continue walking, now chatting about other things as they head back to the office. Jeremiah feels better. Ruby agrees with what he has been considering. Still, he will see what Kate and Robbie think, not expecting anything different.

A few hours later, Jeremiah is home, preparing to head out to the gym. He goes into the living room, where Kate is working, and says, "I think it's time to quit."

"What are you talking about?" she replies. Kate has soured on The Way Home ever since the management change. They do not seem to appreciate or value all of Jeremiah's hard work.

"The job, what else? My marriage?"

"Not funny, Jeremiah!" reacts Kate as she smiles. "You know what they say? If it feels right—do it," is Kate's endorsement.

"Yeah, I think I'll ease into it with Sara."

"You mean 'Say it ain't so, Sara?'" adds Kate. They laugh loudly.

Two hours later, Jeremiah is in his car, returning home from the gym, and dials Robbie. She doesn't pick up, so he leaves a message informing her of his plan to quit his job. He feels it will probably play out with him being a consultant for a while.

When Jeremiah is home and after dinner, he receives a text from Robbie. *Good. Just make sure you have a written agreement. Set exact limits on the use of your time, and make sure your compensation is commensurate with your value! Every hour you spend on job-related matters is more time taken away from your more important interests.*

Jeremiah says to himself, "God, she's good!" and then replies, *Yup! Good suggestions!! TY!*

Chapter 58
Surprise!

Flipping on the light switch in her office, Robbie sees there are new

voicemails. She puts her tote and handbag on the chair next to her desk and removes her coat. Sitting down, she plays them. The first one is a spam call, but the other two are from WCBS and the New York Times. She scribbles down the callback information on a pad by the phone.

The CBS caller is Frank Martino; the name is somewhat familiar, but she can't place it. The Times caller is Joyce Chen. Both want to talk— they have questions regarding the grant. It is early afternoon. Robbie will return the calls later after taking care of a few other matters on her to-do list.

An hour later, Robbie dials the NY Times. She asks the receptionist to speak with Joyce Chen. After introductions, Joyce asks about the RFP. Who is behind it, and what does the donor expect to accomplish?

Admittedly, the announcement lacked substantive details, and Jeremiah had not framed out or expressed his vision or goals. All he said was that the state of affairs in their country was so broken. There was too much struggle, division, discontent, pain, and suffering everywhere and not enough compassion, understanding, and generosity. Sharing the lottery winnings with others in need through an organization equipped to deal with some of those social issues would help immensely.

Robbie makes a note on her pad: *Frame vision and goals for RFP!!* She then explains to Chen her best on-the-fly version of the RFP vision and goals, closing with, "We have a group of individuals interested in making a difference in the social problems afflicting our community."

Joyce replies, "So, you can't tell me exactly who. And it sounds like you are winging it on what you expect to accomplish."

To which Robbie replies, somewhat defensively, "This has been unfolding rather rapidly, Joyce. We are just not ready to go public with a lot of details. We are more prepared to work through our process of selecting an organization that will align with our ideals for this grant."

"That's fair. Do you have any sense of timing? Can you share any details on your process?"

Robbie itches to get off the call. She promises to provide Chen with more details soon. Chen accepts and says the Times will be running an intro piece, nonetheless. Robbie is not surprised. The call ends on a cordial note. This grand idea of Jeremiah's will be a lot trickier than she had imagined, particularly the media relations part.

At CBS, Frank Martino is at his desk surfing the web, looking for nothing in particular. His phone rings. The caller ID shows it's from Robbie Winthrop's law office. He gathers his thoughts and pulls out a pad, then finally answers, "Martino here."

"Mr. Martino, this is Robbie Winthrop, returning your call."

"Please, call me Frank. Do you mind if I call you Robbie?" he replies, trying to break the ice. At the same time, he presses the record button on his phone.

"No. Sure, that's fine, Frank. What's on your mind?"

"We are planning to do a story and wanted to reach out to you for comment."

They want to do a piece on the RFP? That's a bit odd, thinks Robbie. TV news doesn't usually cover this kind of story—this is more a print media piece. She is racking her brain, trying to remember how she knows of Frank Martino. Where had she heard of him?

"You'd like more details related to the grant we've announced?" asks Robbie.

"Yes, that, and..." Franks pauses, leaving Robbie hanging before he says, "Well, I'll get to the point, Robbie."

"Please do," says Robbie, curtly, but a little rattled.

"We have learned that you claimed the November Mega Millions Lottery jackpot. And you are also connected to this RFP thing. It appears that you won and are running the grant. Or it is an unnamed client of yours. So, which is it?"

Surprise doesn't even come close to Robbie's reaction. How did they link the two and so quickly? Someone must have leaked it to Martino. It had to be someone at the lottery. But who? It could be anyone—a clerk or a secretary. There is no way of knowing who. Ultimately, it's the lottery top dog who is responsible. If they leaked and revealed the donor, they would skewer the senior leadership. But winners' identities are usually made public, but not with trusts. She has an affidavit guaranteeing anonymity. Robbie's head is spinning.

"Robbie, are you still there?" By now, Martino knows she is not the winner and is considering how to protect her client. Without outright denying she claimed the winnings, she is confirming it.

"Robbie, who is the winner? Listen, we learned it was you who claimed the prize. It doesn't matter how. Our source has full deniability—no one explicitly singled you out, we just connected the dots. We can easily send out a truck and crew with a picture of you and snoop around and we'd get the same result."

"Alright, Frank. It was me. I claimed the prize on behalf of my client. But I cannot tell you who my client is. I just can't."

Frank gets it. But he now has confirmation that the lottery winner and grant are linked. He has enough for his story. That's good news. The bad news is, he has missed the deadline for today's news cycle; it will have to wait until tomorrow.

For Robbie, it finally registers. Martino is the guy who broke the lottery story back in November. He seemed like the relentless type. She'd have to stay on her toes to protect Jeremiah.

"Frank, whatever you do, please remember, we are trying to do something good here," offers Robbie.

"Yeah, I know. I'm just doing my job."

"I understand. I'd be happy to share more with you soon. But I doubt my client will ever want to reveal their identity—certainly not anytime soon."

"Okay. Whatever you can, whenever you can, would be great," says Martino.

"I'll be in touch," Robbie closes and then hangs up, as does Martino.

Wow. Tough stuff. No interest in why the grant, just who's behind it, thinks Robbie, annoyed. Grabbing her cell phone, she shoots Jeremiah a text: *CBS knows it was me.*

Her iPhone rings immediately. It's Jeremiah, wanting to know what had happened. She explains everything that took place, emphasizing that someone at the lottery must have leaked it. "I am linked. But they didn't know anything about you," she explains.

They conclude that it isn't the worst thing and end the call.

Chapter 59
Press Time, Again

The NY Times RFP piece ran as expected. It contained no surprises, no revelations. It was light without any significant details concerning who the players are, the Rising-Up grant's vision, or goals. But the Times had scored the scoop in the mainstream media. The public had just learned about the RFP and the one hundred million earmarked to the NYC non-profit world.

When Robbie arrives at the office, there are a few messages on her phone. One is from Newsday. Depending on who you spoke to, Newsday is Long Island's equivalent to the Times. Leaving a callback number, the caller had read about the grant and wants to know if it is true.

Robbie will decide how to handle this call. For now, she has enough on her plate. A callback, if at all, will have to wait.

It's ten past five when Jeremiah walks into the house. Like most days, Kate is working with the TV's sound muted in the living room. Jeremiah changes into workout clothes and sits on the couch facing Kate. They exchange details about how their respective days have gone.

The conversation wanes, and the room goes quiet. Endless commercials advertise repetitively. None are of any interest to Kate or Jeremiah. Kate then asks Jeremiah if there are any developments with the RFP. He gives her a brief account of what they have received so far: a few applications, some letters, and a bunch of phone messages. Jeremiah qualifies the results by reminding Kate that it has only been a week since they went public with the announcement. He also shares that Robbie has received numerous inquiries from the media.

Returning to her work, Kate unmutes the TV. The late afternoon CBS news is on the screen. There is an oversized graphic displayed: EXCLUSIVE LOTTERY UPDATE. The reporter is standing in front of a kiosk in Manhattan with a mic in hand. He continues with how CBS has an exclusive regarding the recent unclaimed four hundred and thirty million Mega Millions Lottery prize. From anonymous sources, CBS has learned of a connection between the winner and a Long Island group planning to donate one hundred million to an NYC non-profit organization.

Kate looks over at Jeremiah, stunned. He had not mentioned details of the media calls Robbie had received. Both Robbie and Jeremiah saw little impact on the connection between the Rising-Up grant and the lottery winner. Plus, there was even less they could do about it. The reporter shares nothing more about who the actual winner is and invites viewers to stay tuned to CBS for further updates in the coming days.

Kate mutes the TV. "Is this bad?" she asks.

"Not really. I think it somewhat legitimizes what we are doing. Let's face it: it was only a matter of time before someone connected the two. I would have preferred it to be after we had completed the process and made the grant. But sometimes, things are out of one's control. I am not concerned."

Chapter 60
Hey Google

Home alone, Danny sits in his kitchen with his laptop open to Google. The first result from his search for Jeremiah Baldwin is The Way Home's leadership page. In the administrative section is Jeremiah's name, prominently displayed as the head of the IT department. Other search results reveal that Jeremiah had a running career years ago. More results point to a Facebook page and sites to perform identity checks. Nothing is coming up that makes Jeremiah look like anything other than your average Joe.

Who is this guy? thinks Danny. *Why is he the beneficiary of the second trust?*

He Googles "Phoenix Warehouse." Results appear for either Phoenix or Warehouse, but nothing for both words. Then Danny Googles "Rising-Up"—and a stream of web addresses pop up. The Chronicle of Philanthropy, Philanthropy New York, and the New York Times are listed. Rising-Up's website is also displayed. Danny reads all the content. So, Rising-Up is an organization that plans to give away a lot of money to some lucky non-profit charity! The only name associated with Rising-Up is an attorney, Robbie Winthrop, with no references to Baldwin.

He scrolls the results and discovers a CBS news video clip titled: *CBS Exclusive—Rising-Up & Mega Millions Linked*. Danny clicks on the link, and the video slowly loads and then plays the news item that aired previously. The reporter states that someone from the Rising-Up organization had claimed the Mega Millions Lottery jackpot from early November.

"The plot thickens," mutters Danny quietly. "So, what's the deal here?"

Getting up and pacing the room for a few minutes, he stops and looks out the window. A man sits on a bench across the street with a dog; its leash tied to a pole a few feet away. It hits Danny like a bolt of lightning: this Rising-Up thing claimed the lottery jackpot. Phoenix Warehouse and Rising-Up are associated. And this guy Baldwin is connected to Phoenix.

Phoenix is the beneficiary of Rising-Up, and Baldwin is the beneficiary of Phoenix; hence Baldwin is the beneficiary of Rising-Up. So, Jeremiah Baldwin is the lottery winner, and the two trusts are masking his identity to claim the money anonymously! *That sneaky son-of-a-bitch*, rails Danny to himself. *Who does he think he is?*

Chapter 61
You've Got Mail

As the week winds down, Robbie is looking forward to a slower-paced weekend. It has been a tough week with all the media BS. Her office hadn't been this busy since interest rates bottomed in September 2012 when everyone was scrambling to refinance their mortgages. In less than a week, the Rising-Up project has received one carton full of mail. That evening, she and Jeremiah are going through the mail to organize it. Jeremiah had created a spreadsheet to track the correspondence received.

They had decided on three major categories:

- Completed applications, separated into two sub-groups: qualifying (moving on to second round) and those eliminated

- Letters of any kind

- Phone messages

Rising-Up has received seventy-eight qualifying applications, eighteen letters, and thirteen phone messages. The applications will be reviewed and evaluated by the selection committee. Jeremiah will read the correspondence later and determine if any of it might be worthy of further consideration. Unfortunately, Robbie's cursory review had not identified anything relevant from her perspective.

Of the thirteen phone messages, ten were inconsequential, but three were from media outlets: The NY Times, Newsday, and WCBS-NYC.

Stepping away from the conference room table, Jeremiah turns to Robbie after they finish sorting the applications, saying, "Not bad for a week. I bet we'll get double this in the next."

"We should schedule a selection committee meeting for next Saturday to determine who should get the second application. We could do that here, no?" he continues.

"Sure, that'll work. I'll send a meeting invite tomorrow to the group," replies Robbie.

"Interesting, the calls from the media," says Jeremiah.

"Yeah, I know. The media are so quick to pick up on things. I still can't believe the leak at the lottery—it pisses me off! I should go after Granson. I don't know. We will need to be extra careful in the future if we are to keep you anonymous. I should be the only person to have any contact with them," answers Robbie.

"Agreed. You are right, on all counts," finishes Jeremiah.

"Right. Now let's get out of here and call it a day."

Jeremiah salutes Robbie as they pack up. Jeremiah grabs the letters, which he will review at home. Finally, they both head out for the weekend. Thank God it's Friday!

What's a good secret worth?

Danny continues to research Jeremiah Baldwin, Rising-Up, and Phoenix Warehouse but cannot find much of any substance. All he can surmise is that this sneak Baldwin is getting all that money Scot-Free without anyone knowing that Jeremiah Baldwin is the winner. And all the while, Danny is up to his ears in debt. It just isn't fair!

Wondering, Danny whispers to himself, "I bet he'd like to keep it all a secret. How much would it be worth to him that no one finds out? Ten, twenty, fifty grand? I bet he'd pay handsomely."

Alas, a vague conspiracy is hatching in Danny's mind. Nothing definitive yet, other than a possible way to get out from under his debilitating financial obligations. Of course, there is no consideration of consequence with such a scheme. It just seems like a way out. He sits there in a daydream, letting the notion of being debt-free fester.

Chapter 62
Drama Central

It's another dreary wintery day in the northeast, not too cold, but dirty gray everywhere. On days like today, Florida seems so appealing. Ryan is home for the weekend and sitting at the kitchen island, having breakfast.

Jeremiah is at the stove making an omelet when Ryan starts, "So Dad, now that we have all this money, when are we going to split it up? When am I going to get my share?"

"Your share? Are you kidding, Ryan?" replies Jeremiah.

"No, really, Dad?" persists Ryan.

"Listen. Things will stay pretty much the same around here for a while, maybe some slight changes. I will continue to manage the finances, just like before, but it'll be more comfortable for us. No Bentleys, though. I want a house in Florida. Hopefully, we'll leave you kids a nice inheritance down the road," says Jeremiah flatly.

A debate ensues. Ryan cannot wrap his head around the notion of charity on the scale of what Jeremiah is considering. Nevertheless, he wants his piece of the prize.

"Enough, Ryan," Jeremiah finally says. "It is my ticket and therefore my decision. I'll consider any reasonable suggestions or requests, but no 'Crazy Rich Asians' lifestyle for us. Got it, mister?"

"So not cool, Pops!"

Kate is out getting her nails done and running errands. While heading to the cashier at the Stop & Shop, she runs into Julie Stevenson, Kate's childhood best friend from Jericho. Julie picks up where she'd left off about how crazy it is for them to give away so much money.

"I couldn't believe it when I saw it on the news the other day—I wanted to call them and tell them that you are the idiots behind this whole dumb grant idea."

"Jesus, Jules, have you lost your mind?"

"Me, what about you? I'm not throwing away a hundred million!"

There is no explaining any of this to her. It is literally like a Democrat trying to explain the reality of global warming to a Republican.

Finally, Kate says in the most controlled and stern way, "If you screw this up, Julie, I will never, ever talk to you again. Just mind your own business and stay out of ours. We clear?"

Julie nods meekly. They stare at each other, and Julie then slips away with her tail between her legs. Kate never gets this excited, but this is too much. And it felt pretty good to let off a little steam. The past few days have been so intense.

Jeremiah left the house for a workout at the gym, so Only Harley and Ryan are home. Ryan is still disturbed by his father's gullibility. He walks into Harley's bedroom, where she is texting on her iPhone and watching TV.

For the first time, Ryan is revealing his true feelings, similar to Julie's. He says to Harley, "I can't believe Dad would give away all that money. If we split up one hundred million four ways, that would be twenty-five million each. I can't believe he'd do that to us."

"First of all, it's not ours. It's Dad's, and he should be able to do whatever he wants with it," replies Harley. "And second, there's still a lot for us afterward."

"Yeah, but he isn't going to split that up either, at least not now. He's talking about an inheritance someday. Completely ludicrous, if you ask me. What a control freak!"

"No one's asking you, Ryan. You're such a douche."

Ryan walks out in a huff.

In his car on the way home from the gym, Jeremiah's phone rings. It's Robbie. "You gotta sec?" she asks.

"Sure, what's up?"

"Well, when I was speaking to the reporter from the Times last week, it was pretty obvious that we need to have a vision and goals for Rising-Up. At least something we can go public with."

"You're right. We need to define what we see as the outcome of making this grant. In broad terms, we need to articulate what we want to accomplish. So much of it will be aspirational, but we do need something."

"Exactly. We need to frame how the grant will help even though we don't know who will be receiving it."

"I will play with this tomorrow. Robbie, thank you."

"Talk soon."

Chapter 63
Short and Sweet

The next day, having slept on his fantasy about a big payola for Jeremiah Baldwin's secret, Danny decides to approach Baldwin blindly. He has nothing to lose. *The guy is smart—he'd surely be open to buying some "insurance for his secret,"* reasons Danny.

How do I get to him? Maybe through that attorney for Rising-Up. They did publish her name and address. He could send a note to Baldwin through the attorney, he concludes—nothing too much, something short and sweet.

Something like:

To: Jeremiah Baldwin

I know what you have done, and I know who you are.

I am offering you some insurance to keep your secret.

I will be in touch.

Looking at the message, Danny figures it should do the trick, failing to realize that blackmail is a felony. A crime that not only could derail his budding legal career but one that could land him in jail for a long time. He prints the letter and addresses an envelope to Robbie Winthrop at her office, with no return address. He will mail it in the morning.

Chapter 64
Logan Aldrich

Jeremiah is in the den with a cup of tea. He is going through the stack of letters received with the applications. There are eighteen, but only one stands out—it's from someone named Logan Aldrich.

Her letter apologetically begins by acknowledging that she is not a CEO or grant writer or a fundraising expert at a health and human services organization. However, she is a graduate from The New School, having majored in Sociology (first in her class), and has also received a master's degree from Columbia in non-profit administration. Currently, she is working, remotely in NYC, for the Geller Institute, headquartered in Washington, DC, as a policy research analyst. She continues with:

> I don't know who will read this or if at all. But I want to share my thoughts on what $100 million means to me in making a difference in providing more opportunities for those in poverty.
>
> That is my theme: "Equal opportunity for the poor."
>
> One might ask, "What does this mean, and why is it significant?"
>
> Since the dawn of time, we have been a culture of "have's" and "have-nots." The nature of our society has changed dramatically

from agrarian days. Every person today can be either a contributor or otherwise in our global digital community.

Economic disadvantage is doing the world a tremendous disservice by limiting the participation of bright, capable, economically challenged citizens. If these people cannot participate in our communities, they risk being a drain on our economic infrastructure and resources. Therefore, it is in our interest to empower and enable the poor and mitigate those dependencies and resource drain risks.

Our community can no longer afford to enable the scourge of poverty. Creating genuine opportunities for all is the solution, and your grant could be a considerable step in fueling dramatic change in reversing poverty in New York.

Our poor are underutilized national resources. We need to create programs and advocacy for social and political change to provide equal rights for the poor. Increased access to higher education, housing, career opportunities, and healthcare is essential.

To this extent, my theme for more equity for the poor resonates with the vision of your philanthropy: I want to be a part of it.

She has written some "manifesto," but Jeremiah likes it—he likes it a lot. It embodies many of his deepest feelings. She sounds so liberal, so Bernie Sanders. Such passion and energy in her words. Here is a young person who wants to be part of the solution, not the problem. It might be half-baked, but it sure does engender hope in Jeremiah.

He doesn't know what response he and the committee might have for the letter, but for now, it is worthy of more in-depth exploration. As Jeremiah rereads the letter, his thoughts turn to what Robbie said about Rising-Up needing an articulated vision statement and goals. He jots down some ideas:

The Vision: This grant will enable a non-profit organization to address a social problem affecting those living in poverty by creating new programs or enhancing existing ones.

The Goal: The grant will have maximum impact with visible and measurable outcomes.

He has a good start. Jeremiah will present it at the upcoming committee meeting for feedback and ideas for expanding it.

Chapter 65
More Applications

It's only been three days since the last mail Robbie received on Friday. Sixty-four new applications, four letters, and two phone calls.

The days roll on, and by Friday, an additional one hundred twenty-seven applications arrive, of which thirty are bogus scams, bringing the total legit apps to two hundred thirty-nine.

The media exposure didn't hurt and undoubtedly boosted application submissions with more correspondence and phone calls. None are of any concern—except one, which will require a sober discussion with Jeremiah in person.

The media has quieted down, too. They are about to close the qualifying application process, and Robbie intends to give Martino and Chen updates after the selection committee meeting on Saturday. Soon, they'll be moving into the real work: finding the right grantee.

Chapter 66
Now What?

When Robbie had called Jeremiah earlier in the morning, they agreed to meet up later in the day at a diner on Jericho Turnpike. But discreetly, she had not given him any heads-up on why she wanted to meet. Often, they would get together to hash out details concerning the RFP. They are now seated in a secluded booth in the rear.

"How could this happen?" asks Jeremiah after hearing about Dan Carson's letter. "How did someone link me to Rising-Up?"

"Well, we did know that any ingenious deviant with access to the trust documents could piece it together," replies Robbie caustically, trying to diffuse Jeremiah's angst.

"Yeah, but still," whimpers Jeremiah.

"I know. Regardless, it couldn't have been the lottery—they weren't aware of the Phoenix trust's beneficiary. They only knew that Phoenix was the Rising-Up beneficiary."

Jeremiah listens quietly. He's annoyed with this wrinkle and distracted—something he did not want or expect.

Robbie continues, "It had to be someone at the County Clerk's Office. They are the only ones with access to both documents. So, someone there had to have linked them. But who? They are so swamped with work. Who'd have the time to connect the two?"

"Yeah, and who would have the audacity to attempt to bribe us?" questions Jeremiah. "Don't you love the last line: 'I'll be in touch,' without any mention of how much this 'insurance' is going to cost."

"Listen, Jeremiah. Be prepared—you may have to pay this guy off," warns Robbie.

Jeremiah shudders at the thought; it is utterly contrary to his values. Finally, they agree that they will have to wait and see.

Chapter 67
The Selection Committee Meets

Now that two weeks have passed since the official RFP announcement, Jeremiah has convened his "selection committee." This group of trusted friends will advise him in selecting the right charity for the Rising-Up grant. Ruby, Eli, and Morgan have taken the LIRR from the city, and Jeremiah has picked them up at the Hicksville station and driven them to Robbie's office in Plainview.

Everyone is seated in Robbie's conference room. The space is tight but not uncomfortable. The session will not take more than three hours, and refreshments and coffee are available.

Jeremiah has prepared an agenda. It is brief and direct.

AGENDA

Introductions

Opening remarks – Ruby

Goals for the day

Vision for Rising-Up

The evaluation/selection process

Next steps

The mood is upbeat while everyone introduces themselves. Finally, Jeremiah asks Ruby to say a few words.

Clearing her throat, Ruby starts, "I was thrilled when Jeremiah told me about his winning, and even more so when he shared his thoughts about Rising-Up. How cool to be involved in selecting an organization that fits best in fulfilling his wishes to create positive social impact in our community. I have worked with social services agencies serving the poor for many years, deeply yearning to see more improvement in the conditions that exist for the less fortunate. Progress has occurred, but only in small steps. Oh, how wonderful it would be to achieve some quantum leaps in this fight. What Jeremiah is doing is bold, and bold leadership will accomplish miraculous outcomes." Looking at Jeremiah, she says, "Thank you for asking me to be a part of this! Thank you all for being here today."

There are soft applause and a warm feeling in the room. Kate is taking it all in, now feeling some pride in what Jeremiah is attempting to do. For the first time, it is registering that they are on the verge of doing something profoundly good. There can be no downside—their hearts are in the right place. She is beaming.

Jeremiah expresses his thanks to Ruby. He is lifted by what she has just said. It's one thing to have those feelings in one's head, but when someone else echoes them, it's startling. He is about to continue when Robbie interrupts with, "I, too, am thrilled to be a part of this."

And Eli joins in, "Me too!"

Morgan, who had been observing everything, says, "I, too, have been in the social services world for many years and have worked with

Jeremiah. But, I have never seen anything like this before. This is amazing!"

With everyone having had their opportunity to share, Jeremiah moves to the next agenda item. The day's goal is to filter the qualifying applications down to a group of candidates who will receive a second, more detailed application.

Next is the vision for the Rising-Up grant. Ruby begins with, "Jeremiah and I have been talking a lot about this." She then hands out a piece of paper. At the top is a title and four bullets:

Rising-Up Grant – Vision Elements

- Improve self-sufficiency, economic capacity, and social wellbeing
- Transform the lives of those living in poverty
- Enable those in need to create productive lives of purpose
- Empower them to realize their potential

Jeremiah follows with, "These are the major themes or aspects that I think are important for a vision for the grant." Handing out another piece of paper, he continues, "Taking them all together, this is my thinking for a vision statement for the grant." And he points to the sheet in his hand, which reads:

Rising-Up Grant – Vision Statement

To improve self-sufficiency, economic capacity, and social wellbeing for those living in poverty and enable them to realize their potential and to create more productive lives.

Proceeding, he says, "It is important to have these values down on paper to be our guiding principles in this selection process. The vision statement and its elements are not cast in concrete and can be tweaked if necessary. Also, as we move forward with the grant, there may be times where we will need to speak publicly about our process. This vision statement will be useful in that respect. Lastly, the vision statement will also help us arrive at specific grant goals for the winning candidate."

The group studies the vision statement and elements, followed by a bit of murmuring, whispering, and head bobbing. After a few minutes, Jeremiah asserts, holding up both pieces of paper, "So for now, if there are no changes or suggestions, let's agree that this represents the Rising-Up vision."

Unanimously, everyone declares, "Agreed."

Eli stands and reaches for the ceiling. "I need a little stretch break," he says.

Ruby also gets up, walks to the room's side, and begins texting someone. Kate and Morgan are chatting while Robbie, checking her email, has drifted to the other side of the room. This impromptu intermission lasts for only five minutes.

When everyone is back in their chairs, Robbie resumes the meeting by describing the evaluation process. She then points to a stack of forms to be used to capture each reviewer's findings.

"We will evaluate each application on the organization's culture, vision, potential impact, organizational excellence, and leadership.

We will be ranking each evaluation category on a scale from 1 - 10, then tabulating the scores. An application will pass with a score of 36 (out of 50) or higher. Those proposals with at least two "passes" will advance to the next application."

The applications, two hundred thirty-nine in total, are sitting in the center of the table, and the group begins taking apps, reviewing, and evaluating them. Each person completes a proposal, then passes it to their right. After two hours, the original stack of apps has become a new stack at the head of the table. Jeremiah informs the group that Eli will score them. Additionally, he discloses that if anyone wants to leave at this point, they are welcome to do so. No one does.

Eli reviews each evaluated application. He scores each one, as Jeremiah had outlined. Of all the apps, twenty-three scored thirty-six or higher. And of those, sixteen apps had achieved a thirty-six or better score from two of the evaluators. Thus, sixteen applicants will receive notification to complete a second application.

After Eli has announced the results, everyone cheers lightly. They have accomplished their primary goal for the day and are ready to move on to the next phase. Robbie looks over at Jeremiah with joyful eyes; she is relieved—it has turned out as envisioned.

As the group gets ready to leave, Jeremiah shares the next steps:

(1)   The committee will notify the selected applicants of their advancing to the next phase to complete a second app.

(2)   They will also notify those who did not advance and

(3)   They will need to create another selection process for picking the three or four finalists.

Jeremiah cautions that he is undecided about whether a similar group approach for the second evaluation will be the same as the first. In any event, he will notify the committee of what the selection process will be in a few days.

They completed the evaluation in under three hours, just as Jeremiah had predicted. Kate volunteers to drive Morgan, Ruby, and Eli to the railroad station for the next train to the city. In the parking garage, hugs all around, a happy group. Robbie is staying behind to finish up a few work tasks. And Jeremiah is heading home—he slides into his car alone, a bit exhausted but completely pleased. Another step closer to the finish line, but still with many miles to go.

Chapter 68
Out of the Blue

Later that night, Jeremiah is in his bedroom, having read the insurance letter for the hundredth time, when his iPhone rings. It's 9:30 at night—who could be calling now? He answers tentatively, not recognizing the caller's number. It's Ava Starling, Jeremiah's psychic astrologer friend.

"Hi, Jeremiah. I hope I'm not disturbing you," starts Ava.

"No, no, it's okay," replies Jeremiah.

Ava continues, "I just had the strangest vision of you. I saw you surrounded in much darkness. I had this impression of you with a noose around your neck and a gun to your head. Is everything okay?"

"I'm okay, but I am dealing with a situation with my lottery secret. Someone has found out I won and wants money to keep quiet. I received this letter. It's disturbing, to say the least," responds Jeremiah.

"Read it to me. Maybe I can 'see' something," directs Ava.

Jeremiah proceeds to read the letter as Ava listens in a trance-like, meditative state. There is silence for about fifteen seconds when she finally says, "I see a shiny new sportscar, bathed in blinding sunlight. The images of the car and the sun keep alternating: car, sun, car, sun. It's a name—Carson! Not sure if it's a first or last name. Wait! I now see the letter D. It's the first name starting with the letter D. D Carson is the sender's name. The D bleeds into an image of a dam on a river. I think it means Dan. Yes, the first name is Dan or maybe David. No, it's Dan. Sometimes he goes by Danny, but hardly ever Daniel. The sender of the letter is Dan Carson."

Jeremiah can't believe it. "Are you sure?" he asks.

"Definitely the Carson part, and pretty sure on the first name too."

"Wow, that's too much. Now we must find this Carson guy. I'm going to ask Robbie if she can work with this," Jeremiah declares, feeling a bit better now.

"You hang in there, Jeremiah. Everything will work out fine. Let me know if I can help in any way," reinforces Ava.

"I sure will. Thank you so much, Ava!"

Chapter 69
I Know a Guy

Jeremiah's night sleep was fitful; he kept waking up with haunting visions of his blackmailer. Finally, unable to sleep, he rolls out of bed and tries to calm himself by meditating. Not surprisingly, it works, and he can think more clearly—certainly, Robbie will come up with a plan for dealing with this, now that the blackmailer has a name.

Although it's early, he gets her on the phone. Their conversation is challenging, but it ultimately quiets Jeremiah's anxieties. He shares the full extent of his call with Ava. Robbie probes and throws questions out, demonstrating her initial skepticism of Ava's findings. In the end, she relents. Dan Carson is the guy who sent the insurance letter.

"What should we do?" asks Jeremiah.

"First, we will confirm he is real, and then we will locate him and get more information on who he is. The more we know about him, the better we will be able to identify his weak spots. Knowing his identity is big! We will then devise a plan to turn him from going any further with his shake-down scheme. Then we approach him. I know a good investigator, and he owes me. His name is Tony Calabretta, and he's smart, relentless, nearby, and six-six—very intimidating! Once we get more on Carson, Tony will visit him." Robbie pauses. "Oh, and one more thing, Jeremiah. Don't discuss this with anyone! It could get nasty."

Chapter 70
Jeremiah's Big Idea

Having completed some errands, Jeremiah gets comfortable in the den after lunch. Scrolling through the DVR recording, he clicks on CBS Sunday Morning. This show is one of Jeremiah's favorites, always interesting with uplifting stories. On the couch next to him are the sixteen applications from yesterday's meeting, as well as Logan Aldrich's letter and the Rising-Up vision statement. They had made much progress in selecting candidates for the next phase. He feels good.

Jeremiah reads through the proposal summaries again. Each has fascinating stories and visions for what they will do with the money if they are the selected recipient. It is too early to predict which of the proposals will win. It could go in many different directions. Three things, though, are rattling around in Jeremiah's mind:

- The Way Home had outlined a "digital divide" plan for Wi-Fi and connectivity for all its homeless shelters that included laptops, tablets, and staffing for implementation. He liked their proposal concept, mainly since it involved technology.

- Logan Aldrich's letter focused on the poor, an underutilized national resource. She asserted that to provide more equality for the poor, they needed to create advocacy and political/social change programs. In addition, increased access to higher education, housing, career opportunities, and healthcare was essential.

- How did the applications and Logan's letter measure up with the grant's vision? Did they intersect in any way?

Earlier in the morning, when Jeremiah awoke, he meditated again, easing himself in the best way he knew how. As he sits in the den, ignoring the TV, his thoughts turn to how they can combine the three proposal concepts. Ten minutes flash by in an instant when suddenly Jeremiah's intuition whispers a gentle, encouraging impression: *Just Do It.*

That's it! Merge the three concepts into a broader initiative. It is a stark departure from the initial RFP plan of identifying one worthy non-profit recipient. This more comprehensive digital divide initiative will need to be larger in scope, involve other non-profits, and most likely government and corporate support.

Jeremiah does not know how all this might come together. It doesn't matter; the bigger idea is what matters now. It is bold. Very bold, and it resonates with Jeremiah. He will play with it and see if it will gain any additional traction.

A pad and pen rest on the side table. Jeremiah starts making notes. He draws triangles, boxes, and arrows, not exactly a flow diagram. After numerous sketches and notes, things are starting to click.

He starts writing down some bullets:

- City-wide
- Access
- Technology
- The poor

That's it: an initiative to provide city-wide access to technology for the poor. Jeremiah will let it simmer. The idea is marinating, taking shape.

The Rising-Up grant will provide technical assistance funding for city-wide "access ramps" to the digital superhighway in all homeless shelters and public housing in New York City. It will be a public-private partnership involving multiple non-profits, city government, and corporate sponsorship.

Looking at what he has just written, Jeremiah keeps reflecting. He is not doubtful, but he's unsure what to do next. His advisors will need to weigh in on this. And he will also speak to Logan Aldrich for her take, if for no other reason than to let her know how moved he was by her letter. But, for now, he will coin the access ramp idea as Plan B.

Before dinner, Jeremiah emails Morgan to see if they can meet for coffee or lunch tomorrow, suggesting a diner near her apartment in the '50s. Jeremiah intends to use their time together to obtain feedback on his new idea. But, of course, there is no telling what she might think.

Wherever she comes out on this idea, though, there is a rational case for it. Jeremiah will have to wait and see.

Chapter 71
Do Access Ramps Connect?

The next day, Jeremiah checks his email—he has received a reply from Morgan. Yes, they can meet around noon for lunch at the Mercury diner on Second Avenue. With that settled, Jeremiah turns his attention to his other work items for the day. He has a brief meeting scheduled for eleven. Afterward, he'll head out to meet Morgan.

Precisely at the agreed-upon time, Jeremiah walks into the diner. Morgan is sitting in a booth with a cup of tea and the NY Times open. She greets him warmly as he sits across from her. The waiter asks if Jeremiah would like a menu. He declines, saying he only wants a cup of black coffee and some tuna salad.

As the waiter drifts away, Morgan asks, "So, what's up?" He describes how he is thinking about a much more ambitious project with his lottery winnings without hesitation. An initiative that would dwarf the original plan to find one charity for the grant.

Before Morgan can reply, the waiter returns with Jeremiah's order. He slowly takes a sip of his coffee as Morgan sits there, processing what he has just shared with her. She is conflicted. On one level, the idea sounds great. But, on another, she feels there are too many opportunities for things to go wrong. And she tells him so. She further describes where she thinks the potential choke points are and the areas where breakdowns could arise, specifically when attempting to coordinate such a large project with so many diverse stakeholders.

Jeremiah is disappointed but did want some honest feedback. He'll have to re-think this idea. It was only Plan B, distant at best. He will continue, for now, with the original RFP concept: Plan A. With nothing further to discuss, he scarfs down the rest of his tuna and coffee. As he places a ten-dollar bill on the table, he says to Morgan, "Gonna bolt on you, hon; got a lot of stuff waiting for me back at The Way." She smiles, and he gives her a peck on the cheek before he is out the door.

Twenty minutes later, Jeremiah is back at his desk. He logs into the RFP website and begins cloning it. He is going to create a sister site for the second application candidates. It is a quick set of tasks with minimal content changes. He then reviews an email he had drafted earlier; Robbie will send it out on his behalf to preserve his anonymity. He does the same for the mail to the candidates who did not advance. Both are brief and cordial. When he is satisfied, he forwards the drafts to Robbie.

Now it's time to connect with Logan Aldrich. Jeremiah opens his Gmail account. In his drafts folder is an email he had composed the night before. It expresses his positive reactions to her letter and his desire to meet with her to explore further how his grant could be more aligned with her vision. He suggests a few times and places. Finally, after rereading the draft three or four times, he presses the send button.

Fifteen minutes later, his cell phone rings. It's Logan. Her voice is firm yet friendly, and she'd be happy to connect in person. They agree to meet at a Starbucks near Penn Station at eight a.m.

Before calling it a day, Jeremiah flips through his folder of applicants who will receive the second application email. Of the sixteen, Bronx Family Services is one that resonated thoroughly with Jeremiah. BFS is located a few blocks from Yankee Stadium in the South Bronx; their CFO is an old contact of Jeremiah's. BFS has diverse social programs, including permanent housing, shelters, housing protection, social work, job readiness, and entry-level technology job training. They are well run and have an excellent reputation.

Another non-profit selected is The Life Recovery Center, headquartered in lower Manhattan. They, too, have a wide range of social programs, good financials, and a respected community presence. Either of these two candidates would make a worthy recipient of the grant, should the original RFP plan remain intact.

Chapter 72
Coffee Time

Jeremiah arrived at the office early the next day in advance of his meeting with Logan. After reading some of the overnight emails, he heads out to the Starbucks down the street. There, sitting alone, is an attractive young woman typing on her cell phone. He goes over to her, inquiring, "Logan?"

She smiles. She has a coffee, and Jeremiah signals he is going to get something for himself. She nods. When he returns, he sits down across from her. They exchange pleasantries and details about themselves, getting better acquainted. Jeremiah wants Logan to know how moved he was by her letter. He had sensed a sincere desire on her part to make a difference. It is as if she was a kindred spirit of sorts. Who better to engage with on Jeremiah's Request for Proposal mission?

As he elaborates upon the RFP history to date, Jeremiah tries to gloss over the lottery part. Nonetheless, Logan politely interrupts, "So that was you? You are the winner?"

Somewhat bashfully, he concurs with a shake of his head. Continuing, he offers vivid details, including how they had collected the funds anonymously, the press and the story linking the RFP to the lottery win, the selection committee, and finally arriving at the point where he intends to share his thoughts about the digital divide. He pauses.

Logan has been listening carefully. Jeremiah can tell she is impressed. The RFP had accomplished much in a short time. She comments, "That's some story. So much of it seems like a fantasy. It's hard to believe someone would do this. Why? Don't answer. I get it. I could imagine doing something so selfless if I were in your shoes."

There is a pause in the conversation. Nothing uncomfortable.

Logan continues, "So, why are we here now? What's on your mind, and how does it concern me?"

Her directness strikes Jeremiah. She is sharp and to the point. He replies, "I have this idea and think you could fit into it very nicely. It is a bit of a departure from my original concept for the Request for Proposal.

Let me explain. When I read your letter, you mentioned 'greater equity for the poor' and more access to essential services and resources. It resonated strongly with me. I then read a proposal we received that suggested funding for technology infrastructure to bridge the digital divide.

These two ideas merged in my mind. Bridging the digital divide was the way to increase access to services and resources for the poor. It could be the best way to create more equity. What if we took this one agency's proposal and expanded it city-wide? Thus, a bolder vision was born for my grant for city-wide access ramps to the digital superhighway in all homeless shelters and public housing."

Logan is entranced. She had had no idea what to expect from Jeremiah when he had asked to meet. His concept is so over the top. How could this be achieved? He has one hundred million, no small fortune, but a project of this magnitude would require so much more. Yet—it is incredible.

Finally, she replies, "That is something. It's huge. But how are you going to pull it off? And why am I here?"

She answered enthusiastically yet reservedly. Jeremiah has nothing specific in mind. He only feels that she might bring a certain amount of energy to the project to get it off the ground. He says, "I'm not sure. I felt Ramp-Up—that's what I'm calling this idea—might appeal to you, that you might want to be a part of it in some way."

"It is certainly compelling. Game-changing. Who wouldn't want to be part of something as groundbreaking as this?"

"Well, do you want in?"

She pauses, wondering, *What am I getting into here?* Then, finally, "Yes, I want in. What do you want me to do? How can I help?"

"Well, we first need to determine if this is viable. Can we pull together the needed resources to make this happen? We need to do a little research and analysis. We need to frame out the scope and participants and their roles. We also need to figure out the leadership and governance aspects. Those elements should reveal if this is realistic. Could you do that?"

"Yes, of course. Analysis projects like this are part of what I do regularly at work."

"Good, give some thought to how you would proceed and what compensation you would like. We need to act quickly, though. I want to make a decision sooner than later on this."

"I can map this out within a couple of weeks, probably much quicker, and then I will get back to you with the details. And I assume this is all on the down-low."

"Good, and correct, completely confidential."

Chapter 73
It Doesn't Take Long

Tony Calabretta lives in Garden City, only a couple of miles from 240 Old Country Road. He has a stylish, three-bedroom house not far from the Roosevelt Field Shopping Mall, and the smallest bedroom on the second floor is his office. One of the many tools in his investigator's toolbox is his incredible technical skills. If he couldn't hack into it, he knew someone who could—and would. There is no one he can't find.

Dan Carson is going to be easy! A quick Google search brings up the usual websites: a LinkedIn page, the Hofstra student forum, a Facebook page—he also finds information from a Nassau County employee site. Tony scrolls through the site's pages and finds Carson, a part-time clerk at the County Clerk's office. Bam! So that's how he put together the Rising-Up/Lottery/Jeremiah connection.

Now for the good stuff—Tony finds his driving record, bank records, credit history, family background, a criminal check, and more. Tony uses a standard profile template he had borrowed from his FBI days. With all the data he's obtained, he will merge it and identify Carson's psychological makeup, motivators, and tendencies. This analysis will reveal how to pinpoint the ideal triggers to neutralize the blackmail scheme. Then they can take action to disarm Carson as a threat.

It doesn't take long for Tony to complete his analysis. Carson is laden with family issues, is passive-aggressive, and is financially stressed; he should fold under the slightest amount of pressure. Tony will visit him at his job as the next step. He scribbles a note on a nearby pad to call Robbie by the end of the day to update her.

Chapter 74
Pivot Time

It's late afternoon, and Jeremiah is on his usual train home. He has had all day to reflect on his meeting with Logan. She had agreed to drill down further on the viability of his RFP Plan B—Ramp-Up—for access ramps to the digital superhighway for the poor.

Nothing is more apparent to him than that this could be a tangent and dissolve into extinction. Yet, he feels compelled to pursue it until it is obvious it will not fly. In the meantime, Plan A will continue to move forward.

However, based on the second application results, Jeremiah will also be trolling for potential Ramp-Up partners. He plans to share the Ramp-Up possibility with the team soon, either at the next meeting, by email, or separate phone calls.

Plan B's focus will be on homeless shelter providers, supportive housing, and government public housing.

A second application for government and housing provider non-profits is not feasible, as they haven't completed the first application. Government agencies and supportive housing organizations would need a different means for consideration. It would be difficult to proceed along these two different paths with the same process. Therefore, it makes sense to focus on shelter providers using the existing evaluation process.

Jeremiah is in wonderland. How can he float Ramp-Up?

Robbie called, but it went to voicemail. "There were more 'first' applications in today's mail. Maybe you could look them over before the holidays?" Jeremiah's mind turns to thoughts of curiosity on how his team members will react to this different approach for the grant. How would they feel about Plan B? He is impatient and needs to get some sense of how acceptable Plan B would be with his committee. He pulls out his iPhone and hastily begins to craft an email to the group, providing few details, but offering that he is thinking about a broader initiative for the grant. The expanded focus is on bridging the digital divide for all by providing "access ramps" to the digital superhighway.

He closes by saying that he doesn't want to get into a long email thread but only wants to share his current thinking. He'll supply further details, and they will discuss this at their next meeting after the holidays. He knows he'll get reactions but has no idea of the type or by whom.

Chapter 75
"You can take this job and—"

Jeremiah has scheduled a one-on-one with his boss, Sara. He wants to test the waters concerning his forthcoming departure, not that he needs to; he is now a millionaire. Jeremiah just wants to ease out smoothly from his existing responsibilities. The last thing he wants is to leave The Way Home high and dry.

At last, Sara comes into her office, where Jeremiah has been waiting for almost half an hour. It is so typical of Sara and no surprise to Jeremiah. Sara sits down at her desk and not at the small conference table where Jeremiah is seated. She gazes at the computer screen with her right-side facing Jeremiah and starts typing at her keyboard as if no one else is in the room. Jeremiah just sits there, waiting patiently. Eventually, Sara turns and looks over at Jeremiah, and immediately Jeremiah declares, "Sara, I'm thinking of leaving."

She doesn't respond, trying to process what she just heard. Finally, Sara wonders, *is Jeremiah going home early or what*. She then replies, "What do you mean?"

"I mean, I'm thinking of leaving The Way, you know, quitting, retiring, whatever you prefer," answers Jeremiah.

"When?"

"Hmm. I am thinking as soon as possible. Soon. Very soon."

"Why?"

"I've been doing this stuff for a long time. There are other things I'd like to do that I have been putting off. Now seems like as good a time as any for me."

"What about our HQ relocation project? And what about that system of yours?"

"That's why we are having this conversation, Sara. I know those are important projects, and I will do what I can to make the transition smooth, but I intend to leave as soon as possible. Frankly, no time ever seems good for big changes like this, right, Sara?"

"Do you think you can push this off a couple of months?"

"No, I want you to put this into motion now and figure out what needs to be done so I can move on. First, you need to create a transition plan for reassigning my responsibilities. Second, you may need to hire some temps or something."

"Damn," complains Sara.

"Stop, Sara. Change is a good thing. We'll work something out. Of course, I can always be reached by phone if needed. But I can no longer be here twenty-four-seven. There is much I want to do and working here will not allow me to focus on those other things that are important to me."

"What kind of things? Oh, never mind. I get it, I think. It's just we recently submitted a proposal for a huge digital divide project, putting Wi-Fi in all our facilities. If we get it, you'd be an important part of the implementation team to make it happen."

That is interesting; Sara is showing cards she usually keeps under wraps.

"Okay, let's talk in a few days. You are going to have to come up with some very creative alternatives, Sara. In the meantime, I suggest you inform Len of my intentions to leave. And please start working up a draft consulting agreement and a transition plan, regardless of your possible pending project."

Jeremiah begins to get up to leave, knowing full well that Sara will do nothing on this except probably tell Len of their meeting. As he heads to the door, Jeremiah says, "Thanks, Sara, see you later."

Chapter 76
Follow Up from Logan

The clock on the DVR reads 8:58 p.m., two days after meeting with Logan. Jeremiah is reading work emails. Then, he shifts to his Gmail account, where a message from Logan is in his inbox. Its subject line reads: Follow up from our Tuesday morning meeting.

With a combination of anticipation and apprehension, Jeremiah opens it and quickly scans the email. She has prepared a preliminary outline of the project elements and what she has discovered thus far.

The outline lays out potential partners in the non-profit, government, and corporate sectors. It also specifies the likely types of housing facilities that could "ramp up." And Logan has itemized the different kinds of possible technology grants, including infrastructure, devices, and training. Lastly, Logan touches upon the need for framing out leadership and governance structures.

Jeremiah is pleased by the quick response but does not feel moved in the same way when he'd first read Logan's letter. Her outline isn't much more than something he could have composed. It is a good start, but Jeremiah had expected more, much more. And from her research, Logan did not reveal much about the landscape for such a project. Perhaps that was forthcoming in the future.

Ramp-Up is going to be much more ambitious, he fears. Nonetheless, he replies, thanking Logan for her efforts. He tells her he is taking some time off but will be in touch over the holidays.

Bringing Logan into the mix would either require paying her or engaging her on the selection committee—or both.

Chapter 77
Where Can We Talk?

Tony is prepping to confront Dan Carson. He has done his research and conjured up his next moves. Dressed in black trousers with a matching silk shirt and cashmere blazer, Tony exits his also-black Mercedes, parked in the rear lot behind 240 Old Country Road. His .45 caliber Glock is snugly fit in his shoulder holster hidden under his blazer. Entering the building from the back entrance, he follows the signs to the County Clerk's reception desk.

An attractive woman behind the counter politely asks how she might be of service today. Tony says, "I'd like to see Dan Carson, please."

She smiles, picks up the phone. and presses a few buttons, then softly conveys, "There is someone here to see you, Danny." She tells Tony that Carson will be with him shortly.

A couple of minutes pass, and from the reception area's back door walks a young man, clean-cut but with disheveled hair. He can't be more than twenty-five and saunters up to the counter, where Tony is waiting patiently.

"How can I help you?" asks Danny, looking up at Tony.

Staring back at Carson and in a somber no-nonsense voice, Tony states, "I'm interested in some insurance."

Danny goes white for a moment with instant fear. Continuing, Tony asks, "Where can we talk privately?"

Dan's mind is racing like a thoroughbred—where can he escape? There are no real options here. Finally, he stutters, "Follow me," and moves to the left to a door to let Tony in. Tony follows into the service area and continues after Carson into a small conference room.

After the door closes, Tony demands, forcefully, "Sit!"

Danny obeys and asks, "What's this about?"

Tony sits down across from Danny, showing no emotion, and says, "I think you know what this is about. We got your letter."

Danny does not confirm or deny it or say anything at all—he only stares back, not knowing what to expect next.

"Where in the world did you ever get that absurd idea to blackmail a philanthropist who wishes to be anonymous? How selfish can you be? How stupid and desperate are you?"

Beads of sweat surface on Danny's forehead; he never expected a confrontation like this. He figured there'd be some secret communications and ultimately an agreement, and he'd walk away with a sweet bundle of cash. *How'd they ID him so quickly, and who is this big fixer guy?* Danny is in no position to direct anything now. He is screwed!

"Dan, you seem like a nice enough kid. I'm sure you hadn't thought this out much. You didn't even tell us what your insurance would cost," continues Tony. "So, what do you want?"

Danny is like a block of cement, frozen with fear. Stammering after an awkward lapse, "Um, I uh, I don't know—maybe a million?"

Tony starts laughing. "Are you fucking crazy?" After Tony's laughter subsides, he continues, "I tell you what—you think about this some more," giving Danny some degree of false hope. "And you send us another letter when you know what you want exactly. Then, when we get your 'proposal,' we will arrange a sit-down. We clear?"

Danny nods.

"And no one else is to know about this—understand?"

Danny whimpers, "Yes." Quiet again, Danny meekly asks, "How'd you know it was me?"

"We have resources. We know people. We know everything about you, Dan. You just let us know what you want," concludes Tony as he gets up. He leans forward over the table and opens his blazer, and his gun moves forward about six inches, directly in Dan's field of vision. "You know, Dan, if you were smart, you would just drop this whole thing. You are not in a good position on this, capiche?"

With a tinge of bitterness and frustration, Danny finally blathers, "It's not fair that Baldwin gets all that money! I'm entitled to something."

"Really? I don't think so!" Then, tapping his Glock, Tony continues, "Think about what I just said and don't be stupid. This can end nicely."

And without another word, Tony turns toward the door, buttons his blazer, and walks out, leaving Carson shivering in a pool of sweat. Putting his head in his hands, Danny, in disbelief, lets out a deep sigh, bewildered and scared. But his sense of greed is still alive, although on life support; *this is only a speedbump,* he rationalizes to himself.

226

When back in his car, Tony retrieves the recording device in his breast pocket and turns it off.

Chapter 78
Christmas Break

Every year, usually during the week between Christmas and New Year's, the Baldwins head to North Miami for vacation. Kate's mom's condo is in Aventura, due south of Hallandale. This year, Kate and Harley flew down the week before Christmas, and Ryan and Jeremiah followed a few days later.

"Vacation" is an overstatement for these excursions. Kate calls them their annual retreats getaways. They don't do much except lounge around the pool, play cards, go to movies, shop at the mall, walk around the adjacent golf course, and dine out. It is a well-deserved respite with no frills, and usually, everyone needs it. And depending on the weather in New York, the Florida sunshine and warm weather are a blessing.

This year, the break is especially appreciated; Jeremiah has too many balls in the air. Between the RFP, his work responsibilities, and his efforts to extricate himself from The Way Home, he needs some time off.

On the flight down, Jeremiah mulls over Logan's email. She has suggested the creation of a non-profit for managing the Ramp-Up program. It would entail project oversight, funds distribution, and fundraising to obtain additional money from other partners. Rising-Up would fund technical assistance and technology grants. Simultaneously, the Ramp-Up operations would need to find more funders like the Robin Hood Foundation to sustain its administrative functions.

The great thing about holiday recesses is that everything goes quiet for a while. Although it is never one hundred percent, one gets the opportunity to disconnect in this era of remote devices. However, detaching means time slows down, and there is space to work through things with fewer distractions.

As soon as Jeremiah is in the condo, he drops his bags in the foyer and transitions. He changes into a bathing suit, gathers his iPhone, headphones, a book, and heads to the pool. The sun is shining brightly, and the temperature is perfect. He eases into a chaise lounge chair and lets out a long sigh, and then he is fast asleep in five minutes.

The ripples of laughter of children splashing water in the pool playing Marco Polo reach him. He rouses and slowly sits up, refreshed from a twenty-minute power nap. What a gorgeous day!

The minutes slowly tick by, and it doesn't take long for Jeremiah to become fully immersed in his new surroundings. He has been napping all afternoon in the warm, comforting sun and has left the stress and bustle of New York behind. Here in Florida, he can be more himself, and the relaxed climate does wonders for his imagination and contemplation.

The next day while preparing for the upcoming day's activities, Jeremiah receives a call from Robbie. She's just checking in to see how the trip went. More applications have been arriving, and they all look good. It will be hard to filter them down—there are many good candidates with varying needs and plans for the prize money.

Jeremiah shares with Robbie what has transpired with Logan; he tells her all about Plan B. She likes the idea and the name Ramp-Up but feels the undertaking may be too ambitious. Jeremiah agrees; he has second thoughts as well for the same reasons. Nonetheless, he will float it further with the others.

Having had some time to shift gears to south Florida's slower pace, Jeremiah's stress levels are melting. He decides to talk with Eli, Morgan, and Kate tomorrow and get their feedback about Ramp-Up. After he has processed their feedback, he will reach out to Logan to iron out potential next steps.

That evening everyone heads to the mall for dinner. They have been going to Bella Luna in the Aventura mall for years, a family favorite. Once they have been seated, they place their drink orders. Ryan shares that he plans to Uber down to South Beach later to meet up with friends. Harley intends to watch a movie on her computer. And Kate and Jeremiah will probably watch something on cable that is mutually agreeable.

Their meals arrive, and other than forks clinking against plates, silence descends upon their table. Jeremiah begins telling anyone who will listen about the letter Logan had sent and his thinking to expand the RFP grant to a broader initiative. Ryan and Harley think it's exciting. Jeremiah states he thinks it's too exciting, too ambitious, and Kate agrees with a nod while taking a sip of her Pinot Grigio. That ends that discussion as they begin considering what they might do tomorrow; the weather forecast is sunny, warm, and beautiful.

Back at the condo, Harley retreats to the bedroom with her laptop and headphones in tow. Kate and Jeremiah move into the living room and scan the TV programming choices available. They find a recent movie they hadn't seen back home and settle in. Halfway through, Kate has lost interest and disappears into the bedroom while Jeremiah is snoozing comfortably.

In the morning, Jeremiah makes coffee and has breakfast. Then, changing into workout clothes, he will walk the three-mile loop around the Aventura golf course. The weather couldn't be more beautiful as Jeremiah exits the building. It's just another day in paradise. His headphones are attached, and Jeremiah surveys his usual podcasts and music library. Nothing jumps out at him. He decides to call Eli to get his take on Ramp-Up.

Eli picks up in his usual cheerful manner. They exchange updates, and Jeremiah then shares his thoughts on Plan B and how he'd arrived at the access ramps idea from Logan's letter. Eli is ambivalent. He says it sounds good. However, the idea of finding one winner, the original grant strategy, appeals much more to him. That comes as no surprise to Jeremiah; when Eli is going in one direction, it's hard for him to change lanes. As they close, Jeremiah explains that after the holidays, the selection committee will regroup, hopefully somewhere in the city, if they can find a place.

The days pass like pages in a well-written novel that you cannot stop reading—nothing special—just pleasant, relaxing time spent. Jeremiah kept in touch with his office, and fortunately, things in New York have also slowed down.

The Christmas vacation is quickly waning. Tomorrow Jeremiah and the family will be on a flight home to New York. Where did the time go? It has been a good break; very little work to deal with and lots of relaxation time. Before calling it a day at the pool, Jeremiah phones Logan to update her on the conversations he has had with his "advisors." Logan is also on break, visiting her sister in Ohio.

They chat about how they each have spent the past week before Jeremiah gets into the details. He tells Logan the reaction to a digital divide initiative is mixed. Feedback is positive, negative, and some in the middle. Jeremiah concludes the topic by saying that a decision about the digital divide initiative is still pending, but ultimately it will be his decision. He reassures Logan by telling her he still likes the idea very much. Logan thanks him for his honesty, but she is feeling a bit deflated. Jeremiah then states the committee will be meeting within a week to go over numerous agenda items, including the digital divide initiative.

He asks Logan, "Have you given any thought to what your potential role in all of this might be, regardless of which direction we go in?"

Logan says she hasn't. Jeremiah then asks her to give it some consideration. He also asks if she'd like to attend the meeting. She says she will let him know soon.

They say goodbye. Jeremiah gathers up his things and heads upstairs to their unit.

Chapter 79
Wait and See

Dan Carson's meeting with Tony Calabretta had completely rattled him. Though he was intimidated beyond reason, Danny is still desperate to ease his student debt. So desperate that he has lost all sense of what he's doing. Regardless of whether he pursues further with his blackmailing of Jeremiah, he has already committed a crime. Attempted blackmail is as much of a felony as executing it. And his letter, admission to Calabretta secretly caught on tape, could ruin him. And then there was the gun. That was only a scare tactic; they'd never use it. Or would they?

Blindly, Danny sees only one direction—follow through with the original blackmail scheme and hope for the best.

Tony had called Robbie that night after he had met with Carson. He related what he had dug up on Carson, his analysis, the meeting, and how he had left it with Carson.

"So, what do we do now?" asked Robbie.

"We wait and see if he follows through or not. If we do not hear from him in a week, I'll stop in on him to make sure it's dead," replied Tony.

"And if he sends us another letter?"

"It will probably be for how much he wants and how to pay it."

"You know if we pay him, there is no guarantee he won't go public or want more. And if we do pay him and he keeps quiet, we can't have him prosecuted. Prosecuting him would expose Jeremiah to the authorities, and who knows how long that would stay private. So the only viable option for us is to get him to drop it."

Tony added, "Well, I'm not so sure we couldn't prosecute him. We'll have to look into that more. But, for now, our best shot is to turn him into a quitter, somehow."

"Exactly," Robbie agreed.

"But how?"

"We will need to get him in a one-on-one with Jeremiah. Jeremiah will inspire him not to disrupt the Rising-Up vision," asserted Robbie.

"You think so?"

"Oh yes—Jeremiah is quite passionate, articulate about his mission, and can be most persuasive. And who knows what other ideas he may have. Besides, if he can convince his wife to go along with giving away one hundred million, he can persuade a kid to drop the blackmail scheme," added Robbie with a chuckle.

"Okay—we'll wait and see."

"Yes, we will."

Chapter 80
Back in NYC

It's the day of New Year's Eve, 2018, and the holiday vacation is practically over. *To where has the year evaporated,* wonders Jeremiah as he drives up Route 1 to Fort Lauderdale International Airport. It is five o'clock a.m., and he and the family are heading back home taking a seven a.m. American Airlines flight into LaGuardia. Both Ryan and Jeremiah plan to go to the city—Ryan to his apartment and Jeremiah to his office. The girls are taking an Uber home.

Jeremiah will spend only a couple of hours at the office, going through a batch of emails and seeing if anything significant needs his attention. That night, he and Kate are going to a dinner party at Bo and Patty Henderson's house, where the friends plan to dine and usher in 2019. Bo is quite the master in the kitchen; his passion for cooking and entertaining is legendary. Even to those who are not into dining, these events and theatrics are a spectacle to behold.

The office is a ghost town. Almost everyone has taken the day off. Jeremiah putters around his office until he no longer can justify being there. He darts out to catch the next train home, having read all his emails with nothing pressing in his queue. He gets to Penn, and the next scheduled train will depart in eight minutes. Excellent. He charges down the stairs and walks to the middle of the train, where he finds the car eerily empty. Sitting in a seat by the window, he settles in for the ride home.

As the train exits the East River tunnel, a bulb lights up in Jeremiah's head. What if they scale back Plan B, the digital superhighway access ramps plan—what if they just did it for homeless shelters? That could work. That could certainly work!

Now, Jeremiah has three options:

- Plan A – one non-profit winner for the entire $100 million

- Plan B – a citywide initiative to bridge the digital divide in all public housing (homeless shelters and government-funded/supported housing facilities), aka RAMP-UP

- Plan C – "Plan B-lite" – which is Plan B, but only in homeless shelters

Jeremiah feels encouraged, not locked into a specific strategy or initiative yet. What matters is how each grant option will fit best with his vision:

- Would the grant enable an organization to create a new program or enhance an existing one that would address a social problem affecting those living in poverty?

- Would the grant have maximum impact with visible and measurable outcomes?

Jeremiah's advisors will need to help him determine which strategy aligns best. He is very confident about this; he has assembled a good group. Though they might not be experts in social services and all the ills plaguing the community, they are responsible, caring, thoughtful, and reliable individuals. In Jeremiah's mind, there is no doubt they would get to a wildly successful endgame.

The train is gently rocking as it pulls into the Jamaica station. Jeremiah's iPhone buzzes—he has new emails; Robbie is checking in. They have received more mail, more applications, and a slew of letters. Jeremiah replies, suggesting they meet soon to review. They agree to meet up after work at her office in a few days.

The email exchange reminds Jeremiah of something he'd had on his mind. He wanted to connect with an old friend from The Community Fund, Jenelle Jansen-Abrams. Jenelle had been the Vice President in charge of programs. When it came to social issues, she was one of the most knowledgeable people Jeremiah knew. She was incredibly gifted and connected. Since leaving The Community Fund, Jenelle had become the CEO of a highly respected anti-poverty policy and advocacy organization in lower Manhattan, The Faith-In-Motion Alliance, aka FIMA.

Jeremiah composes a short email asking for a fifteen-minute meeting with Jenelle at her office. Within ten minutes of sending the email, Jeremiah receives an invite with a date and time in two days. He accepts. With their meeting scheduled, he'll brief Jenelle on the events to date and get her feedback on what she'd do if she were in his place.

Chapter 81
"Buddy, can you spare a dime?"

Following her call with Tony from before the holidays, Robbie had crafted an email to Jeremiah. She had minimized her phone call details, informing him that they would need to turn Dan Carson into an ally and get him to abandon his plot. How? Time would tell. In the meantime, they would just have to wait for Carson's next move.

The next day, Robbie opens Jeremiah's email response, acknowledging her report. He is not overly concerned, agreeing that they should "turn" Dan Carson, if possible. Jeremiah intends to preserve his anonymity without succumbing to blackmail. He closes with: "What will be, will be."

About a week later, Robbie finds a letter in her office mail from Carson; it is like the first one, addressed to her with no return address. She rips it open. It is the same as the first letter, but with two additional lines:

Cost of insurance: $100,000

Await instructions

Tapping her fingers on the desk, Robbie wonders: *What next—another letter or a phone call? One hundred grand—not that much. But they are not going to pay, that's for sure!*

She calls Tony and relays the "proposal." Laughing, he declares, "What a joke. This kid is too much. Guess we'll have to wait some more."

Chapter 82
Harley Invades Philadelphia

The evening at the Hendersons had been exquisite; a delicious meal, lots of stimulating conversation, and much good cheer. It is not much past eight o'clock the next morning, and Kate and Harley are moving in and out of the house, finishing packing the cars while Jeremiah sips his coffee. They are going to Philadelphia to move Harley into a sublet.

Harley landed her dream job. She is going to be working in the camp's winter office in a suburb north of Philadelphia. Her new apartment is near the University of Pennsylvania, where there are more housing options available. They are taking two cars, both stuffed with boxes of Harley's many things. Kate and Jeremiah will drive one, Harley in the other.

With no traffic, Philadelphia is only two and a half hours away. When they arrive at Harley's new apartment, no one is there to greet them. All the student residents are still on Christmas break. They enter the quiet, unlit foyer and proceed slowly through the hallway to Harley's locked room. On go the lights, and the move-in process begins in full force.

Jeremiah and Harley start retrieving boxes from the cars and deposit them in her room. After completing close to twenty trips, the cars are empty, and Harley's room is cramped with belongings. Now, the fun part for Kate and Harley: unpacking and arranging things. They are pros at this, and in no more than an hour, they have completed this phase. The room now looks like Harley's.

The first item for Jeremiah to set up is the TV. The apartment has a cable modem. Harley will use Hulu and Netflix for TV and cable channels over the internet. It doesn't take long to remove the new forty-six-inch flat-screen TV from the box. Quickly, they set it up, plug it in, and it's ready to configure. With a bit of trial and error, *voila!* All cable TV systems are a go.

While Harley and Jeremiah have been playing with the TV, Kate has been rearranging the unpacked items, deciding where they logically should be put—intermittently getting Harley's direction and authorization. As she is doing this, she is also making a shopping list of supplies and other things that are still needed, such as more paper towels, a new shower curtain, and door hooks to hang clothes on.

Everyone is tired after a couple of hours of these move-in activities and the long drive. It's time for a break. They grab their coats and the shopping list and head to Target in Kate's car. The trip is short, and the scenery foreign. There are street names of trees and presidents and buildings of differing architecture. Philadelphia is your typical east coast urban city. Smaller than New York and much less dirty. It has a charm of its own, much like Boston but grittier.

Jeremiah finds a parking space right across the street from the Target on Chestnut Street. Parking in Philly is a bitch, but today, New Year's Day, not so much. The store is empty. A few store employees are mingling in their signature red vests. This Target has two floors, not like the single ground floor types on Long Island. They move about the store as if on a treasure hunt. Finally, they head to the cash register with most of the items on the list found. Kate pulls out her Target credit card; she will get a five percent discount on everything in the shopping cart.

The drive back to the apartment is as uneventful as the one to Target. They pull into a spot right by the entrance, empty the car of their newly acquired purchases, and then schlep them into Harley's room. Harley signals where each item should go as they are removing them from the bags. Five minutes is all it takes. Kate and Harley survey the apartment; it is looking good. Jeremiah smiles, too. Feelings of satisfaction all around. Time to call it a day—at least for now.

It is after three, and now they can check-in at the hotel. It's back into the car and to the Hampton Inn a few miles away. As they head to the hotel, Jeremiah reminds everyone that he is taking Amtrak to the city in the morning. "We know, Dad. You have that meeting with that lady you worked with," acknowledges Harley.

The hotel check-in process is smooth; they are in a room on the third floor. There are two queen-sized beds with a large window facing a vacant lot across the street. Taking off his shoes, Jeremiah flops down on the bed nearest the window and prepares to take a little nap. Within minutes, he is out. Kate and Harley are chattering about the outstanding tasks needed to complete their move-in mission. The TV in the room is playing sitcom reruns, providing a familiar soundtrack to dull the room's quiet.

As Jeremiah stirs from his nap, an hour has passed; Harley announces that her stomach is growling. "When can we go and eat?" she demands. Kate and Jeremiah nod in agreement, and they get ready to leave. Not far from the hotel is a burger place, highlighted on a list of restaurants provided by the hotel.

In no time, they are walking into Bobby's Burger Palace, Bobby Flay's hip burger restaurant in "University City," Philadelphia. It is the ideal place to go for a quick, tasty meal. The seating area is practically empty, except for a young couple with a baby in a stroller. The family orders their meals and finds a table in the middle of the restaurant. The dining area is very bright, with walls painted in different yellow and orange shades, a warm atmosphere.

The server brings over three trays and places them on the table. Kate repositions them to match the orders correctly. Everyone has fries—they are golden brown, cooked perfectly, and delicious beyond description. As they devour their food, the conversation quickly reverts to what else they need to do for the apartment.

After they have eaten, they will make a stop at a different Target a few miles away for the remaining items on Kate's list. Kate confirms she'll drive Jeremiah to the train station to catch the 9:50 a.m. Amtrak to NYC.

Chapter 83
"If you were in my position?"

In the morning, Kate drops Jeremiah off at the Thirtieth Street Station. His train will arrive at Penn Station in NYC around 11:15 a.m. As he boards the escalator to the platform below, the train pulls in. Jeremiah finds a seat in a sparsely occupied car after numerous passengers exit.

The doors close. In minutes, the train is at cruising speed. Jeremiah is traveling light; all he has is a backpack containing a book, a laptop, and a Wi-Fi jetpack. Removing the computer and connecting to his Wi-Fi, Jeremiah opens Gmail and scans his inbox. Robbie has confirmed the date, time, and place for the next selection committee meeting. A law school friend of hers has offered up conference space at his firm. Jeremiah quickly crafts a meeting invite to the committee members and Logan. The address for the meeting is:

The Law Offices of Tucker & Townsend, LLC

115 W28th Street – 4th floor

Friday, January 4, 2019 – 1:00 p.m. to 3:00 p.m.

Jeremiah has always loved trains. As he puts aside his laptop, he drifts off into his memories. There were those trips taken as a child with his grandmother to New Haven to visit family. When in high school, he would train into the city and take the bus up the Hudson to his boarding school. And the holiday excursions from college to home, in Connecticut, he'd take the Amtrak to Berlin. The train was like a sanctuary. It provided a quiet place to read, relax, and nap. There was something about the steady rocking motion that had a therapeutic effect.

With a slight jolt, the train comes to a stop in Trenton, New Jersey, returning Jeremiah to the here and now. It would be another fifty minutes before he'd be in the city, so Jeremiah retrieves his laptop again and opens a Word document containing his work project list. He identifies needed tasks that he can tackle now. Fully engrossed in his work, Jeremiah has lost total sense of time when he hears the conductor announce that they will be arriving at Penn Station in three minutes.

The walk from Penn to his office takes the usual five minutes, and by 11:30, Jeremiah is at his desk. It will soon be lunchtime, and before long, he'll need to get ready for his meeting with Jenelle Jansen-Abrams.

Jenelle's offices are in the financial district on Pearl Street. It has been probably ten years since they last met in person—however, they did stay in touch via Facebook, email, and an occasional phone call.

Jeremiah enters Jenelle's office after being escorted by her secretary. The small talk lasts only a minute when Jenelle asks directly, "So, what's up, Jeremiah?"

Jeremiah decides he'll reveal as little as possible about the lottery part if he can. Frankly, the lottery is irrelevant—what he is seeking is guidance on the right strategy for distributing the money.

"Well, Jenelle, I wanted your take on something. I have an incredible opportunity and wonder what you would do if you were in my position. I am part of a group with a sizable amount of money. We are considering granting this money to a worthy organization, cause, or initiative. I am interested in learning what you might do if you were in our place."

"Wow! That sounds so exciting! How much is a 'sizable' amount of money, if you don't mind me asking?"

"Millions, Jenelle. Tens of millions. One hundred million, to be exact," answers Jeremiah, unable to hold back. "Holy cow, Jeremiah! You are a part of that Rising-Up grant, aren't you," she charges. Jenelle knew of the Rising-Up grant, as her team had submitted a proposal a week ago. Jeremiah nods slowly.

"Don't tell me—and you are also the winner, aren't you?" she speculates, referring to the Mega Millions jackpot.

Jeremiah tries to find the right answer. He does not want to admit he is the winner, nor does he want to lie about it outright. Finally, he says, "Let's just focus on the issue at hand and why I came to see you, Jenelle."

Their eyes lock for only a moment—she knows it's him.

Their conversation stops for no more than ten seconds. It's not an uncomfortable delay. Finally, Jenelle continues, "So, you have a hundred million to play with, right?"

"Right."

Jenelle ponders for a bit, then says, "I have the perfect solution—you can give FIMA the grant. You know, we submitted our proposal last week," she says with a big smile.

"Well, that would solve our dilemma," responds Jeremiah. They both laugh, and after a slight pause, Jeremiah continues, "There are three options we are considering. One, we can give it all to one organization or maybe two, our original plan. Two, we can donate it to a group of housing providers for technology to access the digital superhighway. Or three, we can give it to only non-profit homeless shelter providers for digital access for their shelter residents."

They continue to discuss the rationales behind the digital divide strategy in-depth, with Jenelle acknowledging it sounds like a good idea, very inspiring. Finally, she says, "You want to know what I would do, right?"

"Right. What would you do?"

Another pause, and then Jenelle answers, "I would set up a foundation or a non-profit to make grants on a case-by-case basis. Perhaps, the digital divide initiative might drive most of the grants, but I'd also like to grant other organizations that resonate in other ways. I would do a foundation because it would enable me to be much more involved. I wouldn't want only to give the money away—I'd want to nurture my giving and watch it grow, close-up, and see the fruits of my dreams. That's just me. That's what I would do."

Jeremiah is deep in thought, saying finally, "That is interesting. Now, we have four options!"

They laugh again.

"I need to digest this and review it with my group," Jeremiah says.

"Certainly, I would too. Feel free to reach out to me. I am happy to help however I can."

They finish up, and Jeremiah starts to leave, saying, "I'll be in touch soon. And thank you for your insights and your time; I appreciate it."

As he walks to the subway a few blocks away, Jeremiah's thoughts are in overdrive. With Jenelle Jansen-Abrams involved, it gives Rising-Up credibility. How can he use Jen? How does FIMA's anti-poverty work fit into what he wants to do? Will he give FIMA a grant?

Chapter 84
Listen Carefully

When Robbie returns to her office after a brief holiday respite, she has a hang-up among her phone messages. Forty-five minutes later, the phone rings as she is reading the newspaper at her desk. After three rings, she picks up and says, "This is Robbie Winthrop. How can I help you?"

Following a short delay, the voice on the other end quietly orders, "Listen carefully to these instructions for delivering your insurance payment."

Robbie rolls her eyes—this sounds like something out of a 50s B-movie.

The voice continues, "Get a gym bag and fill it with ten packs of unmarked one-hundred-dollar bills. Tomorrow, meet me in the Target parking lot at the Broadway Mall in Hicksville."

"No, Carson! That's not happening. You are going to have to come here for the money, understand?"

Carson interrupts, "No, I'm not doing that."

"Yes, you are. You have no choice. If you want the money, you will have to come here. Are we clear?" commands Robbie.

Finally, after a long pause, barely audible, comes Carson's resignation: "Alright."

"Now, *you* listen carefully, Dan. I will text you in a week with a date and time to come here and discuss this in person. Until then, you sit tight and keep quiet. I assure you we will put this to rest, agreeable to both you and us—just be a little patient. Understand?"

With a little bit of hope of getting his big payday, Dan replies, "Understood, Ms. Winthrop."

Chapter 85
More with the Media

Jeremiah is at Speedy's, seated in the back on the second floor, gazing blindly at his lunch. He has been here for a few minutes, just thinking about his meeting with Jenelle the day before. Her idea of creating a foundation made a lot of sense. But did it mean Jeremiah would have to manage it? Did he want a second career as a foundation administrator? Later that afternoon, when he would meet up with Robbie, they could go over this and determine if a foundation is a sensible way to realize the Rising-Up vision.

In the meantime, Jeremiah's lunch beckons. He grabs a plastic fork and tastes the different selections on his plate. Remembering the many things waiting for him at the office, he picks up his pace, and when he has had enough, he quickly prepares to return to work. Phone messages needing call-backs, a meeting to attend, and a bunch of lingering paperwork await. When he has done all he can for the day, he sets his sights on his upcoming visit to Robbie's office.

On Long Island, standing by a file cabinet in her office, Robbie has a term sheet for a new client's real estate transaction she is reviewing. The phone on her desk rings. The caller, Frank Martino from CBS, wants to know if there are any new developments related to the RFP. He is fishing for something to support another follow-up segment.

Robbie decides to be as forthcoming as possible. Why not? They have nothing to lose. She gives him an updated count of applications received: two hundred thirty-nine to date. She qualifies the number by saying there are more in the unopened mail. In a day or two, they will have a better total.

In addition to the new applications they have received, there have been countless inquiries. Lastly, Robbie informs Martino that the selection committee has met and will be meeting again tomorrow. There are multiple grant options on the table, and interviews will start the following week.

Martino asks who is on the committee, to which Robbie answers that she can't tell him. He then asks when they will complete the selection process and when they will announce the winner.

Winging it, Robbie thinks the end of the month is reasonable. "January 31st," she affirms. "But that could change."

"Will there be an announcement?" asks Martino.

"We are still deciding whether there will be a public statement or not."

Robbie promises to call Frank in two weeks with more after the committee meets and when interviews are underway.

They hang up. Frank knows he doesn't have enough for a story. But he wonders—maybe he can get an exclusive if Robbie's group makes a public announcement.

As Robbie sits at her desk, considering her call with Martino, she decides to call Joyce Chen at the Times. To be transparent and fair, Joyce had been very professional when they have spoken previously. Her call with Joyce goes pretty much the same as the one with Martino.

Afterward, Joyce reflects on the call and determines she has enough for a follow-up. Print media has more latitude in what they publish versus TV. She hastily transforms her notes into a piece worthy of submission to her editor, with hopes of making the next edition.

Jeremiah's commute from the city seems instantaneous. In what feels like a flash, he is knocking on Robbie's front office door. It is almost five o'clock—exactly when Robbie scheduled them to meet. He walks in with his backpack over his shoulder and gives Robbie a peck on the cheek.

After they get caught up on personal matters, the conversation turns to developments associated with the RFP. Jeremiah relates what had occurred in his meeting with Jenelle Jansen-Abrams. Robbie listens intently, throwing in a question here and there.

Finally, Jeremiah concludes by stating that they now have four options, Jen's foundation idea being the newest. Robbie agrees that they all seem viable. They exchange their views on the positives and negatives of each. They reach no conclusions, only that they will need to stay open. The appropriate strategy will surface at the right time.

Now it's Robbie's turn. She tells of her call with Frank Martino from CBS. Robbie explains she had shared with him as much as she could and stressed that there weren't any dramatic changes—just that the process was moving along.

"Martino wanted to know our expected date for selecting a winner. Making an executive decision, I said our target was the end of January, but subject to change," informs Robbie.

Jeremiah remarks, "Perfect."

Robbie continues, "Martino also asked if we would be making an announcement, to which I answered that we were still deciding if and how best."

Jeremiah follows with, "We have a few paths we can take for an announcement. We can inform just the recipient—or recipients—with no public statement, do a press release, or schedule a live press conference."

"Or a hybrid of the three," responds Robbie.

"I am not so sure about a press event. Do you think that's a good idea, Robbie?"

"I'm not sure, either. We'll have to think it through. And maybe have the committee weigh in on it." After a slight pause, Robbie continues, "By the way, I had a similar call with Joyce Chen at the Times. I thought it only fair to share with her what I had with Martino. She was surprised to hear from me but was appreciative. I wouldn't be surprised if the Times puts out a short update piece."

Jeremiah nods with tacit approval. As they continue to chat about how far the RFP project has come, Robbie smiles and points to a large file box in the corner, saying, "There's some more mail to go through."

The carton is packed. Jeremiah moves it to the desk, and they start removing items and placing them in logical stacks of letters or applications. The pile of proposals is over a foot high, and there are about twenty-five letters.

Over the next hour, they sift through each pile to weed out the irrelevant solicitations, identifying the proposals worthy of further review. Robbie is keeping score—the box contained one hundred seventeen new applications and twenty-two letters, bringing the total number of applications received to three hundred fifty-six. And the number of letters received to date now totals forty-six.

Most of the new letters are insignificant. However, there is one from the Citizen's Community Foundation of New York. It is from its president, Natalie Perkins, pitching their services to assist Rising-Up however they can. There is also a proposal from FIMA, Jenelle's agency.

It's getting late—they've been at it for almost two hours. Jeremiah signals that they should start wrapping up; there is always tomorrow. Robbie agrees, but they don't immediately begin their exit process. Jeremiah expresses that they should discontinue having second applications for candidates who advance, and they should directly interview the qualifiers. The interview should suffice in place of a second application.

Robbie agrees and resurrects the four grant options, reinforcing her take on their distinct positives and negatives. Jeremiah is paying only half attention—he'd been pondering grant options incessantly. He and Robbie are both spent from their respective long days, so they call it quits for the day.

Chapter 86
The Faith In-Motion Alliance Application

The Faith In-Motion Alliance (FIMA) is a small organization compared to the other ones identified as possible recipients by the selection committee. Their annual budget/revenues are dramatically below the fifty-million-dollar threshold, somewhat arbitrarily set as an RFP requirement. Nonetheless, that did not stop them from applying.

FIMA has programs related to supporting faith-based organizations and services for children, seniors, and well-being for those living close to the poverty line. One distinguishing aspect of FIMA's application is its poverty policy and advocacy expertise. When Jeremiah had read the proposal in Robbie's office, there were three parts.

The first addressed funding their member partners, thirty-five small, faith-based non-profits that supported those in poverty with soup kitchens, food stamps, and more. They featured a few of these partners and their programs with anecdotal success stories. The second part dealt with specific existing FIMA social services programs to be enhanced. These included their programs for children and seniors, plus the associated partners who had received funding from FIMA.

In both cases, the FIMA proposal went into painstaking detail on how they would use the funding and the processes they would institute for monitoring outcomes. Though Jeremiah was impressed with their professional management style, FIMA's service areas lacked attraction, according to his leanings.

However, the last part of FIMA's proposal resonated with Jeremiah. FIMA wanted to use a third of the grant to intensify its poverty policy and advocacy work. Again, they offered a convincing case with supporting details and documentation.

There was definite potential here. Jeremiah felt it deeply. He did not quite see FIMA as the right candidate for Plan A, where the grantee received the entire one hundred million. And he also did not see a good fit in the Plan B or Plan C frameworks for technology to bridge the digital divide. FIMA's partners might need technology enhancements, but that would be a stretch; most did not provide any housing to the poor.

Jeremiah was baffled. What role could the Faith In-Motion Alliance play here?

Besides FIMA's uncertain role, Jeremiah wondered how The Citizen's Community Foundation of New York (CCFNY) might fit into his plans. They had been serving wealthy donors to fulfill their philanthropic goals for decades. Donors drove their business, and routinely satisfied clients would recommend new donors.

CCFNY also has a small development department to identify new client opportunities to win their business. Often, this would start with a letter of introduction requesting the next step of either a visit to their offices or a phone call. Included in their correspondence was impressive marketing material highlighting their successful performance over the years. One such letter had been in the mail Robbie had received.

She had read it a couple of times and reviewed the enclosures—she knew this was something Jeremiah might want to research. Jeremiah had also briefly scanned the material from CCFNY, thinking it interesting. It was just one more thing to explore further. Maybe they could be helpful.

Chapter 87
Agreement with Sara

Jeremiah has not followed up with Sara since first broaching the subject of his "retirement" a few weeks ago. It is somewhat surprising when an email appears in his inbox from her with the subject line: Retirement. He reads the short email—it doesn't say much, other than Sara and Len are open to creating a new transitional role for Jeremiah that will ultimately lead to his full-time retirement.

The email seems typical of Sara—no material substance, but it is going in the direction Jeremiah wants. The Way Home is "supportive" of a transitional role. Jeremiah sits, thinking for a while, before hitting reply. The more profound truth is that he doesn't need any future with The Way; he keeps forgetting he is rich now. But he also poured five years into the systems he had created and wants to see them live on after he is gone.

Jeremiah's email starts by thanking Sara for getting back to him. He quickly types what he feels are the key points that need to be in his new role as a consultant:

- The goal of the engagement
- Time frame

- Scope

- Knowledge transfer

- Effective date

- Written agreement

- Terms

- Closure

These are just high-level points and require further details. Jeremiah would be the one to flesh it all out for Sara's approval. He closes by saying he would frame out the points further with specifics according to his requirements and send Sara a meeting invite soon to work out a final agreement.

Though there is no formal arrangement yet, they did have somewhat of an agreement in principle. Given how Sara had not supplied any details from The Way Home's point of view, Jeremiah feels he could write his ticket however he sees fit. He already has a shortlist in mind of what he wants and would expand it into an agreement that both sides can accept. He is determined to be compensated appropriately, even though he doesn't need the money. His time deserves commensurate compensation. His experience has taught him that when people pay the right price for the services they want, they are vested and committed. Besides, his remuneration is the best metric for how The Way would value him in this "new" capacity.

Chapter 88
The Selection Committee Reconvenes

Jeremiah left for "lunch" at 12:45 p.m., saying that he'd be back around three and headed to Tucker & Townsend offices located only a few blocks from his. As he walks down Sixth Avenue, he wonders how the meeting will go. Will his team provide insights and clarity to make the decision-making simpler? How will they receive Logan? It will undoubtedly be interesting. This meeting will be a big step forward in defining the final tasks for awarding the grant.

As Jeremiah enters the newly constructed office tower, the clock in the lobby prominently displays the time: 12:53 p.m. Many new buildings in NYC are dual-purpose, where the lower floors are for commercial retail and office space, and the upper floors are for residential condominiums. At the security station, he shows his ID. His name is on the attendee list Robbie had sent over. The professionally dressed man behind the desk nods approval, returns Jeremiah's ID, points to the elevator bank in the rear of the lobby, and exclaims, "Fourth floor."

Off the elevator, there is a sign at the reception desk that reads:

Welcome Rising-Up

Conference Room 2

Jeremiah proceeds in the direction of the conversational chatter coming from the corridor to the right. When he gets to the room, Eli, Robbie, and Morgan are seated at one end of a large conference table. There are chips and soft drinks available on a credenza near the entrance. Kate is not attending the meeting—she is having some long-overdue dental work done. Besides, Jeremiah can always get her views at home.

There is a vacant seat next to Morgan. When Ruby arrives right after Jeremiah, she beelines toward it. Jeremiah circles the table, saying hello to everyone, then sits at the head with Robbie to his left and Eli to his right. Morgan is seated at Robbie's right. Jeremiah announces that Logan will be joining the meeting, mainly as an observer, and that they'd wait a few minutes before starting.

To fill the time, Robbie explains how she managed to obtain the use of the conference space. When in law school, she had a study partner named Guy Cleveland. Guy was a good man, and after law school, the two of them had stayed in touch. They would often ask each other for favors and help with various matters. And consistently, they delivered. Robbie was an expert in networking and knew how to maximize the value of her contacts.

From the doorway comes a warm and friendly, "Hello, everybody." It is Logan Aldrich who has finally arrived. Jeremiah immediately goes over to her. He shakes her hand and directs her to an empty chair while introducing her to the group.

In his introduction of Logan, Jeremiah states that he had asked her to observe the "proceedings" because she had made an excellent RFP suggestion. She had inspired him with a broader view of how they might distribute the jackpot to bridge the digital divide. That is significant. And should they move in that direction, well, it only seems fitting for her to be in on it from the start. Plus, any thoughts she might have today could be helpful.

The group is nodding in support. As Logan sits down, everyone introduces themselves and shares their connection with Jeremiah. The team, though assembled somewhat randomly, has gelled tightly over the past few weeks. Now, it is time for the meeting to get started; it is 1:15 p.m. when Jeremiah distributes a sheet of paper that reads:

AGENDA

1.   Introductions

2.   Potential grant options

3.   Proposal recap

4.   Citizen's Community Foundation of NY

5.   Next steps

    a.   No second applications

    b.   Phone interviews

       • Format

       • Candidates

6.   January 31st announcement

With the introductions done, Jeremiah begins by reviewing that the original game plan. He discusses plans A, B, and C, then introduces the latest option: Plan D, to create a non-profit or foundation and make grants to agencies and projects that could positively impact reducing poverty in NYC.

The group starts to digest the summary with occasional head bobbing as they review the different plans. No clear favorite emerges. Some discussions ensue. Have they wasted time and energy by not sticking to the original Plan A approach? Why change now? The dialogue is revealing. Plan A is "one and done." The other options require much more effort, with the chosen strategy most likely taking on a life of its own. Jeremiah concludes the spirited exchange by saying that regardless of which path they select, all four are consistent with the RFP's original goals to reduce poverty. He then turns to Robbie to move on with the next agenda item.

Robbie distributes an outline to each committee member. On the top of the page is printed: RFP Proposal Summary. Rising-Up had received three hundred fifty-six proposals, of which the committee had identified sixteen to complete the second follow-up application. Of those, twelve submitted second applications. The committee selected eight to evaluate further from all reviews of both types of submittals of potential candidates.

Also received were forty-six letters and twenty-two phone calls. Of the phone calls, two stood out: the NY Times and WCBS-TV. Robbie was managing media relations with both, providing regular updates on the RFP evaluation progress.

There are no questions, so Jeremiah takes his cue to move on. He opens a folder and circulates copies of the Citizen's Community Foundation of New York letter. "What do you think of this?" he asks.

The group studies the letter. Without hesitation, Robbie says, "Having a third party might be a practical way to go. They could do much of the heavy lifting in vetting the agencies."

Morgan responds by saying she knows of CCFNY from her previous experience but has had minimal direct dealings. She adds, "They have an excellent reputation for integrity, efficiency, and professionalism. They are very thorough and private."

Eli is next, asking if CCFNY would be potentially part of Plan D, the foundation option. Would Jeremiah be considering handing over the entire project to them?

Jeremiah can only shrug and say he had no idea where this exploratory path would lead. Eli then says, "I can't believe they would be cheap!"

"You're right—we are looking at about one percent a year of funds under management," is Jeremiah's reply.

"Wow! That is a lot and not cheap at all. That's roughly one million in the first year. Holy cow! And what do we get for that? Do they monitor the projects, evaluating outcomes after making the grants?"

"All good questions, Eli," is Jeremiah's response.

Ruby has been waiting patiently to share her thoughts, and when there is a pause, she adds, "What can they do that we can't? I think our pool of money is big enough for us to manage the process more economically."

"We should stick to our original strategy, Plan A, one awardee. We can forego all the extra expense and effort," Eli repeats.

Robbie loves the animated debate. She looks over at Morgan and then Logan. Morgan steps in, saying that Ruby has a good point. Logan nods in agreement.

Jeremiah, half smiling, interjects, "Guys, I only wanted to be transparent. I wanted to share the letter with you and get some feedback, which I am certainly getting. Thank you very much. No conclusions or decisions yet—but more to come, I'm sure."

It seems like the right place for a break, and Ruby walks over to where the refreshments are. She studies what's available, then takes a bottle of water. Logan follows her example, as do the others. After five minutes, everyone is back in their seats, and Jeremiah announces, "Next steps."

Robbie begins by saying that they will be discontinuing the second application. They would only use the first qualifying application. If "qualified," they would invite the candidate for a phone interview. She then states that they are still finalizing the interview format. They plan to invite eight organizations for conference calls. She reads off their names and suggests that the group do some independent research on each of them.

Jeremiah then asks if there are any questions. When no one speaks up, he says, "The last item we have to discuss is how we announce our decision. We have set January 31st as our target decision date, which is not locked in stone. The bigger question is, how to announce? Should we have a press release, press conference, or nothing at all?"

Eli is the first to respond. "I say nothing at all."

Morgan's response is, "Press release."

"A press conference could be cool," remarks Ruby, giggling.

"Great, a consensus. Logan, what do you think?" adds Jeremiah.

"A press conference will heighten awareness on the poverty issue we are attempting to impact. I think it is a great idea, so long as you are prepared and have answers to all the possible questions that might arise. The visibility could also surface additional supporters and others who might want to embrace your vision," responds Logan.

Everyone is quiet, taking in Logan's comments. It is settling in—this is real; they are on the edge of rolling out a philanthropic strategy that could make a big difference.

Jeremiah then adds that they have some time to figure it out—the first thing is to determine whether the grant strategy will be Plan A, B, C, or D, which would drive the selected winner or winners.

It is almost three, the witching hour for the conference space. Quickly, the meeting begins to wrap up, with everyone preparing to leave. In a flash, the team is on their feet and heading in their separate directions.

They had accomplished much in the meeting. The RFP vision is moving forward. This small group is launching a project that will profoundly affect the lives of many. It is the precise dream Jeremiah had in mind.

Chapter 89
Candidate Profiles

So far, six non-profits, serving one hundred thousand New Yorkers yearly, have risen to the top of the candidate pile with appealing proposals.

The potential grant recipients include:

Bronx Family Services' proposal was one of the first that clicked with Jeremiah. BFS is a scrappy organization dominating The Bronx with a broad mix of social programs, including permanent housing, homeless shelters, housing protection, social work, job readiness, seniors' programs, and entry-level technology job training. Founded in the early seventies, BFS is well run and has an excellent reputation.

Community Assistance Connection is a large non-profit, having grown through mergers with smaller struggling agencies over the years. Jeremiah had worked for their CEO, Dana Castellano, at a previous non-profit and highly respected her for her leadership and humanity. CAC is significant in size and scope; it has an annual budget of over two hundred million with developmental disabilities programs, homeless and supported housing services, veterans' programs, entrepreneurial projects, and behavioral programs.

Project Empowerment's main office is not far from Jeremiah's; they had scored high with all the committee members, and their proposal was compelling. Their program focus is on health services, housing, and employment. Annual revenue at PE is close to one hundred million. They operate in all five boroughs of NYC and serve over fifteen thousand people.

The Life Recovery Center, also located in Manhattan and founded in the early seventies, focuses almost exclusively on housing solutions for homeless and struggling individuals and families. LRC has served about nine thousand people the previous year, with yearly revenue of seventy-five million. And Morgan is very familiar with LRC's CEO; he'd attempted to recruit her to run their fundraising area on numerous occasions.

The New York Lifeline, based in Brooklyn, serves all five boroughs in NYC. Jeremiah knows of this organization from his days at the Community Fund, where they participated in an afterschool initiative that used software Jeremiah had developed. Their programs focus on economic development, legal services, education/youth development, housing, health, and family support. They have an annual budget of one hundred and fifty million.

The Way Home, aka "The Way," where Jeremiah works, is in mid-town Manhattan. The Way's sole mission is to eradicate homelessness, and they have shelters and housing facilities in all five NYC boroughs. In addition to housing programs, The Way has support services to enable their "clients" to move up to the next level of independent living, including job readiness, technology training, and childcare. The Way provides its clients with an extensive support network of licensed social workers who work tirelessly to ease the trauma of homelessness. With total revenue of eighty-five million yearly, they serve approximately twelve thousand people annually.

The next day, Robbie is in her kitchen reading the Times with the TV on in the background. In the Metro section, there is a brief story titled: *$100 Million Grant Undecided.* It is the follow-up piece from Robbie's conversation with Joyce Chen a few days ago.

The story is only three paragraphs in length and provides a short recap of how the Times had learned about Rising-Up weeks previously. The article speculates who some potential winners might be, explicitly mentioning The Community Assistance Connection and The New York Lifeline. The closing sentence states that on January 31st, Rising-Up will announce its final decision.

Robbie smiles as she takes a sip of her coffee. She can't believe how hungry the media is for content; they will run with whatever they can dig up. She grabs her cellphone and shoots a text to Jeremiah.

Check out the Times, Metro section, a blurb on the RFP. No Biggie, but now we have a deadline of January 31st. Too much. 😊

Chapter 90
"Hey Jen, what do you think?"

According to Jeremiah's gut, the FIMA application, though excellent as proposals go, is not going to cut it. FIMA is only a ten million organization, and the RFP budget requirement of fifty million should have automatically disqualified FIMA from consideration. Nonetheless, Jeremiah has to give them credit for their moxie. Jeremiah is confident, though, that FIMA could fit in the picture someway somehow. He picks up his phone and dials Jenelle. He wants to test the waters to see how flexible she'll be in some other capacity.

Jenelle is out of the office at a board meeting, so Jeremiah leaves a long message detailing how he feels and how the FIMA proposal will not fit. He wants some sense of how amenable FIMA might be in a scaled-down grant or advisory role. Jeremiah is sure that Jenelle will be happy with a smaller award of any kind, but he wants to make sure they could map out an acceptable way on how that might work.

By the end of the day, Jeremiah receives a call back from Jenelle. She starts by thanking him for considering FIMA and acknowledging that they knew full well they were testing the limits with their proposal, given their size and scope of services. Jeremiah is pleased by Jenelle's opening remarks.

She then says, "Jeremiah, FIMA, and I can help you; we are on board with you. I am not concerned about the grant. We are here to do God's work! However, we can serve—we are down!"

Jeremiah replies joyfully, "That's wonderful! I don't expect any free lunches, though. The pool of funds is large enough to be creative. I am thinking of somehow tapping into your policy and advocacy expertise, leadership strengths, or both."

"I'm sure we can find a way to make that work. As I said, however, we can help," answers Jenelle.

"Good. Let's think more about it, and in a few days, start framing something out," concludes Jeremiah, with Jenelle agreeing.

Jeremiah is psyched. Jenelle is a rock star in social services in NYC. Who better to have on the team?

Chapter 91
Talking to the Foundation

Diane Reynolds, the Director of Donor Services, had signed the letter from the Citizen's Community Foundation. She had included her email address and phone number and requested a return contact to explore a mutually beneficial relationship. Jeremiah decided he would research their services further, and if there were any reasonable value add, he'd seriously consider using them.

It is 9:45 a.m. when Jeremiah calls. After two rings, there is a click, and a warm female voice announces a friendly greeting. Jeremiah introduces himself by stating he is part of the Rising-Up grant selection committee and wants to ask some questions about the community fund and how they might work together.

Reynolds introduces herself, disclosing her role at CCFNY and how long she has been with them. The foundation has had a presence in New York since well before the Depression. Continuing, she says that they have worked with many donors and can custom fit "packages" to suit exact donor needs. The foundation has helped countless individuals and professionals achieve social impact in the community by building lasting legacies for many New Yorkers.

There are no standard programs. The foundation tailors each donor's philanthropy strategy around the donor's specific requirements.

That said, the foundation's basic donor model has two parts: asset management and charity distribution. Also, the foundation can provide various consulting services connected to either area.

Asset management involves the accumulation of assets and investment management. The charity distribution function thoroughly examines donor goals, then develops and executes the distribution plan to specific charities or initiatives.

CCFNY has standard distribution strategies such as health care, seniors, homeless, youth, et cetera. A donor can opt-in for one of these strategies or work with the foundation to develop a more specialized plan.

Charity analysis, a critical strength of theirs, is essential in determining which charities to include in distribution and donor recommendations. Their analysts knew all the pros and cons of most of the non-profits in the city.

Jeremiah had questions before Reynolds made her remarks. However, she has covered most of his concerns. Nonetheless, he asks, "Does the foundation provide a service that assists individuals in creating their own foundations?"

"We can do that. And we have done that for some of our clients. You also have the option of working with your attorney or any financial institution. For example, Fidelity offers donor-advised funds to its clients with nominal fees. Fidelity is a very economical way to go," replies Reynolds.

"It seems that Fidelity's investment management approach versus any other financial institutions' service compared to what you may offer should not be the primary determinant in one's decision. What I mean is that theoretically, each foundation alternative will have investment results that should not deviate significantly. Therefore, it should not drive the decision as to where one decides to set up their foundation."

"Agreed," is Reynolds's reply.

"Let me ask you another question, Ms. Reynolds. Does your foundation's range of consulting services include assistance in framing out governance?"

"Yes, we can assist you with that, too," answers Reynolds.

Jeremiah reflects for a few moments. Finally, he says, "Ms. Reynolds, I'd be interested in knowing what it would cost for a specific consulting engagement. The scope would include charity analysis for ten to twenty non-profits and guidance in creating a governance framework, should we create our foundation. Can you prepare a proposal for us?"

"Certainly, Mr. Baldwin. We can have that for you in a couple of days."

"Excellent. That would be great."

"My pleasure. Thank you for your consideration."

Chapter 92
Candidate Interviews

Robbie and Jeremiah are on the phone early on January 8th. Their goal is to nail down a plan for phone interviews for the potential grant recipient(s).

Instead of secondary applications and cookie-cutter questions, Jeremiah wants the process to be conversational. He wants the "interrogations" to subtly elicit the "feel" of the applying organizations they will interview. Each interview should last only about an hour. They will start with a general question and go from there—candidates may have anyone from their organization on the call. Robbie will set up a conference bridge for all participants to use.

Robbie, Morgan, Eli, and Rudy are the interviewers. Jeremiah will be on the calls but silently lurking and unannounced—just listening and taking notes. They will conduct round-robin discussions. And pepper the exchanges with specific questions to reveal an organization's competency, character, vision, culture, and management excellence. According to established criteria, the team will have a "scorecard" to note their assessments of each non-profit.

Robbie will make calls later in the day to schedule the interviews, hoping to start on Thursday. She adds two additional candidates to the list: The Excelsior Support Network and The Golden Rule Guild, headquartered in Manhattan, offering a wide range of social services. There are now eight candidates slated for interviews. The plan is to complete the interviews by the end of the following week; however, there could be additional interviews.

When the call with Jeremiah is over, Robbie pulls up her spreadsheet containing the candidates, each having one primary contact and a respective email address. She crafts an email inviting each separately for a conference call and states she will be scheduling them the next day. She asks for three dates and time preferences and a list of their attendees.

Before calling it a day, Robbie has one more task to complete: texting Dan Carson with details for a meeting to resolve his blackmail attempt. "Dan, this is Robbie Winthrop. Be at my office next Wednesday, next week, at five o'clock." That's it—short and to the point.

Like Jeremiah, Robbie is an early bird. The next day, she is in her office at 7:30 a.m. After getting a coffee, she proceeds to check her email, which, as usual, is packed with follow-up business emails, spam, newsletters, and more.

To her delight, all eight candidates have replied. She quickly goes about creating a timetable and setting up invites for each interview. With the schedule completed, there is one interview per day for the next week, starting Thursday through the end of the coming week. On the following Friday, they have scheduled two.

Robbie has done her best to schedule the calls for as early in the day as possible. The start time for the interviews is eight a.m., except for the very last one at three p.m., the following Friday.

As of the close of business on Friday, January 18th, it appears they will be complete with the entire interview process. Robbie reflects a moment—there is no way they'd be ready to decide and disclose a "winner" on January 31st. No way! But that was okay—they will figure it out when they are good to go.

Chapter 93
The Transition Agreement

It is a quiet Wednesday right after lunch, and half the staff desks on the floor are vacant. The sound of silence is eerie. Jeremiah sits at Sara's conference table, reading his emails, waiting for Sara to step away from her computer and join him.

Finally, Sara gets up, apologizes for the delay, and sits down across from Jeremiah. His outline is on a pad in front of him. Without any hesitation, Jeremiah launches into it.

"My goal for this agreement is to lay out a framework for a transition role for me. It should provide a smooth transition for The Way Home to assemble the appropriate resources to assume my responsibilities and the workload I have maintained. Specifically, that refers to the work I have been doing with the metrics data warehouse," he begins. "All of the administrative and user support tasks I have been performing will need to be transferred to someone else in-house. I intend to continue maintaining software updates and new functions, but no longer on a full-time, twenty-four-seven basis."

Sara's eyes flash, but Jeremiah holds himself strong. He has rehearsed this to himself many times.

"I will facilitate the transfer of knowledge and deliver assistance during regular business hours. And I will provide support in the event of emergencies. Again, this will be in conjunction with the metrics data warehouse system only. We will need to create a smoother process for handling all the software needs – the current process is chaotic. In the meantime, you will need to find a replacement for me, someone who can do coding and database administration and, eventually, systems design. I will be available to assist in the evaluation process and training of your selected replacement."

"That's reasonable," responds Sara.

"As far as the term of this agreement, I am okay with a one-year timeframe but would prefer far less, say three months. Either of us should be able to terminate this agreement with thirty days' advance notice. The term could be shorter, particularly if my replacement can be brought on board and up to speed quicker."

Sara interrupts, "What do you expect in terms of compensation?"

"Good question—I'm not sure. I don't expect my usual salary, but you need to compensate me fittingly, so you realize the value of my services. What do you think?" answers Jeremiah. It's not about the money for him—how else to assure The Way has skin in the game?

"Well, we could pay you an hourly rate based on the time you put in. You'd need to keep track of your time."

Jeremiah reasons, "I like that ... and the following operational requirements will need to be in place: a PC and printer for working remotely, and connectivity to my current on-site computer at The Way, all-access credentials, and my email account. These are all needed until I am no longer providing services for you. And lastly, I want this to be a quiet transition. No announcements. A seamless change."

Sara bites back her response, then says, "It seems you have outlined everything. I'll come up with an hourly rate. I hope all of this will fly with Len when I run it by him."

"Listen, Sara. I can easily just quit now. I am doing this for your benefit and The Way Home's," Jeremiah emphatically asserts.

Sara does not respond, letting Jeremiah's demand sink in. Jeremiah hands Sara a copy of his outline and stands to leave. "Let's work to get a formal agreement in place within a week—I want this to be effective February 1st, okay?"

"I'll do my best," promises Sara.

Jeremiah pivots and heads back to his office satisfied he is on track for the next chapter in his life.

Chapter 94
The Big Meeting

It's 4:45 p.m., and Tony Calabretta and Jeremiah are sitting in Robbie's conference room. They have framed a strategy to turn Dan Carson into an ally. It is simple: show him that his plan with the blackmail scheme was a dead-end, and the path as an ally would potentially result in a much more favorable outcome.

To accomplish this, Jeremiah has also recruited Ava, who will dial into the meeting. She will 'read' Carson over the phone. The expectation is that the reading will produce a dramatic emotional response in Carson, setting him up for Jeremiah to make his pitch.

Robbie is at her desk when she hears the front door to her office suite open. Then comes a distant, "Hello?" Getting up, Robbie sails into the foyer.

"Dan?" she asks the timid man standing there.

He nods.

She offers her hand and greets him with, "Robbie Winthrop, please come with me."

After a tepid handshake, they move to the conference room and take seats randomly. Tony starts by saying, "Glad you could make it, Dan. I'd like you to meet Jeremiah Baldwin, the founder of Rising-Up, the group who has pledged one hundred million for those in need." Jeremiah and Carson make non-descript eye contact, quietly acknowledging each other.

Jeremiah then leans toward the teleconference phone and presses a button, and says, "We have asked an associate of ours to join remotely."

Dan shows no response.

The phone rings twice when there is a click and a friendly, "Hello?"

Jeremiah responds, "Hi, Ava. Dan, this is Ava Starling joining us."

Then Tony continues, "Dan, you asked me how we knew it was you. Well, let me say that Ava assisted us with our research. She has some very unique gifts and sees things that are not as obvious to others."

It's beginning to sound a little weird to Dan. Not knowing what to say, he just sits there quietly, wondering who these people are and when will he get his money.

Ava jumps in, "Must have been nice growing up in Bellmore—who is Charlotte? A powerful motherly presence. She says you were such a sweet young boy."

Dan tenses with shock and disbelief. *Is this a joke? Did they stalk him?* "That's my grandmother. She lived with us when I was growing up. What's going on here?"

"And who is Louise? She is here too. She says she loved babysitting for you," continues Ava.

"That's my aunt, my dad's sister. She was killed in a car accident when I was seven. What's going on here?" Dan follows, beginning to show some emotion.

"Dan, I can communicate with people who have passed over. They come through when they want to share with their loved ones still here on the earth plane."

"You're messing with me," Dan declares, still somewhat freaked out. *How could this woman know of my aunt and grandmother?*

"Charlotte is your dad's mother. She says for you to forgive him. His drinking was a sickness; he couldn't control it. And your mom had to leave him. She wanted you to grow up in a more positive environment. Despite his drinking, your father loves you very much," Ava reveals.

Dan begins to tear up. *There is no way this Ava person could know all this information unless she really can see beyond the grave!* Jeremiah and the others share acknowledging glances. They are equally amazed at Ava's revelations.

Ava continues, "Louise and Charlotte are both saying in unison, 'We love you very much and are so proud of you and the young man you have become.' Louise, holding up her index finger, is saying, 'Make good choices.'"

Tears are rolling down Dan's face. He achingly says, "She always used to tell me that. Oh, God!"

"Your grandmother is telling me that though you no longer see your dad, he is sorry for all the pain he caused you and your mom," asserts Ava.

Dan can no longer contain himself, quietly sniffling. Finally, he says, "When I was little, we were all so happy together. And then it all fell apart."

Ava then adds, "Charlotte is saying it was the uncertainties and pressures of life that ate up your dad's confidence, driving him to drink. Louise is repeating, 'Make good choices.'"

"I don't see my father anymore. He moved out west a long time ago," Dan remarks.

"He's okay now," returns Ava.

Pulling it together, Dan offers, "This is too much. I feel stupid being here."

Then from Ava, "Louise says to stop beating yourself up. It's okay. It's always okay, no matter what happens. If only you knew how much you are loved. Stop worrying about the future. Everything will be fine. Charlotte and Louise are throwing kisses to you, and they are moving back into the light."

Robbie turns to Dan and asks, "Are you okay?"

"Yeah, but that was too much!"

Ava closes with, "Dan, I am seeing you standing in a meadow. You are on a walking trail that forks. One path leads to a dark area with fences and barbed wire—a prison of sorts—and the other leads to a beautifully landscaped entrance to a luxurious home. Two paths are in front of you, one leading to ruin, the other to success."

Everyone is still. No one speaks. Ava's vision has profoundly affected everyone. There is a click on the conference phone, and Ava is gone.

Chapter 95
Jeremiah's Pitch

Now, it is Jeremiah's turn to speak. He wants to present his thoughts with hopes of convincing Dan that he ought to drop his scheme. Slowly, he begins, "So, with that remarkable display, I can offer very little other than it does suggest the natural direction this affair should take.

There are no coincidences in life, Dan, and it is not apparent to me the reason for our coming together. I know one thing for sure that we all have choices to make, and sometimes, they are not easy, particularly while we are venturing in a specific direction. Please understand that my work with Rising-Up and impacting poverty is paramount. And preserving my anonymity in that regard is equally important. If that's not doable, however, so be it."

Dan is sweating. Jeremiah holds his gaze firm.

"Dan, I hope that you have realized your lapse in judgment here. I do not want to see things go from bad to worse for you because of a mistake. You do realize that you are the one at risk here. You are the one who stands to lose the most if we were to prosecute you, and we do have enough to do that. I am sensitive to your debt predicament and don't wish to be punitive." Jeremiah folds his hands behind his head and leans back in the chair.

"That said, I'm not prepared to pay for silence. Call it a matter of principle. I bet you do not want to be a footnote in my history, looking in from a prison cell. Maybe there is another way?"

Jeremiah pauses briefly, following with, "Dan, I do not believe we are going to solve this today. All I can do now is ask you to reexamine your options and reconsider."

No one says a word as Dan looks down.

"Dan," Jeremiah continues. "I don't mean to sound harsh. I only want you to understand how important this work is for us. Please give some serious thought."

Dan is disappointed; he had not expected the meeting to go this way. He had not anticipated this result: no money, no negotiation, nothing. Still believing he stands a chance in getting something, Dan has not lost hope.

The unspoken cue is that the meeting is over. Tony turns to Dan and instructs, "Let us know what you plan to do, Dan?"

"Yeah," replies Dan as he rises to leave. Robbie reaches over and hands him her business card. Taking the card, he places it in his pocket, scans the room for a moment, and then exits. As the front door closes, Robbie, Tony, and Jeremiah remain motionless, wondering what the outcome will be.

Chapter 96
The Interview Results

The interviews run as expected—there are no surprises; each organization is exceptional. It will be challenging to select just one. The team has performed magnificently—it is a big lift to spend eight hours, over a week, in dialogue with non-profit leadership vying for the Rising-Up grant. Jeremiah's "interview advisors" will need to rise to the challenge of identifying just one non-profit worthy of the entire award if Plan A is the chosen strategy.

With the interview process over, assuming no further candidates surface, the interviewers need to complete their assessments of each candidate. All eight candidates are viable recipients. After the last interview, Robbie asks the team to list their three favorites in sequential order of preference and indicate their reasons. She further requests that they email them to her tomorrow, Saturday morning. She has been keeping score throughout the interviews and already knows how her list will shake out.

New York Lifeline has surfaced as a favorite by Ruby, Morgan, and Robbie. It is one of the larger social services non-profits in New York—they seem to have it all: programs, vision, size, and a CEO who has engendered a high degree of confidence with all the interviewers. They serve about forty-five thousand people a year and already appear to be making a sizable difference in many of the communities where they provide services.

In the interview, Bill Andrews, New York Lifeline's CEO, mentioned they'd been brainstorming around increasing well-being among their clients. They looked at ways to incorporate mindfulness and meditation, belief system therapy, and inner-city sound systems into their programs. Though this was a bit woo-woo, NYL was attempting to think outside the box for solutions and strategies to help their many clients become more self-reliant and well-adjusted.

Another candidate that scored well with the interview team was the Community Assistance Connection. They, too, are a large service provider, serving about thirty thousand New Yorkers a year. They offer a wide array of programs; one is a very innovative jobs program involving urban farming. CAC is also exploring a few other inventive ideas: "foster homes" for adults and pre-fab housing on barges along NYC waterways. Though somewhat controversial, these potential programs illustrate their forward-thinking and motivation in improving the lives of those living in poverty.

Project Empowerment and The Life Recovery Center had also stood out very favorably in the interview process. Both focus on housing and the homeless and offer programs intended to support individuals and families looking to achieve stable living arrangements.

Though liked by the interviewers for their scrappy can-do demeanor, Bronx Family Services was considered too local with their operations and programs solely in the Bronx. They would most likely not make the shortlist.

These preliminary results serve only as high-level feedback and are by no means a final determination of how the award(s) might go. A more formal scoring and ranking will occur soon. This feedback has been illuminating, though—it helped zero in on specific organizations that could be possible recipients. Jeremiah will solicit final recommendations in a few days.

Chapter 97
Reconnecting with Jenelle

A few days had turned into a couple of weeks; funny the way that happens. Jenelle and Jeremiah had agreed to reconnect to discuss consideration for Jenelle's potential role in the evolving vision of Jeremiah's philanthropic quest. The candidate interviews had dominated Jeremiah's focus, and now, he had the opportunity to turn his attention to other things.

Atop that list was following up with Jenelle regarding her role. It is still early, almost eight a.m., and Jeremiah is at his desk. The office is deserted—a typical Tuesday morning for The Way. He decides an email might be best to get the dialogue back on track. Opening his Gmail account, he begins to compose his thoughts.

Dear Jenelle,

Since we last spoke (I can't believe it's been two weeks), we've conducted intensive discussions with potential recipients. We have made no decisions about awardees, or which grant option would be best.

Our biggest question is which grant alternative to pursue. There is an excellent case to award the entire grant to one organization. On the other hand, the foundation and the "access ramp/digital divide" options are equally compelling. We probably won't decide this until the very end of our process.

Regardless of our decided grant strategy, I believe you could be invaluable. Your participation would be significant and add credibility to our undertaking as we roll out. Your experience and wisdom would also be valuable regarding governance issues, award decisions, and overall advisory/leadership.

Here are a few items I'd like your take on:

- *Should we consider outsourcing to an organization like CCFNY or not? How should we decide on creating a foundation?*

- *How might you go about setting up a foundation?*

- *Would an annual budget of $1 million be realistic? Too much? Too little?*

- *Of the following non-profits, do you have any feedback:*
  - *Bronx Family Services*
  - *Community Assistance Connection*
  - *Project Empowerment*
  - *The Life Recovery Center*
  - *The New York Lifeline*
  - *The Way Home*

- o   *The Golden Rule Guild*
- o   *The Excelsior Support Network*
- • *Any other non-profits not on this list that you feel should be?*

These are just high-level questions—no need to get too deep into the weeds. I can't wait to speak with you soon and hear your thoughts!

Many thanks!

Jeremiah

Within an hour from sending the email, Jeremiah's phone rings—Jenelle is on the line.

She wastes no time. Getting to the point, she agrees that a single awardee is the simplest—one and done. But the other three options do offer more impact—they are all pretty much alike, but the foundation approach is more akin to operating a non-profit. She agrees she'd help with the rollout and will call back Friday regarding the other questions Jeremiah raised.

Jeremiah agrees to talk again on Friday after Jenelle has had some time to consider his questions more deeply. Jeremiah is encouraged by her willingness to help with the rollout, and apparently, in other ways. It is going to be a good day!

Chapter 98
That Night

As Jeremiah mulls over the day's events on his commute home, his thoughts keep returning to how he will organize. What will he need to put in place to manage funds distribution should he create a foundation? Or should he go with one of the Tech Connect NYC variations?

Having Jenelle in his corner will help. Jeremiah's uncertainty is vanishing due to his call with her that morning; she has just the relevant experience they need. For the moment, he has confidence, though he doesn't know precisely how his uncertainties will transform into a concrete plan of action.

The next question he wonders is how Ruby, Morgan, and Logan will fit in. Will, any of them, be suitable or even interested in full-time roles, and if so, what would those roles be exactly? More to figure out, and, again, Jenelle's help will be priceless!

As the train careens to a stop in Syosset, Jeremiah moves to the doors, slowly exits, and heads to his car in the parking lot. Tonight, the Baldwins are getting together for a small birthday dinner for Ryan. He should be arriving on the next train. Harley is home. She'd spent the day at a local college career fair nearby, where she was recruiting camp counselors for the upcoming summer.

Dinner tonight will be a family favorite: take-out from Hunan Taste in Glen Cove. Kate has no problem driving twenty minutes to and from for their dinner—it is worth it, as they have the best Chinese on the island.

Over dinner, Jeremiah plans to give an update on the status of the RFP and his job. They have not spoken much about either in some time.

Jeremiah walks into the house, where Harley is in the kitchen, setting the table for dinner. Ryan had texted her, informing her that he'd be arriving in fifteen minutes. Kate has picked up their dinner and is on her way back—she will get Ryan at the train station.

Harley looks over at Jeremiah and exclaims, "Hey, Dad!"

"What's up, sweetheart?" asks Jeremiah. "How was your day?"

Harley elaborates on her day at Stony Brook—all the potential counselors she interviewed and the mundane drive to and from the career fair. She is exhausted but happy. Nonetheless, the long day is over! Jeremiah can tell that working for the camp is elevating her self-esteem.

"And how was your day?" she asks.

"Amazingly awesome—got a lot done today," replies Jeremiah.

The soft sound of chimes coming from the rear of the house indicates that the mudroom door has just opened, followed by footsteps approaching the kitchen. Kate marches in with Ryan, carrying two shopping bags containing their dinner. Rapidly, the containers of food are placed on the table. Harley pours drinks, and Ryan starts picking at the different dishes on the table.

As everyone sits, Kate discusses the goings-on among her circle of friends, bringing everyone up to date. After five minutes, Jeremiah begins to share what has been happening with the RFP and the recent candidate interviews. Finally, he explains the dilemma he is having in deciding the best approach to take.

Kate follows up by saying, "I have watched you for the past two months trying to work through your RFP idea. And I think it's a good thing—I have not wanted to interfere, but there are a couple of things I just don't get."

Jeremiah pauses, listening intently to his wife. She hasn't been this forward in a while.

"Giving away half the lottery winnings is a lot," Kate says. "I know we are still left with a huge amount, but why give away so much? And why go through such an involved process to determine who should receive it? Why not just pick one organization, like Community Assistance, where Dana Castellano is the CEO? You worked with her before and think she is amazing. So why not just hand the money over to her or some other organization or even The Way Home?"

Jeremiah is reluctant to get into a rehash debate but feels he does need to address Kate's remarks. "With all this money, there is no simple way out. I suppose I could turn it over to Dana's agency or a charitable foundation with our wishes for distributing the money, but I'd feel disconnected. There is a reason why this money came to me! We have the right sensibilities to put it to good use. We need to maintain some control over how the money gets distributed and used, and I feel we have the correct mindset and skills to do that very well. And as I have said before—with about half for us—seventy or so million dollars, we will never be in need or run out. It should not be a factor. Is anyone worried that our piece is not enough?"

"I don't fully agree and won't make a federal case over it," Kate says. "I mean, sure, that is plenty of money—it just doesn't seem logical to me to give away one hundred million. I can't explain it. I don't want to see all your time consumed with this, especially now that you can be free as a bird, literally."

"If I enjoy what I'm doing, isn't that the point? I'm not going to take up golf or play canasta or do crossword puzzles all day with my time," replies Jeremiah.

They keep going at it with no actual agreement but no insurmountable divide, either. A few things are for sure: it will be an ongoing contention point for a while, and Plan A still has a chance. However, the talking has stopped, at least for the moment.

After a minute of reflection, Ryan asks about who the non-profits Jeremiah is considering. There is more back and forth with answers and more questions. No longer are they debating—just engrossed in exchanging more opinions. Ultimately a general understanding of Jeremiah's position is reached, though there is still some degree of skepticism over its wisdom.

Jeremiah has never stated his long-held intrinsic belief. Still, when Kate makes another remark, Jeremiah snaps, somewhat annoyed and impatient: "It is my lottery ticket, and therefore it is my call what to do with the money!"

When the subject is sufficiently exhausted, and Jeremiah has chilled a bit, he gently declares, "I have a little announcement." Quiet descends the table, and everyone looks up in anticipation. "As I'm sure you all have been wondering when I will quit my job, I want you to know that I have taken step one. As of February 1st, I will no longer be full-time at The Way—I will be consulting for them until they can find a suitable replacement for me. I decided to stay on to make sure that my work lives on for the foreseeable future."

Harley is the first to react. "Yay—it's about time!"

"Way to go, Pops," adds Ryan.

"I know; no more getting up at four a.m. and schlepping into the city. Instead, I will be able to sleep in—say, until five or six, at least," responds Jeremiah.

They all laugh and continue to devour the remaining food on the table. Jeremiah continues, "Oh, and one more thing." Everyone looks up, waiting. Silence.

"So?" asks Ryan impatiently.

"Who wants some money?" asks Jeremiah with a big smile.

Everyone's faces light up, but no one says a word, wondering if he's messing with them.

Continuing, Jeremiah says, "I know it's been about two months since we received the lottery money, and you all have been great about not pressuring me about spending it. So, I think now might be a good time to start enjoying some of it."

"No argument here," Harley says.

Jeremiah hands out three new American Express cards, saying, "Why don't you guys use these?"

"You rock, Pops," proclaims Ryan. Kate warmly smiles as she gets up and starts to clear the table.

Chapter 99
Thank you, Guy!

Robbie had been most pleased with the selection committee meeting. Guy Cleveland's conference space at his law offices created the perfect atmosphere for a productive event. She decides to call and thank him for his assistance.

Guy says he had been happy to help on the phone, and if Robbie ever needs to use the space again, she should just reach out and ask. Before ending the call, Guy mentions that his firm plans to start a new division focusing on immigration cases. The firm is going to reassign many of its experienced attorneys to this new area. And they need about a dozen first-year associate types to handle a slew of cases already on the books. If Robbie knows of any potential candidates, recent grads, et cetera, he'd appreciate the referrals. He is relying on his contacts to streamline his search process.

When Robbie hangs up, she makes a mental note: this could be the very thing Jeremiah was talking about when he said to Dan Carson, *"Maybe there is another way."*

Chapter 100
Here's the Thing

Jeremiah cannot get over how Kate seemed so fixated in her position concerning how much Jeremiah intends to donate to charity. She is ordinarily a very generous person. No doubt, her viewpoint is not unique—almost everyone in their network of friends and family would probably feel the same way.

A take-home of seventy million is a tremendous amount of money—is it not enough? It should be plenty to live off and do anything one could dream of and still leave behind a legacy. And on some level, Jeremiah feels that even seventy million was too much. Nonetheless, with that money, they would be so well-off.

So, what is it that Kate finds so objectionable about his intended one hundred million giveaway? Like most people, Jeremiah can only conclude that Kate is a victim of social and cultural conditioning. We live in a society where the media bombards us with messages that support the notion of never having enough.

These constant reinforcing messages have created beliefs contrary to our divine blueprint of being kind, loving, and caring souls. And these perverse beliefs have corrupted our behaviors, too. Collectively, we have become a dehumanized industrial civilization.

And if distorted beliefs are not enough, we have been trained to think negatively, big time, all the time! We look out at the world with our biases, beliefs, opinions, and thoughts, and then we "disturb" the world accordingly. If we come with negative—which we usually do—we get negative results.

Jeremiah is compelled to act differently. His compass points up, not down. He is not going to be stuck in that black hole of total self-interest and never having enough. He believes that we live in an infinite universe with infinite possibilities. Thus, his philanthropy will be positive and will produce positive results.

All those external influences (parental, religious, societal, educational, institutional, historical) have shaped our beliefs, thoughts, expectations, and outcomes. Those archaic views may have worked millennia ago, but today the world is transforming to higher consciousness and vibrations. It is moving to fully embody the brotherhood and sisterhood of man, where humanity is returning to a place where we embrace all creatures as sacred.

Jeremiah is growing weary of such heavy thoughts. He'd ignore these weak attempts in his head to justify and verbalize what he knows is right for him. Instead, he will persevere forward as he had intended. It will work out just fine. Family, friends, and anyone else will have to live with it.

Chapter 101
Ready for Departure

Since Jeremiah met with Sara to outline his requirements for a consulting role as he transitions into "retirement," it has been an entire week. After their meeting, Jeremiah framed a written agreement detailing all the points he had laid out when they met. Sara had been very accommodative—how could she not? Jeremiah is in the driver's seat with this exit plan, and he has achieved everything he wanted. The two of them had spent the week going back and forth with revisions—dotting I's and crossing T's.

As he sits at his desk, looking at the four-page document, it finally hits him: he is about to begin his new career as a philanthropist and consultant. Signing this agreement is step one in leaving The Way. It has been almost five years since he came to The Way, and he has accomplished much, professionally, and personally.

It is the personal growth that pleases Jeremiah most. He is a different person now, just as Ava had predicted when she did his astrology chart last summer. He is a kinder, gentler version of the man he was when he had first started at The Way. His heart now motivates him, and he knows that whatever he does, it will be fine. As his grandmother would have said, "It would be bashert," Yiddish for inevitable or preordained.

He turns to the last page, which Sara and the CFO already signed. Jeremiah reaches for his pen and quickly scribbles his name, then dates the agreement. He will give it to Sara later in the morning, and in a week, he will be their consultant, nothing more.

Chapter 102
Jenelle Pledges Her Support

Jeremiah is sitting in Jenelle's office. It is close to noon—he was downtown on a work-related appointment and had arranged to have a quick face-to-face with her.

Jenelle finishes her phone call and turns to Jeremiah, and without any hesitation, says, "The first thing I'd tell you, Jeremiah, is to keep it simple! Creating a foundation gives you a lot of flexibility and discretion in determining who to support. And it is not a complicated process at all. It may involve more work and some added costs, but it will enable you to realize your vision for impact.

If you feel engaging CCFNY in a consulting capacity could be beneficial, fine; they could assist you in creating the foundation. Frankly, though, I do not think you need them. Also, I wouldn't be concerned about an operating budget—a million a year should be more than enough. As far as how to get going, you could ease into it slowly, and I'd be happy to help. FIMA could act as an incubator for your new foundation until you can go off on your own."

Jeremiah is floating as he listens. Jen's ideas are so in sync with what he'd been thinking—and her willingness to step up and support him is a godsend.

"That's amazing and makes a lot of sense," responds Jeremiah.

"Oh yeah—CCFNY could also help you with charity selection and vetting. But I must say that you are on the right track so far from the list of candidates you have. Most importantly, the potential recipients need to be sustainable, organizationally, to the extent they can fulfill your expectations upon receipt of their grants."

Jeremiah nods in agreement.

Continuing, Jenelle says, "Your candidate list is good—there may be a few others, I'd add, but for now, you are good."

Jeremiah is somewhat overcome with emotions. He then inserts, "You know, Jen, I've always admired you—you are such a smart, savvy, committed, and socially conscious professional. Overcoming your health issues years ago was a miracle and seeing you now having risen from that is so heart-warming. I am delighted beyond words to have your wise counsel and support here. I am deeply grateful."

Jenelle is touched; she smiles sincerely. Jeremiah continues, "Two things I want to ask you." He also smiles, knowing full well that Jenelle is one hundred percent behind him and will do almost anything he asks. "Assuming I create a foundation, would you consider being the interim chair of the foundation? And two, since you have suggested FIMA might incubate the foundation, would you consider hosting a small press conference here in a few weeks to announce the RFP results?"

Immediately, Jenelle replies, "Yes, to both."

"Thank you, thank you, thank you!" responds Jeremiah gratefully, adding, "We will spend the next couple of weeks working out the details for a foundation and press conference."

Jenelle nods in acknowledgment while Jeremiah continues, "We had planned to complete all this by the end of January, but I don't see that happening. Too much to do. Maybe more like the middle of February."

It has been a fast-moving conversation—and in only twenty minutes. Finally, Jenelle looks up toward the door to her office, where her assistant is pointing to her watch-it is time for her next meeting.

Jeremiah sees the gesture and knows it's his cue to wrap up. He signals a thumbs up and says, "We'll continue this," as he rises. He walks over to Jenelle and hugs her goodbye, then says, "I can't thank you enough! I'll be in touch."

Instantly, as if transported in some Star Trek machine, Jeremiah is at Pearl and Broad Streets. He is a bit stunned. So much has just transpired. It will take a subway ride to Penn Station to fully digest and integrate the great meeting he just had with Jenelle.

Chapter 103
No Announcements

Jeremiah left his office early, around 2:30 p.m.—he is going to savor his last day as a full-time employee by going to the gym. But, first, he'll stop at Robbie's office. He arrives at about four o'clock, and Robbie is on the phone, speaking with Joyce Chen, who called to follow up on the RFP's status.

Robbie waves to Jeremiah as she speaks on the phone. "Things have taken a bit longer than we had expected. The review and vetting process is very time-intensive, as I am sure you can imagine. It will be a few weeks more before we decide on who the grant recipient will be."

Joyce acknowledges that she understands and asks if Robbie would keep her in the loop. To which Robbie agrees, says goodbye, and faces Jeremiah.

"So, what brings you here, Mr. Baldwin?" asks Robbie playfully. They hadn't scheduled a meeting, but it isn't uncommon for Jeremiah to drop in now and then.

"Oh, I just wanted to check in with you on my last hours as a full-time employee at The Way Home." They both laugh, and Jeremiah continues with, "You know I met with Jenelle Jansen-Abrams last week?"

"Yes, I know, you told me it was very productive," replies Robbie.

"I think so. Jen's thoughts are very much in line with where I have been leaning. I have been thinking the original Plan A grant option is not where we should be going. However, I still don't want to eliminate it from consideration. Publicly, it's still an option, but on the down-low, it's not."

Robbie nods in agreement.

"Her number one piece of advice is to 'keep it simple.' And a foundation seems to be the least complicated while at the same time providing us with a great deal of flexibility in deciding recipients. And she is willing to help big time in getting it off the ground."

Robbie is not surprised one bit—Jeremiah had been sending signals for a while that this was his preferred direction. "Jenelle would be an excellent asset to have on board," she responds.

"Mid-February looks like the time to pull the trigger on all of this. She is also willing to host a press conference for us," adds Jeremiah.

Robbie smiles—this is all coming together nicely.

Jeremiah continues, "So, what do we do with you in the future after we reveal our decisions? You have been my loyal supporter from the start. And what should I do about the others?"

"Those are great questions! I am delighted to continue being your legal counsel, handling all your legal matters as an advisor. I'm certainly not quitting my day job as you did!"

Jeremiah cannot contain himself, laughing vigorously. "Great, I will renew your retainer."

Robbie gives a mighty thumbs-up.

Chapter 104
Your Mother Should Know

Dan has been conflicted for days. He is undecided about abandoning his blackmail plan or following through on it and potentially getting screwed colossally. He cannot believe that he could get caught but quickly getting out of debt is an attractive notion. But inside of him, there is much fear and uncertainty.

"Hey, Mom," he opens after calling her.

"Hi, honey," she replies. "What are you doing?"

"Oh, not much. How are you?" asks Dan.

"No complaints, dear. So, what do I owe this pleasant surprise to?"

Dan begins, "Well, I need a little advice. I have this idea where I could erase all my student debt, but it's not completely kosher."

Swiftly, she replies, "Is it legal?"

Dan is silent.

She continues, "If you get yourself into something that could jeopardize your career, you are playing with fire. You have invested a lot of time and effort to become a lawyer. It would be awful for all that to come undone."

"I know, Mom, but—"

"No, buts, Danny! It's like this. Your current path with Hofstra is slow and steady. If you stick with it, you will be successful over time. It's a proven strategy: get your degree and work hard, and you will be successful. Is your new idea risk-free? Is it proven?"

"No," submits Dan quietly.

"Well, why would you risk everything? You need to be patient and stick with it."

Digesting his mother's comments, Dan abruptly says, "Listen, Mom, I gotta go. Thanks for the advice."

"Danny, decisions are not always easy. Just do the right thing and have faith!"

"Bye, Mom. Love you."

"I love you, Danny."

Dan turns off his phone, thinking, *When am I going to learn? She never makes anything easy for me.*

Chapter 105
Free Willie

It feels like a weekend morning, the kind where Jeremiah gets an additional hour of sleep more than usual. Today, though, is Monday, February 4th, the second day of his consulting career. Day one had been no different than any of the other workdays of the past five years. After shifting positions in bed repeatedly, he decides it's time to get on with his day. He rolls out of bed and stumbles into the den, where he gets comfortable in the plush chair across from the TV.

Here is Jeremiah's preferred mediation space. Quickly he settles in, and within a few minutes, all is black and calm. His breathing is steady and deep. Random thoughts come and go. He has lost all sense of time and bodily awareness; he is in a pleasant state of inner suspended animation.

Some of his friends and family just don't get it—it is too hard, they say. No matter—it keeps getting more and more satisfying for Jeremiah. On every day that he meditates, it seems to set him up for a day that always unfolds as if predestined and completely manageable, no matter what the circumstances are.

An hour disappears like magic. The session ends when Jeremiah opens his eyes slowly. There is no bell or time indicator, just an inner knowing—it's just time to stop. Jeremiah sits quietly, preparing how he will proceed next. It is 7:30 a.m. Coffee seems like a good idea.

With coffee brewed and poured, Jeremiah is at the table with his cup in hand. He is going through his email, thinking that he could get used to this. He laughs to himself—this is his new normal.

He has a Do List with about a dozen tasks. Half are for The Way—some programming changes to reports his former colleagues requested. He also has some calls to make. First, he wants to touch base with the RFP candidates and inform them of where they stand. He will tell each of them that they are still in contention, which they are. And that they can expect a final decision in a few weeks.

He also wants to follow up with Jenelle; she had sent a text with a few additional NP's she is recommending. And he wants to speak with Ruby and Morgan. It is time for them to be on the same page as the endgame comes into focus.

Jeremiah is temporarily distracted by a small bird chirping outside. It's not a Blue Jay or Cardinal—perhaps a swallow of some kind, sitting on the railing of the deck, gleefully singing away, beckoning for attention. In a flash of inspiration, Jeremiah decides at that moment to set the RFP decision announcement and press event for February 22nd: Harley's birthday.

Announcing the RFP winner should not be such a dramatic event—a routine press release could have sufficed. *So why a press conference,* thinks Jeremiah. It is a good question, one that has been plaguing him for days. The only answer he can come up with is that giving away one hundred million is a big deal. And giving it away to help the struggling poor is also significant. Poverty is a massive problem, and this press event would be an excellent platform to heighten awareness. And potentially, new resources and supporters might surface in the fight to create more economic equality.

That makes a lot of sense, and with that, Jeremiah feels certain a press event is essential if he is committed to his vision of reducing poverty. *How should the event play out?* Taking his pen and pad, he starts making notes:

- Who to invite from the press?
- Who to invite—non-profits?
- Who to invite—others?
- RFP team roles?
- Need to secure venue at FIMA
- Event format

What would the event format be? is Jeremiah's next thought. Again, he makes more notes:

- Opening—Welcome—Introductions
- Background
- Founder's message
- RFP decision announcement
- Closing remarks

- Q & A

Over the next couple of weeks, the team will need to address these points and finalize the press conference program.

Shifting gears, Jeremiah turns his attention to the few work tasks he needs to handle. Ninety minutes later, it's time for a break. Perhaps running some errands would be a nice change of pace, and off he goes to the cleaners, post office, and the grocery store. Upon his return home, Jeremiah calls Jenelle. He reminds her that she wanted to recommend a couple of non-profits for consideration.

Jenelle backpedals, saying she has a different topic to propose. At first, she acknowledges Jeremiah's leaning toward technology for non-profits to enhance access to the internet. However, she proceeds by saying that poverty is fundamentally a seesaw. It shifts between not enough jobs to match workers' skillsets and affordable housing options.

Further, by creating more jobs, elevating job readiness, and assisting low-income dwellers with support, a substantial reduction in poverty is achievable. Jeremiah digests this.

Finally, he says, "Assuming I create a foundation, you want me to enlarge the scope of the RFP vision. Grants should not only be for internet access technology but also include non-profits with programs for job creation, job readiness, and income supports like vouchers."

"Exactly," is Jenelle's reply.

"That's interesting. I do like it. But I also like the single-minded focus of what I have been conceptualizing as Tech Connect NYC. Jobs and supports could easily be a secondary avenue for grants. I will need to let this idea marinate for a while. The thing about vouchers, though, is that it would require ongoing funding—we would need to create a fundraising mechanism to sustain it."

"True," replies Jenelle.

Jeremiah then shares his thoughts about doing a press conference on February 22nd. Without skipping a beat, Jenelle reminds Jeremiah that she volunteered to host the event at FIMA. Jeremiah quickly acknowledges and vows to continue their conversation soon. With one tap on the iPhone screen, the call ends. A few more taps, and the phone dials another number. In two rings, Ruby is on the line.

Their conversation is brief; Jeremiah floats the idea of her having the "Chief Program Officer" role with the RFP in its new incarnation. It would be a paid gig, but not full-time—virtual, and she'd be responsible for all related aspects of recipients and potential recipients. Ruby's response is yes; she'd be thrilled to stay connected to the project.

With their phone call completed, Jeremiah is onto his next one: Morgan. He suggests a paid role for her in the new organization after the initial RFP award(s). Her role would potentially be the head of development to raise money from municipal, corporate, and wealthy individual donors. They'd agree upon a fixed compensation amount. And they would need to figure out a legitimate performance-based incentive program. Morgan is open to it and admits they will need to work out the finer points if there is a new organization.

Now, it is time to create and send an update email to the whole team. The email opens warmly, with a marathon metaphor:

We are at mile twenty-four with only two miles to go. Accordingly, I thought it would be best to update you on how those last few miles look as we approach the finish line.

February 22nd is the decision announcement date, and there will be a press event at Faith-In-Motion Alliance (FIMA).

All grant options are still on the table. The future of Rising-Up is open, and there should be no recipient disclosures to anyone. The Citizen's Community Fund of New York is still under consideration for a possible consulting engagement.

The press conference will be open to everyone. And planning the event will be the focus of the group for the next two weeks.

In closing, I want to thank everyone for their help thus far. I am so jazzed about the approaching conclusion of this phase; I promise to share more details when available.

He decides not to mention Morgan and Ruby's potential roles to avoid speculation on which grant option he favors. Within minutes of sending the message to his team, Jeremiah receives an email from Sara:

Can you work on a special report we need for a board committee meeting tomorrow? Are you also available to come in one day during the week?

Jeremiah replies:

Sure. Send the report requirements. I can stop by Wednesday or Thursday.

Then he says to himself, *I think I'm going to like this consulting gig.*

Chapter 106
Press Event Planning

February 5ᵗʰ

Jeremiah's notes from the day before had framed an outline for the press conference. It is straightforward—first, opening statements and introductions by Robbie. Ruby will be next with the Founder's Statement and will read prepared remarks from Jeremiah to explain his motivation and vision for the RFP.

Lastly, Jenelle will close with the announcement of the RFP decision. She will state how they had initially planned on only one recipient but then considered different incarnations in the process. Then, she will announce the decision, the associated goals, and the expected outcomes. And finally, the close will include time for questions and answers.

It is a good first pass on how to frame the event. Jeremiah will refine it later with Robbie. Then, there are more questions to address. They need to identify the specific invitees from the press, non-profit finalists, and whomever else. Should there be any hand-outs, or maybe a Powerpoint? The team could weigh in on this.

The press event's over-arching goal will be to close this chapter on the RFP process and begin the next one: creating maximum social impact.

February 6th

The next morning after coffee and a light breakfast, Jeremiah, sitting in the kitchen with his laptop, opens a blank Word document. He titles it: Press Invite and quickly drafts, in one short paragraph, the invitation to be sent to the invitees:

> *The Rising-Up Grant will be announcing its plans to distribute funding in the NYC non-profit community. This event is the culmination of an extensive review process. It will be occurring on February 22, 2019, at 9:00 a.m., at the Faith-In-Motion Alliance offices located at 56 Broad Street, 4th floor. Kindly reserve your space by contacting Sue Palmer at spalmer@fima.org*

He opens his Gmail account and composes a quick note to Robbie, asking her for comments on the attached invitation. Now, who to invite? There are only three categories that come to mind: media, non-profit candidates, and government—there are no corporations that readily seem appropriate to include. Jeremiah pauses to think a moment; he will also ask Citizen's Community Foundation of NY and ask Jenelle about inviting other foundations or representatives from the mayor's office and city council.

The media invitees represent the usual suspects in TV and print:

- CBS
- ABC
- NBC
- Fox
- PIX
- WOR
- PBS
- News 12
- Spectrum News
- NY Times
- Daily News
- NY Post
- Wall Street Journal
- Newsday

The guest list also includes representatives from the finalist candidate agencies:

- Bronx Family Services
- Community Assistance Connection
- Project Empowerment

- The Life Recovery Center

- The New York Lifeline

- The Way Home

- The Excelsior Support Network

- The Golden Rule Guild

Chapter 107
More Planning

February 8th

It has been a week since Jeremiah left The Way as a full-time employee. Although he remains accessible virtually twenty-four-seven, they are struggling without him. His email inbox is continually receiving messages from staff who need assistance or have questions. Unfortunately, his former IT colleagues are ill-equipped to address all of these "customer" needs.

Jeremiah can only wonder when the volume of email and help requests will stop. When will they get the necessary staff to replace him? He heard from his work buddy, Oscar Rodriguez, that Sara is considering offering Jeremiah a promotion with a hefty salary increase to come back full-time.

For now, Jeremiah can handle it but desperately wants more time for himself and his new life as a philanthropist. It will take some time for Jeremiah to become fully independent of The Way—he will need to be patient.

He had heard back from Robbie yesterday; she thought the invite email was just right. Jenelle had also added a few city government officials' names to include and two foundations who might be interested as future donors. So Jeremiah will spend the next hour creating a mailing list. He plans to send it out by noon and spend the rest of the day on the growing mountain of tasks for The Way.

When he had first started at The Way Home, it was terrific. He could not wait to get to work each morning. His colleagues were authentic and sincere. Each wanted to help one another as much as they could. They might not have been the most elite business executive types, but they made up for it in many other positive ways.

With the new leadership had come a gradual culture shift. The changes were subtle, requiring much mental discipline to adjust to the different, less inspiring environment.

Nonetheless, Jeremiah is grateful for his experience there but happy to be moving forward with his new life. The bittersweetness of this realization is profound, sad, but liberating.

February 10th

After more discussion with Robbie and Jenelle, they have agreed on the format for the press event:

Opening

- Welcome & Introductions   (Robbie)
- Background of the Rising-Up RFP   (Robbie)
- Founder's message   (Ruby)

Reveal

- Grant option decision   (Jenelle)
- Selected non-profit(s)   (Jenelle)

Close   (Robbie)

- Question & Answers

February 15th

It is a week before the event, and the RSVPs are coming in—almost every invitee has confirmed they will be attending. Robbie had suggested a dress rehearsal, which Jenelle agreed would be beneficial. Jeremiah agrees but feels they can do it via a video chat instead of in person. It is ten a.m., and promptly, the dry run begins with Robbie, Ruby, Jenelle, and Jeremiah.

The opening and reveal are estimated to run no longer than ten minutes each. The close should be about twenty to thirty minutes long. In all, it should last forty to fifty minutes and certainly no more than an hour.

The practice run goes smoothly and quickly. No changes seem necessary. Each of the speakers makes notes on their script cheat sheets. As they critique the different sections, the founder's message is one area they dwell on. Robbie thinks it's a bit woo-woo and holier than thou. Jenelle and Ruby disagree; they believe it's perfect, as it reflects just how Jeremiah truly feels and what has motivated him to this point.

There will be critics no matter what is said or who says it. However, they all agree that the program is tight and will achieve the goals of announcing the RFP outcome, closing this chapter, and setting the stage for the next one to come. They agree to talk more over the coming week and tweak the format if need be.

After the call has ended, Jeremiah reflects a bit. He feels comfortable but still undecided about which grant option and recipient—or recipients—he will select.

Chapter 108
A Little Help from Some Friends

Tony Calabretta has kept in touch with many of his friends and former colleagues at the bureau and local enforcement. For example, he has often reached out to Pat Kelly, a lieutenant at the Nassau County Police Department in Mineola, for small favors. The two had formed a friendship after working together on a joint task force a few years ago.

Tony has grown impatient with Dan Carson and wants to give him a little 'nudge.' He's sure Kelly will be willing to assist him. Perhaps a 'routine' traffic stop might do the trick—he makes a call.

Kelly is on board. A traffic stop is no big deal. Besides, favors are what make the world go round. So it is agreed—a patrol car will tail Carson on the Meadowbrook Parkway after he leaves work. They will engage a second cruiser—the first will pull in behind Carson, and the second will cut off any possible escape route in front. All the while, lights flash like the crime of the century.

That is the plan, Thursday after work. Tony hasn't discussed or cleared this with Robbie but knows she is also becoming increasingly impatient too. Thus he decides to call her and give her a heads-up.

"Hey, Robbie," he starts.

"Hi, Tony."

"Listen—I just wanted to let you know I'm going to engage my friend at NCPD to lean on Dan Carson. Not too heavy, just enough to help him decide to drop this thing."

"Okay, Tony, but I don't want any details and don't want this to backfire. And for heaven's sake, please don't hurt the kid!"

"No worries, Robbie. This time tomorrow, he'll be calling you asking for forgiveness."

"I sure hope so. Thanks for the notice, and good luck!"

Chapter 109
Busted

Pat Kelly and Tony had been on the phone throughout the next day, reviewing details around Dan Carson's traffic stop later that day. Kelly had enlisted two cops he trusted and had clued them in on the plan. They are all on the same page—don't hurt the kid but scare the crap out of him and 'encourage' him to call Robbie Winthrop and drop the blackmail demand. It is all set.

Dan is walking out of the back entrance of his office building and getting into his car in the adjacent parking lot at 4:40 p.m. He plans to go home, shower, then grab something to eat.

He is on Old Country Road, signaling to turn onto the entrance ramp to the Meadowbrook Parkway. Dan plans to study for an upcoming exam and then watch some television after he has eaten. Traffic on the parkway is light, and he picks up speed quickly. He is cruising along at about sixty-five, listening to some soft rock on the car's radio, daydreaming about what life might be after he graduates.

There are flashing lights in his rearview mirror—reds, blues, and screaming sirens a few cars back. The commotion is approaching while Dan slows down a bit, not imagining they are coming for him. There are two of them now right behind his car, like annoying hornets buzzing about him. From the cruiser directly behind him comes the command: "Pull over now!"

They've got to be kidding; I wasn't speeding! No matter, he checks in front of his car to locate a place to stop while the second patrol car swerves in front of Dan's, forcing him over. Dan wonders why they are being so aggressive—he has done nothing wrong. He sits there, fumbling for his license. Now what?

The cop in the lead cruiser exits his vehicle first and slowly approaches Dan's. He stops, retrieves his weapon from its holster, and takes a military attack stance, aiming his gun at Dan.

"Crap—this is too much," says Dan out load, now shaking.

The second cop appears at Dan's window, his hand on his holstered firearm. "Dan Carson, show me your hands and do not move," he orders.

In complete disbelief as to what is happening, Dan obeys. "What did I do wrong, officer, and how do you know my name?"

"Shut up, Carson. Get out of the car, turn, face your vehicle, and place your hands on the roof," demands the officer.

Dan complies. The officer grabs Dan's hands and applies the handcuffs tightly as Dan winces from his pinched wrists. Then Dan is directed to the cruiser's rear door and forced into the back seat.

He can't believe what is happening. For a traffic infraction, this is way too much; this can't be real. Then it hits him—his attempted blackmail of Jeremiah Baldwin must be the connection. His life begins to flash before him—he is screwed. Life as he knows it is over. He is going to jail; he should have listened to them; he should have listened to his mother.

After sitting there for a couple of minutes, the door on the other side opens. In steps an imposing figure, Tony Calabretta. He sits down, admiring to himself this devious little drama he just created. Finally, he then turns to Carson and says, "Dan, we gave you a chance to do the right thing, and you didn't."

Sobbing now, Dan rambles, "I never thought Mr. Baldwin would have me arrested."

"He didn't—this is my show. I am in control of your destiny now, Dan. I can make this whole thing go away," declares Calabretta.

Crying, Dan begs, "Please, I'll do whatever you want. Don't put me in jail! Please!"

Tony lets Dan get it all out of his system as his whimpering dies down. "Okay, Dan, you call Robbie Winthrop and tell her it's over, and I'll let you go."

"Okay, I'll do it, I'll do it. I promise."

"You'll do it now," orders Tony.

"Yes, I will."

Chapter 110
I Surrender

Dan is still in the squad car with Tony next to him. They have removed the handcuffs, and Dan has regained his composure. He retrieves Robbie's business card from his wallet and calls her cell. After a few rings, Robbie answers, not recognizing the number on the caller ID.

"Hello, Ms. Winthrop?" asks Dan.

"Yes, who's calling?"

"Ms. Winthrop, this is Dan Carson. Do you have a minute?"

"Yes, Dan, of course," replies Robbie.

"Well, I just wanted to tell you that I am abandoning this whole insurance thing. It was such a stupid idea on my part. I want you and Mr. Baldwin to know how sorry I am for causing any trouble. I was not thinking straight and hope you will forgive me," offers Dan sincerely.

Robbie is pleased and can tell how genuine Dan is, unaware though that Tony Calabretta is sitting right beside him, figuratively with a gun to his head.

"Dan, you are making the right choice here. I will let Jeremiah know of your decision. I'm glad you called."

"Thank you, Ms. Winthrop. You guys have been so understanding, and I appreciate the second chance you have given me."

"I'm happy this has worked out. I must go now, but please tune in tomorrow to watch our press conference. Rising-Up is going to announce our grant decision. It will be on all the networks."

"Okay. Thanks again, Ms. Winthrop."

"You're welcome, Dan. Bye." Robbie hangs up.

Dan closes his phone, and Tony says to him, "Good job, Dan. No hard feelings."

"Yeah," he replies, deflated. He opens the patrol car door and starts to leave.

"Take care of yourself, Dan," closes Tony as Dan steps out and walks back to his car. The police vehicles' flashing lights go dark as they, too, prepare to leave. Tony smirks to himself and says, "I love it when a plan comes together."

The next day, while on a call with Jeremiah, Robbie shares how Tony Calabretta pressured Dan Carson to back down with the Nassau County police's help. Jeremiah is pissed.

"Shit, Robbie! You know that's not my style. I would have never gone along with that," accuses Jeremiah.

"I know, Jeremiah. We just needed to get closure. I made it a point to Tony not to hurt him."

"It was just so uncool and unnecessary and totally contrary to my way of doing things."

"I'm sorry, Jeremiah. I called an audible."

"Okay. Enough, Robbie. It's done," Jeremiah ends and abruptly hangs up.

Chapter III
The Quiet Before the Storm

Almost a week has passed since the planning for the press conference had been completed. Jeremiah has been in continuous contact with Jenelle and Robbie, exchanging minor points regarding the next day's event to consider further.

Jeremiah has still not made any final decisions and is getting a little edgy due to his shifting leanings. He distracts himself by focusing on the tasks that require his attention from The Way. The volume of work has not diminished, but the steady stream is manageable. He promises himself that he'll wake up early on the big day, meditate, make his decisions, and put them down on paper for Jenelle to share at the press conference.

After a quiet dinner with Kate, they go into the living room to watch some television. Within an hour, Jeremiah grows bored and retreats into the bedroom to read. He cannot concentrate, reflecting on what will be unfolding in the morning.

Placing his book on the nightstand, and to no one in particular, he says: "Thank you." He is increasingly mindful of the many reasons he has to be grateful. Then, turning off the night light, gazing up at the ceiling, he slowly fades off into sleep.

Chapter 112
I Have a Dream

Jeremiah dreams on most nights. They are often vivid, colorful, and usually hard to interpret, and within hours of waking, they would vanish from his memory. Nonetheless, as morning approaches, Jeremiah becomes aware that he is dreaming.

His dream begins with Jeremiah walking into a small movie screening room. There is a large TV on the wall with only one chair about six feet across from it. On the screen are big, bold letters: *Jeremiah, please take a seat.*

He obeys. A stately tall, trim gentleman with white hair in an elegant gray suit enters the room from an invisible door. He hands a remote to Jeremiah and instructs: "Please press 222."

Jeremiah again obeys, and the man disappears as oddly as he had appeared. On the screen is the image of an NYC neighborhood, somewhere uptown or in the Bronx. Flashing at the top of the screen is the number 2019.

The image shifts to lines of people with children in tow at a soup kitchen. The place is packed. They are wearing tattered, soiled rags with all their worldly possessions in suitcases. The hungry wait patiently for their sustenance. Sullen, sad faces are echoing with deep despair, some without shoes.

The screen fades to a one-room apartment. There are two filthy mattresses on the floor, without sheets or bedding. In the corners and along the walls are rodent droppings while emboldened cockroaches scurry about the dirty floor. The residents are two adults and three children, the youngest being an infant clutching its mother. There is no kitchen or bathroom in the apartment, only a sink without hot water.

The image dissolves to an alley where randomly strewn garbage is everywhere. Three older teens are imbibing crack by an overflowing dumpster. A few feet away on the ground is a man in his twenties, passed out.

The screen goes dark for a few moments, letting the stark images sink in. These are the images of a world for many who exist in extreme poverty.

The screen then commands: *Please press the green arrow on the remote.*

Jeremiah obeys.

Across the top of the screen are the numbers 2039.

The screen transitions to an image of a young couple of color with a toddler; they are at a "closing" for their new apartment condo. Having achieved the American Dream, their happiness and anticipation are most visible.

The screen fades to a high school senior—she is opening an envelope from Princeton University. The addressee is Maria Alvarez. The address has an Upper Manhattan zip code. She reads the letter slowly, tears streaming down her face, her acceptance letter to the freshman class for the coming school year.

The image then changes to a New York Times headline: The NY City Housing Authority announces it is closing three apartment facilities. Demand for public housing has been steadily declining.

Darkness again, and then the display reads: *Jeremiah, which scenario do you prefer?*

A minute passes, and the gentleman reappears. He is now standing three feet in front of Jeremiah. And in that familiar deep, bellowing voice, he says to Jeremiah, "Only if you come forward and lead the way!" He then repeats more emphatically, the space is vibrating, "Only if you come forward and lead the way!"

Not waiting for a response, the gentleman disappears.

Jeremiah sits up in bed. His heart is racing. Never has he felt such emotion. Finally, as his breathing returns to a healthy state, he rises to his feet. He knows what he must do.

Chapter 113
Pre-meeting

February 22nd

Robbie and Jeremiah are in Jenelle's office half an hour before the press conference starts. They decided they would film the event, and the press could also record it with their shoulder cameras from the back of the room. The room is filling up, and there is an air of nervous anticipation.

Jeremiah retrieves an envelope from his jacket breast pocket. In it are his thoughts, which he wrote down when he woke after the dream. There are two copies, one for Jenelle and one for Robbie, containing Jeremiah's final decisions on the RFP, the grant strategy, and who will receive funding. The last paragraph will be a surprise, one completely unexpected, a total shocker.

Jeremiah hands Robbie and Jenelle a copy. The suspense is slightly akin to an academy award announcement. They gaze at the page, reading it a couple of times. Surprise, indeed, as a soft gasp escapes from both Robbie and Jenelle, their eyes widening. They look up at Jeremiah, speechless.

Finally, Jenelle asks, "Are you sure you want to do this?"

Jeremiah nods and shares with them the dream he had that night. He says it is clear to him beyond any doubt that this is the right way to go, no matter how unorthodox it may appear. He stresses, "I believe my decision is divinely inspired. I completely trust my intuition on this. The reaction, I am sure, will be intense."

Robbie responds, "Jeremiah, I trust your judgment and support you one hundred percent. I hope this is the right way to go. No matter what, I am here for you."

"Me too!" echoes Jenelle.

There are three minutes to go before the scheduled start. Robbie and Jenelle get up to go into the main conference space. Jeremiah will remain in Jen's office and watch from the monitor in her office.

Robbie exclaims, "Okay, Let's get this thing started!" with a deep breath and an enthusiastic fist pump.

Jeremiah sits in silence as Robbie and Jenelle sashay out of the room. It is another one of those days when things will no longer be the same afterward. But it is of no concern to Jeremiah; he's been there and done that so many times before.

Chapter 114
Showtime

It is hard to believe that nearly four months have elapsed since Jeremiah won. So much has transpired in a short time.

The event will probably be over in a flash, and who knows if those attending will completely comprehend the full intent of what is to come? It matters little. What matters is moving forward.

Rising-Up is on its new trajectory now, regardless of those who will be on the sidelines. By the end of the day, Jeremiah's project will have launched. There is no knowing its reception. Saintly or delusionary or somewhere in between are all possibilities.

The reality is inconsequential. It will all come down to the media's sensitivity and their possible need now for a "feel good" story. If Jeremiah's philanthropic vision makes a significant impact on just one person, he will have succeeded.

The FIMA conference space is well-lit and spacious. There is seating for a little more than one hundred in evenly placed chairs, twelve to a row. There are additional seats in the rear of the room. Behind the main seating is a tripod and video camera to record the event and stream it on the FIMA Facebook page. And there is a podium at the front of the room and a large flat-screen TV behind it.

Representatives from all over the media have gathered. All the grant candidates have their representatives present. From New York City's government are a couple of deputy commissioners, one from the Human Resources Administration and one from the mayor's office. And the city council has also sent one of their people. There are no empty seats, and a few loners have chosen to stand in the back.

Joyce Chen is in the first row, and Frank Martino is also in the audience. On the flat-screen TV scrolls upbeat, positive family images. They are images of hope, unity, and well-being.

At precisely nine a.m., Robbie walks into the room and up to the podium. She is carrying a manila folder dressed like the seasoned attorney she is. The room quiets as Robbie begins to speak by welcoming everyone and introducing herself and her role at Rising-Up. She acknowledges Jenelle and thanks her for hosting the event. Robbie also recognizes the officials from the city's government in attendance.

The audience sits quietly and listens intently. After a slight pause, Robbie continues by introducing Morgan, Ruby, and Eli as members of the Rising-Up advisory team. Finally, she nods to the location where the non-profit candidates are seated and recognizes them.

With the introductions made, Robbie begins to give Rising-Up's background. She refers to Jeremiah anonymously as the founder. She explains how he had come to her a few months ago with his idea of donating a large portion of his lottery winnings to a worthy non-profit organization.

Robbie explains how they had had many conversations about the vision and goals for Rising-Up. And the concept of the RFP emerged as the most viable approach to select the best recipient. She provides a summary of the many applications received, interviews conducted, and finalists considered.

She continues her background remarks by stating that there has been much debate about granting only one or multiple organizations. And that there had been genuine consideration to disburse funds on an initiative basis or by creating a foundation.

Finally, she closes by saying, "Today, you will learn the results of this exhaustive process and odyssey we have been on." Again, there is applause as the audience has taken in Robbie's words. She continues with, "At this time, I'd like to introduce Ruby Miller, a member of the Rising-Up selection committee, who will read some prepared remarks from the Rising-Up founder."

Another flurry of applause from the audience as Ruby rises from her seat and walks to the podium.

Ruby steps behind the podium, carrying her printed copy of Jeremiah's statement. She gets settled and looks out over the audience waiting in anticipation. To her surprise, she notices Sara Williams, Jeremiah's former boss from The Way Home. She is sitting a few rows back. There is no eye contact, but she can tell Sara is equally surprised to see her.

Ruby precedes by saying, "As Ms. Winthrop stated, I will be reading a statement from the founder of Rising-Up. There will be copies made available afterward."

She takes a deep breath and then begins in a clear, vibrant voice.

"Why are we here? Not in this room, but rather, why are each of us here on Earth? Is it to grow up, get a job, raise a family, retire? Is it to become rich, successful, and famous? Or is it to fulfill our destiny and work through our soul's evolution? Perhaps that may be a bit out there, but regardless, how might that play out?

"With all the turmoil and troubles in the world today, it seems things are completely misaligned. The chaos, struggle, and disharmony in our lives, reflect that the natural order that God had intended is out of balance. Can anyone honestly deny the poor state of affairs we are in today?"

There is silence across the room—eyes wide and anticipating, inspired by these words.

"We are part of the universe's natural order, and for centuries, have been misled away from our role to be cooperative participants within one human community. Self-interest has misappropriated the infinite abundance available to all, leaving many with nothing.

"Some might say that this is part of the natural order of things— it is the collective consciousness acting out, divine will, but I disagree. Unfortunately, we have been unfairly influenced by corrupted values, based on fear by rich and powerful individuals and institutions, to protect their interests at the expense of those less empowered.

"Forgive the apparent liberal bent in these observations and stop for a moment to look at our world from thirty thousand feet up, not as members of different political parties or special interest groups, but as members of one human community. Can anyone say that our world, our country, is working like a well-oiled, unified system? Can anyone say that critical changes and shifts are not needed now to bring us back into greater alignment?

"In nature, as within herds and flocks, there is an orientation of inclusion—they do not compete. Notwithstanding Mother Nature's food chain, there is a win-win structure within nature's framework within species with no winners or losers, just members. People are a part of that natural framework, but we have not acted appropriately or consistently with nature's blueprint.

"My personal goals for the Rising-Up effort are simple.

To help increase the growing shift in human consciousness to a more loving, caring, and cooperative community.

To inspire those watching this to comprehend that the universe provides and sharing what you have is part of our charge.

To inspire those in need to believe in a higher purpose for themselves.

To inspire others to awaken to their calling to be more socially responsible.

"No doubt, there is much curiosity as to who is behind this. Who is the lottery winner? Who am I? I have chosen to remain anonymous because I believe the mission here is much bigger than who I am. It is not about me—it is about creating more balance in the world and focusing on me would only be a distraction from that more meaningful purpose.

"As the winner of this lottery jackpot, I do not need all of the money. I am left with plenty, more than enough. My happiness, security, and fulfillment are not defined externally by lottery winnings.

"Having looked deep within that place of quiet and persistent guidance, I feel compelled to donate most of these winnings. In so doing,

I believe it will make a significant difference to those in need and achieve the goals I have shared.

"I believe with the greatest certainty that we all have a moral imperative to make this world better off than the way we found it. Therefore, as I have decided that this is the right path for me to pursue, please consider for yourselves: What would you do?"

There is no applause. A long, quiet lull lingers over the room. Like a church sermon, there is much for reflection. Faces are blank, studying their thoughts, not with regret or guilt, but more like thoughts of wonder and possibility.

Ruby softly steps away from the podium and heads back to her seat. Then, the quiet begins to shift from silence to a hush of conversations erupting among a few. Robbie quickly steps back up to the podium for the next segment, saying, "And now I'd like to introduce Ms. Jenelle Jansen-Abrams, CEO of the Faith-In-Motion Alliance, our generous host today."

There is loud applause breaking the gentle tension lingering from Ruby's reading as Jenelle makes her way to the podium.

Chapter 115
The Reveal

The applause is still ringing as Jenelle steps behind the podium. She is a favorite of the press, having a distinguished career in public service in non-profits and city government.

When the applause dies down, Jenelle starts by saying, "Thank you. Those were very uplifting comments from Rising-Up's founder, and I completely embrace his vision and goals. These are the same reasons why I have devoted my life to public service, and I encourage everyone here and in our great city to do the same."

The audience, without restraint, vigorously applauds again. The Rising-Up team is delighted. The mood of the room is upbeat. The press conference is unfolding perfectly.

Sara Williams is not altogether paying attention. She is distracted by having seen Ruby. *What is she doing here?* She keeps wondering. *What is her connection with all of this?* It is bothering her. It makes no sense.

As the room grows quiet again, Jenelle continues, "As Robbie Winthrop explained in her opening remarks, there had been much consideration around the best-giving strategy to create the most impact on helping those in poverty.

The grant selection committee had initially pursued a single recipient strategy. However, upon deeper examination, we conceived other approaches. One was to create a foundation. Another possibility was to launch an initiative around bridging the digital divide with funding to increase technology use for internet access for those living in poverty. These digital divide ideas were affectionately dubbed Tech Connect NYC and would provide 'access ramps' to the digital superhighway in public housing and homeless shelters.

I would like to acknowledge Ms. Logan Aldrich for her extraordinary contribution in helping hatch this innovative approach, which would empower those economically challenged to connect with resources and opportunities. Please stand, Logan," directs Jenelle, pointing to Logan in the front row.

Complying, Logan rises, turns to the audience, and waves. More applause erupts. When the clapping stops, Jenelle goes back to her comments and asks with a big smile, "Wouldn't it be great to do all of the above?" Rippling through the audience are widespread signs of approval.

"Well, I am happy to announce that Rising-Up will do exactly that. We will be creating a foundation that will be known as Tech Connect NYC. It will focus on technical assistance and resources to expand and enhance access to the internet for New York City non-profits who provide housing, initially in homeless shelters."

The audience response is overwhelmingly positive, with loud applause and cheers. Without a doubt, those in attendance approve—obviously, a surprise to the invited non-profits, who look on for further clarity. Their feelings are mixed. Those providing homeless shelters are decidedly pleased—the others, not sure if they will benefit.

Jenelle continues, "After Tech Connect NYC gets going and makes significant in-roads in shelters, the vision is to expand to other public housing, such as supportive housing and government facilities. The foundation will also make grants on a case-by-case basis to organizations whose missions or initiatives resonate with the vision of the foundation."

Jenelle continues with additional comments about the foundation's start-up and the progress thus far. As she ends the details about the foundation, she pauses and looks over at Robbie. Their glances at each other are indiscernible to anyone in the room. It is non-verbal communication between only them. Only they can comprehend the message: *"Buckle your seat belts!"*

An unexpected, professionally dressed gentleman casually walks up to the podium from the back of the room. He is wearing a dark suit and a white shirt without a tie. He has cleanly cut salt and pepper hair and wearing glasses.

As he reaches the podium, Jenelle steps aside, and he replaces her, turning and facing the audience. No one in the audience recognizes Jeremiah, all wondering who he is. No one except Sara Williams, who immediately is turning vibrant shades of red.

The unidentified man looks up at the audience and confidently announces, "Good Morning, my name is Jeremiah Baldwin. I am the founder of Rising-Up and Tech Connect NYC. I am also the winner of the lottery prize that has made this vision a reality."

A loud gasp of shock and surprise descends upon the room. The audience's press representatives are frantically texting away on their cell phones while the other guests look at one another in complete disbelief and awe.

"There are two things I want to say to you all: why I am up here and the names of three organizations who will be receiving the initial grants from Tech Connect NYC. It had always been my intention to remain anonymous. I did not want to be the subject of unsolicited requests or demands on my time and attention. Coming forward would have only meant an extreme invasion of privacy for not only myself but my family, as well.

"And then I had a dream, a dream that was profound, clear, and very specific. A dream that I could not overlook, one that if I tried to ignore, I would not be able to live with myself. My intuition firmly resonated, instructing me to do this. And so, here I am today, coming forward.

"My coming forward serves a few purposes. First, I hope this foundation and the grants it makes will set an example of doing what is right. The conditions in our city require more acts of generosity and selflessness. To be a compelling example of compassion and charity, I had to be here. I hope it will inspire others to perform similar acts and lead the way.

"Without repeating earlier remarks, please understand, as difficult as it is for many rational people to embrace, this entire experience is living proof of how the universe works in mysterious ways. This is the universe at work."

Jeremiah stops speaking and looks up. The audience begins to applaud in affirmation. A steady sound of hands clapping in harmony with beating hearts. There is a mood of hope and resurrection.

Robbie looks up at Jeremiah; there are tears in her eyes. Their gazes lock for a moment. She then smiles as he nods, acknowledging her support.

"And now, I'd like to continue by announcing the three winning non-profits selected to be the first recipients of grants from Tech Connect NYC. Many factors went into our decision. We concluded that these organizations have the necessary attributes and qualities to succeed: excellent management teams and operations, with strong abilities to create maximum impact in the community. We are still finalizing the amounts and scope of the grants. And the winners are Community Assistance Connection, Project Empowerment, and The Way Home."

The room erupts with cheers and applause; it is deafening.

As the distracted audience reacts to the announcement, Jeremiah quietly walks off the dais toward the exit in the ensuing pandemonium. Robbie moves back to the front as attention shifts to her. Jeremiah slips out of the room unnoticed.

Smiling, Robbie states that the floor is now open for questions and answers. Across the TV screen behind Robbie, the display flashes:

What would you do?

Epilogue

Dan had taken the morning off from his job at the County Clerk's Office. He is "fully recovered" from his episode with Tony Calabretta and Nassau County's finest. Before heading to work, Dan would renew his driver's license at the DMV. While sitting in his living room, he recalls that Rising-Up had scheduled a press conference to announce the one million recipients. It is 9:05; the coverage was to begin at nine. Quickly, he turns on the TV, and in a moment, he finds the live press event on Channel 4.

There is Robbie Winthrop at a podium, speaking to the audience. He watches intently as the event's agenda unfolds. *Wow,* he thinks. *This is the real deal. All those people and speeches!*

It had never occurred to him the magnitude of what Rising-Up was all about. One hundred million to support charities to help poverty-stricken people in New York. Rising-Up is a big deal; it is finally sinking in. And what a good thing the lame blackmail scheme of his died.

Then, suddenly, there is Jeremiah Baldwin standing in front of the crowd. He looks so sincere, professional, and inspiring. Whatever happened to his most pressing need for anonymity? Dan listens to his comments about a moral imperative to do the right thing, et cetera et cetera. He begins to feel blessed to have met Jeremiah and thankful for how Jeremiah and Robbie had dealt with him. Others like Calabretta would have done him in big time. And then Robbie is there taking questions. How surreal, like some futuristic movie.

Sitting quietly, Dan reflects further, finally realizing how blessed his life is. The room is still—he hears the clock ticking in the hallway, and it is time to get moving. He gets up and rushes about in preparation to head to the DMV and then work.

There is no traffic, and soon, Dan arrives at the DMV and, surprisingly, is in and out within twenty minutes. Then, he stops at a deli to pick up lunch and proceeds to work. While on his way to the office, Dan decides to call Robbie. He takes out her business card and dials the cell number on it. After two rings, Robbie answers in her car with Jeremiah on the LIE heading home from the press conference.

"Ms. Winthrop?" asks Dan.

Recognizing the voice, Robbie responds, "Yes, is that you, Dan? What's up? Did you happen to catch our press conference?"

"Yes, yes, I did. I had no idea how big a deal this thing is. I am so sorry for trying to profit by knowing Mr. Baldwin was behind it all. It was so stupid and thoughtless."

Jeremiah is sitting close enough that he can hear everything. He reaches for the phone and says, "Hey Dan, this is Jeremiah. Stop apologizing. We know you are sorry. It's us who should be sorry. When I learned how the police stopped you, well, it upset me greatly."

Surprised, Dan says nothing.

Jeremiah continues, "It's time for us all to move on. Focus on the future and what you plan to do with all that you have gained from this experience."

"Yes, sir, Mr. Baldwin. I saw you today, and well, it was amazing. I hope there is some way I can be of service to you in making your vision real."

"We'll see, Dan. You never know," responds Jeremiah, smiling at Robbie as he hands her back the phone.

"So, Dan, I was going to call you today anyway to let you know that I recommended you for a position at a friend's law firm. It should be an excellent opportunity for you."

Astonished, Dan replies, "I don't know what to say, Ms. Winthrop. That is so generous of you, particularly after everything that has happened."

"True. It just shows you've got to be positive and always do the right thing. Make the best of this opportunity, Dan."

"I will and thank you both."

"Good luck, Dan!"

The traffic on the LIE is light, and Robbie is making good time. She turns to Jeremiah, saying, "That was some surprise, going public as the winner!"

"I know. I never wanted to, but I felt I had to for greater Rising-Up legitimacy. It will make going forward from here much different."

"Yes. It will be interesting. We sure have a lot more work ahead of us."

Jeremiah smiles at Robbie's use of 'we.' "This whole thing is like a dream, so surreal."

"And a miracle, too."

"Yeah. I'll say."

"Fortunately, we have a weekend to rest up before we dive into the next chapter of this adventure."

"Thank God—I can use the rest; it's been draining. This next chapter should be exciting, planting our 'grant seeds' and seeing where it all goes."

Robbie nods in agreement.

"I wonder where it will lead, how long it will take, and what's next," continues Jeremiah.

"Let's stay focused on making the grants and deal with what's next down the road."

"I'm just saying. I wonder what my Rising-Up afterlife will be like."

As they turn onto the LIE exit ramp for Jeremiah's house, Robbie chirps, "Only time will tell."

Acknowledgments

Writing a book is no simple undertaking. It takes time, patience, and motivation. Most importantly, it takes an idea that grabs the writer so that the writer and unfolding book are linked in an unyielding quest to reach completion.

Over my life, I have read many books focusing on self-help and spiritual matters. Initially, I thought that writing a book about such topics might be the direction I would take. However, on further reflection, I concluded that my contributions would pale compared to those I had read. So why reinvent the wheel with my re-hash of their ideas?

And then it came to me: tell an inspirational story that embodies the principles and values I have gained from authors and teachers who shared with me their wisdom and insights on personal transformation and self-realization.

Thank you for the inspiration, insights, and teachings from Dr. Christiane Northrup, Dr. Wayne Dyer, Deepak Chopra, Michael A. Singer, Oprah Winfrey, Eckhart Tolle, Paramahansa Yogananda, Pam Grout, Gabrielle Bernstein, and Alan Cohen.

I am most grateful to my family and friends who have given me the space to pursue this dream. Their support has been a tremendous source of encouragement.

ACKNOWLEDGMENTS

Thank you to those who offered me their time, advice, support, and assistance so generously: Lori Pappas, Jennifer Mount, Dian Zirilli-Mares, Margot Steinberg, Betty Steele, Brandt Aidikoff, Roger Mummert, Randi Brett, Bonnie Stone, and Monte & Anna Sugarman.

Special thanks to Taylor Hale for her development suggestions and indispensable editing assistance.

Cover & formatting by Kerry Watson.

About the Author

A native of central Connecticut, Ira Bellach currently resides on the north shore of Long Island. He has held numerous technology-related positions in naval architecture, banking, computer services, and not-for-profit organizations in metropolitan New York over the past forty years. He is a Pratt Institute graduate, where he majored in industrial engineering/operations research and has an MBA from Pace University. He is married with two grown children, a son and a daughter.

Made in United States
North Haven, CT
11 December 2021

12500384R00224